PRAISE FOR

A Timely Vision

"Grabbed my attention on page one . . . Puzzles are unraveled and secrets spilled in a fast-paced paranormal mystery full of quirky characters you'll want as friends."
— Elizabeth Spann Craig, author of *Pretty Is as Pretty Dies*

"A delightful yarn . . . Kept me turning pages until it was done."
— Patricia Sprinkle, author of *Friday's Daughter*

"Filled with likable (if eccentric) characters and boasts a vividly realized small-town setting."   —*Booklist*

"This opening act of a new amateur sleuth is a wonderful mystery due to memorable eccentric characters including Duck. The whodunit is complicated enough to keep readers entertained and stymied . . . The heroine is sassy and spunky . . . Joyce and Jim Lavene have . . . another hit series."   —*Midwest Book Review*

"A leisurely mystery that had me guessing almost 'til the very end . . . It was fun and the characters were likable . . . I could almost smell and feel the salty sea air of Duck as I was reading."
— *A Cup of Tea and a Cozy for Me*

"This is a mystery with strong characters, a vivid sense of place, and touches of humor and the paranormal. *A Timely Vision* is one of the best traditional mysteries I've read this year."
— *Lesa's Book Critiques*

continued . . .

Fruit of the Poisoned Tree

"I cannot recommend this work highly enough. It has everything: mystery, wonderful characters, sinister plot, humor, and even romance." —*Midwest Book Review*

"Well-crafted with a satisfying end that will leave readers wanting more!" —*Fresh Fiction*

Pretty Poison

"With a touch of romance added to this delightful mystery, one can only hope many more Peggy Lee Mysteries will be hitting shelves soon!" —*Roundtable Reviews*

"A fantastic amateur-sleuth mystery." —*The Best Reviews*

"For anyone with even a modicum of interest in gardening, this book is a lot of fun." —*The Romance Readers Connection*

"The perfect book if you're looking for a great suspense." —*Romance Junkies*

Perfect Poison

"A fabulous whodunit that will keep readers guessing and happily turning pages to the unexpected end. Peggy Less is a most entertaining sleuth and her Southern gentility is like a breath of fresh air . . . [A] keeper!" —*Fresh Fiction*

"A fascinating whodunit with unusual but plausible twists and plenty of red herrings." —*Genre Go Round Reviews*

Berkley Prime Crime titles by Joyce and Jim Lavene

Peggy Lee Garden Mysteries

PRETTY POISON
FRUIT OF THE POISONED TREE
POISONED PETALS
PERFECT POISON
A CORPSE FOR YEW

Renaissance Faire Mysteries

WICKED WEAVES
GHASTLY GLASS
DEADLY DAGGERS
HARROWING HATS

Missing Pieces Mysteries

A TIMELY VISION
A TOUCH OF GOLD
A SPIRITED GIFT

A Spirited Gift

Joyce and Jim Lavene

BERKLEY PRIME CRIME, NEW YORK

THE BERKLEY PUBLISHING GROUP
Published by the Penguin Group
Penguin Group (USA) Inc.
375 Hudson Street, New York, New York 10014, USA
Penguin Group (Canada), 90 Eglinton Avenue East, Suite 700, Toronto, Ontario M4P 2Y3, Canada
(a division of Pearson Penguin Canada Inc.)
Penguin Books Ltd., 80 Strand, London WC2R 0RL, England
Penguin Group Ireland, 25 St. Stephen's Green, Dublin 2, Ireland (a division of Penguin Books Ltd.)
Penguin Group (Australia), 250 Camberwell Road, Camberwell, Victoria 3124, Australia
(a division of Pearson Australia Group Pty. Ltd.)
Penguin Books India Pvt. Ltd., 11 Community Centre, Panchsheel Park, New Delhi—110 017, India
Penguin Group (NZ), 67 Apollo Drive, Rosedale, Auckland 0632, New Zealand
(a division of Pearson New Zealand Ltd.)
Penguin Books (South Africa) (Pty.) Ltd., 24 Sturdee Avenue, Rosebank, Johannesburg 2196,
South Africa

Penguin Books Ltd., Registered Offices: 80 Strand, London WC2R 0RL, England

This is a work of fiction. Names, characters, places, and incidents either are the product of the author's imagination or are used fictitiously, and any resemblance to actual persons, living or dead, business establishments, events, or locales is entirely coincidental. The publisher does not have any control over and does not assume any responsibility for author or third-party websites or their content.

A SPIRITED GIFT

A Berkley Prime Crime Book / published by arrangement with the authors

PRINTING HISTORY
Berkley Prime Crime mass-market edition / December 2011

Copyright © 2011 by Jim and Joyce Lavene.
Cover illustration by Robert Crawford.
Cover design by Annette Fiore Defex.
Interior text design by Laura K. Corless.

ISBN: 978-0-425-24502-6

BERKLEY® PRIME CRIME
Berkley Prime Crime Books are published by The Berkley Publishing Group,
a division of Penguin Group (USA) Inc.,
375 Hudson Street, New York, New York 10014.
BERKLEY® PRIME CRIME and the PRIME CRIME logo are trademarks of Penguin Group (USA) Inc.

PRINTED IN THE UNITED STATES OF AMERICA

10 9 8 7 6 5 4 3 2 1

We'd like to dedicate this book to Chris and Jamie, who helped us know Duck better—and find out where all the skeletons are buried.

Thanks! J & J

Chapter 1

"I'm nervous."

"There's nothing to be nervous about. Just hold my hands and close your eyes."

I did as my friend Shayla Lily said. We were seated at an old rosewood table that had once served as a spot where Thomas Jefferson ate breakfast and attended to his morning business. In the candlelight, the aged patina glowed, making shadows and depth in the wood.

"I can't help it," I said, even though I knew I was supposed to be quiet. "It's been a year."

"It's just like riding a horse, sweetie. Except you're on back this time and I have the reins." Shayla tossed her rich black hair and took a deep breath. "Are you ready now?"

I wasn't really sure if I was. It had become ritual for Shayla and me to meet on my mother's birthday, October 15. Shayla was a medium who'd lived in Duck for the last few years. Contacting my dead mother was what had brought us together originally. Now we were friends—even though our personalities were very different.

I had already decided, as the month of October approached, that this was the last time I would try to raise the ghost of my mother.

It was a big decision for me. I'd desperately wanted to talk to her after her death more than fifteen years ago. There'd been no time to say the things that needed to be said before her car went off one of the bridges that connect the Outer Banks to the mainland of North Carolina. I just wanted that last opportunity to tell her that I loved her. And that I was sorry.

"Spirits of the air—hear my voice." Shayla began the ritual while I tried to decide if we should even do it. "We seek Jean O'Donnell. Her daughter is here to speak with her. Hear me, spirits. We ask your blessing and to speak to Jean O'Donnell."

I squeezed my eyes closed—wanting so much to see her and, at the same time, afraid that I would. I'd never seen a ghost. Shayla had told me it was a lot like seeing a living person. I had a feeling that wasn't quite true. I wanted to believe that my mother could come back to me. I wanted to hear her voice one last time.

"Is anything happening?" I whispered. I could hear the wind battering the house outside. I knew Duck might be catching the tail end of a tropical storm that was headed up the coast after hitting Florida.

"Nothing is gonna happen if you keep talking, Dae." Shayla's voice seemed loud even though she was whispering.

The candle on the table between us flickered as though some errant breeze had filtered through the room. There was a scratching sound at the window beside us. I rationalized it as a tree branch, clawing at the glass.

Shayla invited the dead to join us again. Her plaintive cry was made poignant by the not-so-subtle overtones of her New Orleans accent. I wondered if anyone was listening to her.

It seemed to me as though my mother must not have anything to say to me. Maybe she was still angry. Maybe she blamed me for her death. I knew she was upset when she left me at college that day. We'd argued, as we frequently did. She'd left early for Duck because a storm was brewing in the Atlantic. I'd let her go without telling her that I loved her. She'd left me without looking back.

Was I to blame for her state of mind? Had she been crying when she lost control of her car and skidded off the bridge into the Croatan Sound? Her body had never been found.

If guilt were a necklace, mine would be ten feet long and weigh a hundred pounds. I didn't know if she blamed me, but I blamed myself. I was a stupid, selfish, thoughtless kid who didn't know any better. But that was no excuse. Which was why I was sitting here, hoping to talk to her and make amends.

But it appeared it was going to be just another night. A flickering candle and an eerie feeling didn't mean my mother was with us.

Shayla sighed. "I'm sorry, Dae. But I don't think you should give up."

"It's been a long time." I opened my eyes and glanced around the room. A prickly tingling went up and down my spine, but that was all. About what you'd expect when you're sitting in a dark room trying to call back the dead. "I don't think she wants to talk to me."

"Listen, it's not always that cut-and-dry. The dead have regrets too. Sometimes it isn't that easy to come back. Maybe your mama just can't get here to you."

I smiled at her, took my hands back and wiped the tears from my eyes. "Thanks for saying that. But I think this is it. I'm not trying again."

As though my words were a signal to some unseen source, the wind outside began whipping up even harder. The candle on the table not only went out—it, and the candleholder, fell over. The tree branch that had been politely tapping on the window broke off and smashed into the glass. Rain and wind blew in on us from the cracks.

Shayla and I moved quickly away from the broken window that overlooked Duck Road. "Help me move the table," I said.

"Never mind that," Shayla argued. "I think we might have created a breach in the spirit plane. That kind of stuff doesn't just happen with a normal séance."

I dragged the Thomas Jefferson table away from the rain and pushed it into the center of the room. Shayla might not appreciate the importance of the piece, but I did. I'd done the research on it—which in this case consisted of touching it to learn its history.

Shayla might see ghosts and be familiar with the spirit plane. I have a gift too. Nothing so fancy—I can find lost things that people are looking for and learn about those things by touching them.

"It's just the storm," I assured her. I'd been born and raised on the Outer Banks, the strip of barrier islands that lies between the Atlantic and the various waters that separate it from the North Carolina coast.

"Look at those," Shayla whispered, pointing. "Do *those* look like something the storm dragged in?"

I followed her finger and saw three balls of light floating across the dark room. The practical aspects of my Banker (Outer Banks) heritage made me go over and try to touch them. That same Banker heritage made me stop short of actually connecting—we were superstitious too.

"What are they?" I asked my specialist on the spiritual realm.

"Spirit balls," she answered, clearly awed. "I've personally never seen them before, but I've heard stories from my ma and her gran about them. Spirits sometimes travel like this when they don't take form."

I swallowed hard. "Can you talk to them?"

"I don't think so. They're pure energy."

"Do you think one of them is my mother?"

As if in answer, one of the balls flared out like a sparkler, then disappeared. The other two continued their leisurely pace across the room.

Shayla took out her cell phone and started taking pictures. The flashes seemed to disturb the balls—they fled into the wall and disappeared.

"Did you get them?" I figured photos were the only way anyone would ever believe us.

She checked the camera function on her phone. "They don't look like much. No wonder pictures of phenomena like this are always fuzzy. Who's prepared?"

"But we saw them." My whole body felt like it had been immersed in a vat of static electricity. Shayla turned the lights on. They flickered a few times but eventually stayed on. We laughed at each other—our hair was standing straight up on our heads.

"We did," she agreed. "I think this means you shouldn't give up trying to talk to your mother, Dae. The spirits are trying to reach you. You have to give them more time."

I couldn't argue with her. The whole experience had left me trembling and ready to jump—which I did when my cell phone rang a moment later.

Heart pounding, I answered and tried to focus. It was problem number 347 for the Duck Mayor's Conference. Who'd have thought so many problems could come up for a two-day event? "I'll be right there," I promised our town clerk, who sounded on the verge of collapse.

"You can't go now," Shayla said after I got off the phone. "We're so close—I can feel it. You might still be able to talk to your mother tonight."

"As exciting as that sounds, if I don't get over to the Blue Whale and sort some things out, the town staff might all be dead from stress. Think how much guilt I'd have then, since the conference was my idea."

"You shouldn't play around with the dead," Shayla quoted with dark intent.

"I'm not. Really—maybe you could tell them how serious I am. We could try again after I get things settled down." I hugged her and smiled. "Thank you for being here with me."

She rolled her expressive dark eyes. "Go on then. Go do your mayor thing. I'll try to get this place cleaned up. You know, I think this storm might be worse than the TV weather people are expecting."

Chapter 2

I'd brought the golf cart and my umbrella to Shayla's house for the séance. Neither of them was any good at protecting me from the hard rain and high winds that were sweeping across the island. It was hurricane season—but not anything to panic about.

My storm knee that I'd injured surfing when I was fourteen ached like crazy, telling me that Shayla was right about the tail end of this tropical storm. It would surprise me if it wasn't upgraded to a hurricane before the end of the day.

Most stores and houses were locked down, windows already boarded up or protected by heavy shutters. Storm debris was being pushed across Duck Road, our major thoroughfare.

But people were still out, dressed in colorful ponchos and boots. A few restaurants and shops were open, including Game World, our gaming arcade. Most people took bad weather for granted. Only the worst of it got our attention.

That made it difficult sometimes to protect the population. Most Bankers flatly refused to evacuate in the face of hurricanes, much less a tropical storm. Even though I was the mayor of Duck and understood the emergency protocols, I was just as bad. I couldn't imagine what kind of storm would make me and my grandfather leave our home on the Currituck Sound.

As far as I knew, an O'Donnell had never left Duck for something as unimportant as some rain and gale-force winds. My family had lived here for several generations. Stubbornness was bred into our Banker bones.

I turned down the side street that led to the Blue Whale Inn. Rain almost blinded me, but I hunkered down behind the plastic windshield and kept my foot on the accelerator. The battery-powered golf cart responded with its usual sluggish movement. It was lucky to go ten miles an hour. But it was better for the environment than a gas-powered golf cart and cheaper to run. A lot of people here used carts instead of cars.

Though, in times like this, Gramps's old car might've been better.

The Blue Whale Inn sat squarely facing the Atlantic side of Duck. Its three stories, tall turret and sweeping verandah welcomed guests into a wealth of comfort and Southern charm. It had been built in the early 1900s and had been the scene of many major events in Duck—both legal and illegal—down through the years.

It was owned now by ex-FBI agent Kevin Brickman, who'd labored long hours to make the place livable again after it had sat empty for more than thirty years. Between his wonderful cooking and painstaking refurbishing, the Blue Whale was again a hub of activity year-round.

I pulled up through the circle drive and parked by the old hitching post. As I got out of the golf cart, I spotted a set of keys on the ground. I stooped down and picked it up, thinking someone would miss it. There was only a single key—a car key—on the key ring, and a fob—maybe a dolphin?—broken in half.

Immediately, I was swamped with emotions that came from the object. I couldn't make out the woman's face as she threw the key ring at someone, but I felt her anger and frustration. Whoever the key ring belonged to was having a very bad day. I pocketed it, then turned to go inside.

"Where have you been?" Nancy Boidyn, the town clerk, demanded in an uncharacteristic tone of panic. She was waiting for me on the verandah. Normally she was an unflappable Banker, unmoved by any outside force. "This place is going crazy! We have to do something."

I was drenched, and my teeth were chattering. "You have Barbara and Althea helping you. What can I do?"

Nancy's eyes flared with anger for an instant. Her narrow lips pressed tighter together.

I realized we were all under a lot of stress. I didn't know what was going on that they couldn't handle, but I knew Nancy didn't get upset over just anything. "I'm sorry. I should've been here. I'm soaked and freezing. I was with Shayla. It's October 15."

Her pretty face softened instantly and she hugged me, totally disregarding my wet clothes and hair. "I'm so sorry, Dae. I completely forgot the date with all this rushing around. Did you hear anything?"

Nancy wasn't surprised by my attempts to contact my mother. Most people from Duck believed having the dead in your life was part of living. Ghosts weren't a big deal. Curses and pirates were our daily fare.

"No. Not really." I didn't go into the spirit balls. I'd probably tell her about them later. Right now, the living needed attention. "So, what's going on?"

She took out a large pink notebook. "The mayor from Elizabeth City needs seltzer water with a twist of lemon, not lime. The mayor from Manteo needs a room with a bigger window. The mayor from Virginia Beach needs a bigger room—with a view of the Atlantic. Some of the schedules were blurry. There may not be enough wine, but it's too late to get any more."

"Why aren't Kevin and Marissa handling these problems?" I wiped away streams of water that kept dripping down my face.

"He's cooking for the reception tonight and getting the ballroom set up. Marissa is in there running back and forth, trying to keep things organized. I thought this was why you assigned me and the girls to the event. Kevin and Marissa can't do everything." She smiled in a more Nancy-like fashion. "But whatever Kevin's cooking smells divine! I can't wait!"

"Let's make it to dinner first. Where are Althea and Barbara?"

Nancy walked me into the crowded lobby of the old hotel. I felt a little out of place, dripping water, my clothes plastered to me, and my sun-bleached brown hair hanging in wet rat's tails all over my head. But I put on my big mayor's smile and began to put things in order.

The first thing I did was drop off the broken key ring with Marissa at the front desk. She was the new manager Kevin had recently hired. Her parents had moved away from Duck before she was born, but she'd come back to take care of her ailing grandfather, Joe Endy.

She was a beautiful young woman, probably in her late twenties, who dressed well and seemed to have an affinity for getting along with people. But there was a sadness about her—something in her eyes that was unspoken—that made her seem like more than just another pretty face. I didn't know her well enough to ask questions.

"Do you have any idea who this belongs to?" she asked, swinging her long blond hair out of the way as she handed out Duck brochures to the people attending the conference.

I told her about finding the key ring outside. "I guess someone will need it before they can go home. We'll see."

I kept glancing back at the key ring until she put it away. Sometimes, I feel emotions for the things I find—it can be hard to set them aside. I had to focus on something else, like changing clothes before too many people saw me this way.

It was warm and dry inside, with a pleasant fire in the old hearth. I avoided people I recognized who were drinking coffee and talking quietly. The old iron-lace elevator was moving slowly up and down, taking guests from the lobby all the way up to the recently completed third floor.

I'd helped in a lot of the renovation—even helped coat the outside of the old hotel in its original blue color. Most of the work was Kevin's, though. He'd done a great job restoring the 1930s atmosphere and charm while modernizing everything for his guests.

I was prejudiced, of course, since Kevin and I had been dating for several months. Sometimes it seemed as though he'd lived in Duck forever even though he'd been here less than a year. He'd blended in as a Banker, joined the chamber of commerce and the volunteer fire department.

But he was more than a responsible Duck resident, or even a boyfriend, to me. He understood my gift in ways even my grandfather didn't. He never seemed to be surprised by anything that happened. Pirate curses and ghost stories left him unphased. He might not have been born in Duck, but he belonged here.

I popped my head in the kitchen. Kevin had four other cooks working with him. They all wore white jackets with cute little chef's hats—except for Kevin, who wore an apron over his tuxedo. I watched him as he directed, tasted, and got everything ready for the reception. He was like a conductor with a kitchen full of gastric musicians.

"Dae?" He looked upset and unhappy when he saw me. "What happened?"

"Bad storm outside. I suppose you couldn't hear it." If I'd forgotten how awful I looked, his face reminded me.

"But you're speaking at the reception."

"True. Not to worry. Nancy always prepares for the worst. She brought my outfit over earlier. I'll be polished and ready to go when it's time."

He took my arm and we moved away from the frantic energy of the meal preparation. "How did it go with Shayla?"

"Nothing new happened." I shrugged. "At least not message-wise anyway. There were these strange balls of light that floated around the room and disappeared."

"That's different. What did Shayla say?"

"That we should keep trying." I rubbed a spot on my head that was beginning to throb. "I don't think I have the heart for it anymore, Kevin. I don't know."

He managed to kiss me exactly on the spot that was beginning to ache. "I'm sorry I couldn't be there with you. Somebody set October 15 as the day for the conference and then nominated the Blue Whale to hold it."

I smiled, since that somebody was me. "That's true. Believe me, I would've done it another day if I could have. Has it been terrible?"

"I'm not complaining. The money will look nice on my balance sheet."

"Then I'm glad I could help. Anything else I can do?"

"What you need to do is change clothes." He pushed me toward the kitchen door. "You don't want people to see the Honorable Mayor of Duck looking like she rode over in the rain in her golf cart. Then get out there and network. That's why you did this, right?"

He was right, I thought, heading up the stairs instead of trying the elevator. I don't know why, but looking at it always made me queasy.

The conference was my baby. Twenty mayors, two days talking about our problems and strengths, getting together to make important things happen. I was ready for it—despite the strangeness of the day. I wished it wouldn't have been this particular day in October, but that's the way it had worked out.

I took a long hot shower and pushed the séance and the storm from my mind. I was the first elected mayor of Duck, North Carolina. That meant something to me because this was my home. I wanted to leave my mark here—to have people remember me as more than just a picture on the wall in town hall.

I wanted sidewalks to make walking safer going up and down Duck Road. I wanted community watchdog groups that would help fight bad development, the reason Duck incorporated in the first place. I wanted this to be a good, safe place to live during the summer when we were swamped with fifty thousand tourists and in the winter when there were less than six hundred of us.

As I gazed at myself in the lovely antique mirror, I thought I looked like that mayor in my black floor-length gown, my short hair swept back from my face. I added a touch of makeup and lipstick to enhance my after-summer tan. I was ready to go.

I smiled my big mayor's smile—and in the reflection, saw something move. Well, it was *almost* something. But when I turned and stared at that area of the room, there was nothing there.

I surveyed the room. I was on the second floor of the Blue Whale in a suite Kevin had set aside for bridal parties to get ready for the big occasion. Again, I saw nothing.

Nerves. I grabbed my black clutch and headed out the door. I still felt that little bit of static electricity flowing up and down my arms and against the back of my neck.

It was the storm, I told myself, as thunder rumbled outside, shaking the old inn. But my Banker instincts told me to beware.

Chapter 3

The reception was a great hit. People were smiling, enjoying the good food and talking to each other. The ballroom was filled with twenty mayors, some of their families, and Duck residents I'd pressed into being there.

The town council was up to the task of impressing our visitors. They'd left the Hawaiian shirts and cargo shorts they usually wore to town meetings at home for the night. They cleaned up pretty well—especially Randal "Mad Dog" Wilson. At six foot four, three hundred pounds, he was visible from any corner of the room. He was smiling and giving out campaign buttons for his run against me next year. He was all over the place, wooing constituents and nonresidents alike.

"Seems like a good party," my grandfather said.

"I can't believe you're here, Gramps!" I turned and hugged him. "I thought you were playing pinochle tonight."

"I didn't want to miss the festivities. It's not every day we have a big party in Duck."

"I'm glad you came."

"Looks like Mad Dog is pulling out all the stops to run for mayor."

"I could put a hex on him." Shayla joined us, wearing a beautiful black silk gown. Shayla never wore anything but black.

"Please! Don't even joke about that or I'll be known as the mayor who won because she used magic. A reputation like that can stick around for a few hundred years." I said it in a joking manner—but I was serious. Either I could win an election against someone or not. The first time around, no one ran against me. A competitive election was bound to be much harder. I just wished Mad Dog wouldn't get so personal.

"Don't worry about it," Gramps said. "Mad Dog already had his time. This belongs to you, Dae. I don't think anyone is unhappy with what you've done while you've been mayor."

"What about those ladies who wanted her to put up umbrellas on the boardwalk and hand-washing stations in the park?" Shayla asked. "I don't know how happy they are right now."

Gramps changed the subject. "How did the séance go?"

"Not so good for talking to Dae's mother," Shayla said. "But we saw ghost lights. You don't see those every day."

"I'm not sure what those are," Gramps remarked. "But I'm sorry there's still no word from Jean. I believe she'd come back if she could."

"I think so too." I said it, but I didn't really believe it. She'd died angry with me. How long does that take to go away? I didn't want to argue the point with Gramps—especially tonight. It was almost time for me to give my little welcome speech.

I saw Kevin trying to get the microphone and podium set up across the room. I excused myself from Gramps and Shayla—good thing too, since Mad Dog was headed our way. I wondered if he really thought I'd wear one of his campaign buttons. He'd already given me one. I'd left it in my desk drawer in town hall. I figured fifty years from now, it would be an antique that I could sell in my shop.

Kevin looked up, eyes scanning the crowded room. I met his gaze and waved to let him know I was on my way. A loud clap of thunder managed to get everyone's attention as I moved toward him. Several thick bolts of lightning tore through the dark sky outside the large windows on the back side of the inn, overlooking the turbulent Atlantic.

The crystal chandeliers above us flickered and swung a little from side to side, the large teardrops tinkling loudly. The power stayed on—but a sense of uneasiness crept into the big room.

I managed to avoid Mad Dog and get through the crowd to reach the podium. Despite the storm's furious pounding, I knew no real warnings had gone up across the Outer Banks. Chief Ronnie Michaels of the Duck Police and Fire Chief Cailey Fargo were standing together, both in their dress uniforms. They were drinking punch and acting like nothing was wrong. This wouldn't be the case if the storm was really serious.

"I thought that last one was going to do us in," Kevin said as I reached him. "I remembered that I only have a handful of candles. The generator is ready to go out back, but somebody would have to go outside and start it."

"And in the meantime, we'd have some panic going on in here." I watched the crowd. Most of them were either from the Outer Banks or from one of the cities along the coast. They could probably handle any problem from the storm without too much fuss—not that I wanted to find out.

"Are you ready?" Kevin smiled and adjusted the microphone for me.

"I think so. Thanks."

I waited for him to step back, then addressed the group. People stopped talking and everyone looked up at me. "Before I launch into my welcome speech, I thought I should point out that our police and fire chiefs are here with us in the ballroom. You all know what that means—the weather sounds bad, but it's really nothing to worry about."

Everyone laughed and applauded. The thunder and lightning continued to pummel the outside world around us, but we were okay. I started into my often-rehearsed speech— our guests laughed and applauded at just the right spots. I could see Nancy out of the corner of my eye mimicking the words as I said them. She'd heard the speech often enough.

As I spoke, I thought about the steel gray ocean churning and spitting at the edge of the sand. Trees were blowing, pushed around by the harsh winds. Debris was flying everywhere—the town needed to issue a memo about taking in or tying down lawn furniture before a storm. It would take days of overtime for our maintenance department to pick up all the chairs, cushions and grills and find where they all belonged.

I finally finished speaking—it seemed like it took forever. Despite my words of assurance to everyone else, I still felt the storm raging outside. Maybe it didn't look so bad, but I was beginning to feel something more coming toward us.

I looked out at the faces of people I knew and those I'd never met before. They all seemed calm and relaxed, enjoying the party. Wine and food flowed freely—maybe that helped.

Or maybe I was the only one ill at ease.

I couldn't seem to shake that feeling that had come with the séance. I could only describe it as a feeling of dread. I kept smiling anyway—that was part of my job as mayor. I forced myself to relax and eat something. I chatted and sipped some excellent muscadine wine from one of the local vineyards.

I wished the reception was over and I was home in bed.

That was unusual for me. Normally, I loved these situations. But not tonight. I wanted to pull the covers up over my head and listen to the storm rumble by in the night. I lived with my grandfather in the house several generations of our family had owned and loved. I'd feel safe there—not just from the storm but from the strange uneasiness lurking at the edge of my brain. I couldn't quite put my finger on it. But I knew it wasn't just my imagination.

"Dae!"

I heard my name in a high-pitched, girlish voice and looked around to find another mayor waving to me. It was Sandi Foxx, the redheaded former TV weather girl from Manteo. She'd left the Outer Banks and gone to live in Virginia Beach, becoming a local celebrity there. Everyone knew her around here. There aren't many local channels.

She'd come back a few years ago and been elected mayor of Manteo, which was the county seat for Dare County. I liked her the few times we'd met at other local events.

"Great speech!" Sandi said when she reached me. She gave me an air kiss and her fabulous mayor's smile. She was dressed in bright red—always flamboyant. "Love this place! The Blue Whale certainly has an interesting and accomplished new owner. Is he spoken for? I think I'm about to be between men, if you know what I mean. But they never last long, do they?"

Sandi was also working on her third marriage. She was a determined woman who liked to have her way. She also enjoyed the company of younger men who frequently weren't her husband. It sounded like she might be about to break up with one of them.

"Thanks. Yeah, we love the old Blue Whale, and Kevin has done a great job with it." I didn't necessarily see her as a rival for Kevin's attention. She was only here for a couple of days. But I didn't want to talk about Kevin—it's hard for me to share my life with people I don't know well.

"How about an introduction?" she continued, smiling and nodding to people she knew. Her green eyes zeroed in on Kevin. "He's my kind of appetizer."

All right, maybe it was hard laying claim to Kevin, but

hearing her talk about him as a food made me a little more forthcoming. "As a matter of fact, Kevin and I—"

"Ladies." Kevin joined us, smiling. He slipped his arm around my waist. "I don't think I've met your friend, Dae."

Sandi sipped her wine and gave me an ironic smile. "So that's the way it is, huh? You always were kind of lucky, Dae."

I was relieved that I didn't have to explain about Kevin. He had a knack for showing up at the right time and place. "Kevin, this is Mayor Sandi Foxx of Manteo. Sandi, this is Kevin Brickman of the Blue Whale Inn."

He nodded to her. "Nice to meet you, Sandi. I hope you're enjoying the reception."

"I was." She finished her glass of wine. "Excuse me while I go look for more wine—and someone *available* to drink it with."

"She's . . . nice," Kevin said when she'd disappeared back into the crowd. "Have you known her long?"

"A few years." I related her history. "She's a good mayor. I like talking to her. She's always coming up with new ideas I can steal for Duck."

He laughed. "It's all about taking care of Duck, huh? That's the only reason you agreed to go out with me—you wanted to make sure I kept the Blue Whale open."

"It must be those FBI skills that make you so smart." I hugged him a little tighter and kissed his chin. "As much fun as you are, I have to mingle. There are ideas to steal."

He held me to him a moment longer. "Are you okay? You seem a little worried. Is it the storm?"

"I'm not worried."

"Yes, you are. Your forehead wrinkles up when you're worried. Don't try to lie to me. I have formal training spotting liars, you know."

"Really? You know, Gramps says the same thing. You two are cut from the same cloth."

"In other words, mind my own business. Okay. I can

take a hint. I'll just mingle and try to get people to have other parties here so I can stay in Duck and do what you tell me to do."

"You're so good. See you."

I actually began to relax and enjoy myself as I made the rounds of the room and reacquainted myself with the mayors and their families. The whole feeling of dread was just left over from the séance, I decided. Something about trying to call back the dead probably had that effect on most people.

Just as I was chiding myself about my imagination working overtime, I noticed Chiefs Fargo and Michaels grab for their cell phones at the same time. The devices didn't make a sound, but I knew there was a problem. I started to reassure myself again that things were all right—they'd let me know when that wasn't true anymore.

A loud rumble of thunder cracked over us, followed immediately by the power flickering and dying. Something big was thrown against the two-story window, smashing through it—gusts of rain, wind and some glass following quickly behind. Everyone in the room was soaked.

"Looks like we're catching a bigger part of that storm than we originally thought," Chief Michaels yelled, his voice booming over the shrieks of the frightened crowd and the howling from outside. "We're going to move everyone to the lobby. No need to panic. We all know storms around here. Just move quickly and no one will get hurt."

Chapter 4

Everyone did as the chief asked. We were escorted to the lobby and asked to sit on the floor. There was only one window. It was another large two-story plateglass window that faced the front entrance. But we were seated well away from it, almost tucked behind the stairs.

Kevin and the two chiefs walked around handing out towels, making sure everyone was as comfortable as they could be, reminding us to put our heads down and protect them with our arms.

It was an unusual way to wait out a storm—even for someone who'd been through many of them. All the men and women were in their formal attire, stretched out across the floor. Most were calm about it, trying their cell phones and PDAs to see if they had service. Kevin handed out a few toys to frightened children in the crowd. Some people prayed and urged others to pray with them.

We were probably one of the best-dressed, least panicked groups across the island. Too bad there was no award in that category. Nearly every adult had attended emergency protocol briefings at one time or another and knew what was expected from them. We'd all worked to keep large groups of residents calm through problem situations. It was part of our jobs as mayors.

Voices were subdued as the wind moaned and clawed at the inn. I could hear objects hitting the walls and roof as trees and other debris were tossed around like the toys Kevin had given out. I saw him wince as we heard more glass breaking upstairs.

This storm would probably be costly for residents because we hadn't realized its severity. The weather service wasn't a fortune-teller. Storms didn't always follow the tracks laid out for them. Their unpredictability left people in their paths powerless in the face of fury.

Maybe this was what I'd been feeling. Not just another storm but something worse. I prayed no one would be hurt. We could repair roofs and windows. It was terrible to lose people.

"This was a surprise." Kevin finally came and sat down close to me. "Guess you can't always trust the weather service to predict which way a storm will go."

"You're better off trusting your bunion, if you have one." Mayor Barker Whiteside from Corolla laughed. "Wonder if anyone saw one of the warnings?"

"Warnings?" Kevin asked.

"Spirits that walk the beaches before a bad storm." Gramps was sitting next to me on the other side. "Some of them are specific—they only walk if the storm brings death. Some walk for any major storm."

"Portents of trouble," Barker explained. "We have several around here. Of course, we have the horses. They always seem to know."

"They're better than the weather service any day," Mayor David Manning of Elizabeth City added. "Not much good, though, if you're not out there with them. But they know what's happening."

"If we had a direct line to Tom Watts's place, he'd be able to tell us. He lives out there in an old trailer so he can be near the horses. He knows everything about them," Mayor Whiteside said.

"We're always making fun of the newbies who board up at the first sign of a storm." Gramps chuckled. "Maybe they have the right of it. Living here for a long time might make you careless."

"If my new bay window blows out at home, I'll amen to that, Horace!" David agreed.

I studied the window in the front of the lobby as they spoke. It was at least twenty feet high and a dozen feet wide. It had been there since I was a kid. We used to sneak down and hang out at the old Blue Whale, never guessing it would be occupied again someday. The window faced away from the ocean, so it was probably a little more sheltered from damage. But there was no way to know. It would be expensive to replace. I hoped Kevin had good storm insurance.

Of course, with a group like this, it was a good chance to talk about all the terrible storms we'd lived through. There were tall tales of hurricanes that had lasted weeks, tidal waves three hundred feet high, hail as big as soccer balls and lightning that went on for days.

Flooding was always a problem here because we were caught between several large bodies of water that rose up regularly around us. The whole hundred-mile-long series of islands was well below sea level. We lost coastline every year. We added sand, put in plants to hold it, but it was a constant struggle. It had always been this way for residents of Duck. I didn't see any way it would change in the future either.

"Storm's passing," someone said from across the packed room. "It's getting lighter."

"Or it's the eye," an assistant supervisor from Kitty Hawk said.

"That's no hurricane out there, folks," Chief Michaels

told everyone. "We just got some feeder bands from Hurricane Kelly. The weather service says it's moving away from the North Carolina coast. We'll hole up here a little while longer, then take a peek outside."

Everyone tried their cell phones again, but there was still no service. That was one of the first things we always lost out here—one reason the ham radio club was so popular. They always communicated the latest updates to Chief Michaels and other emergency workers.

I hoped everyone was safe and that property damage was minimal. It was all I could do. The Blue Whale was still standing around us. We were blessed to be here.

The crowd was starting to get restless—the chief said he didn't feel comfortable letting anyone go to the next room and use the bathrooms. Most of the kids had been complaining about it for a while. When we finally got the all-clear notice, a large group ran for the facilities. I hoped the water was still working. There had been times after a storm when it wasn't.

"Well, that wasn't so bad," Kevin said as he helped me off the floor. "We seem to be in good shape."

Anyone who didn't go to the bathroom headed out the front door, including me, Kevin and Gramps. Outside, the bright moonlight made the devastation more apparent. There was a car in what was left of Kevin's mermaid fountain in front of the inn. Several picnic tables were in the driveway—undamaged—as if someone were about to eat lunch at them.

Trees, bushes and plants were tossed across the landscape. There was a tree on top of the roof. I realized as I looked up that all the windows were gone from the top floor on this side of the inn.

"I was a little quick to judge," Kevin commented.

Gramps patted him on the shoulder. "Don't feel too bad. It's easy to misjudge. I've done it before. You get used to it."

Kevin left us to make his way behind the inn so he could

turn on the generator. People walked around outside, looking dazed and continuing to try and reach family and friends with their cell phones. A few guests started for their cars. Chief Michaels stopped them—the roads out of Duck were blocked by debris.

"Everyone calm down." His loud voice got attention. "We're safe here for now. There's plenty to eat and drink and the bathrooms are working. Let's give the cleanup crews a chance to get started. No reason to make matters worse."

Despite close acquaintance with past storms, most people grumbled and complained that they weren't happy about being trapped here, even though they would have been here for the conference anyway. People seemed to be that way about most things.

I got Nancy, Barbara and Althea together. We ushered everyone back into the hotel, promising food and drinks to ease the pain.

Emergency calls for workers were going out across the island. Kevin had been called—along with Gramps—to join the volunteer firefighters who would act as the cleanup crew for Duck. Marissa, still trying to dry her long blond hair, promised to look after the guests and the Blue Whale while he was gone. I promised to help her.

While Marissa tried to get everyone settled down, I went to the ballroom to lock the door so none of the children could wander in and get cut on the broken glass from the shattered window.

The room was a wreck—but the emergency lighting was working. Once the window had broken, torrents of rain had flooded the beautiful wood floor. All kinds of debris had followed, including some confused seagulls that were flapping their wet wings and trying to fly.

I grabbed some towels from the kitchen and managed to get the birds back outside before they caused too much damage. It was still going to be a mess to clean up. I didn't want to think what that big window would cost to replace.

As I was sloshing through the water to reach the door (in my good shoes—there was glass on the floor, so I couldn't go barefoot), something caught my attention. It glittered in the water with the sand and tree limbs, like pirate treasure. I stooped down—it was a diamond and ruby ring. Fear flooded through me.

She'd meant to have the ring sized—it had always been too big. When the rain broke into the ballroom, it had slipped from her finger. She walked through the water looking for it, finally finding it. She dropped it when she saw the gun pointed at her.

"Dae? Are you all right?" Nancy shook me and broke the emotional tie that bound me to the ring. "What are you doing in here? You could get hurt on all this glass."

I took a deep breath and released the feelings from the ring. Kevin had taught me that. After all the years I'd had a gift of finding things, I didn't think there was anything else to learn. I was wrong.

"I know," I answered her, putting the ring on my thumb—it was still too big even for that digit. "I was trying to close off the room so no one would get hurt. But there were birds in here. I didn't want Kevin to have to clean that up too."

"Well, you've done your good deed for the day." She smiled and hugged me. "Let's get out of here. Thank goodness the kitchen is still in one piece and there are leftovers that don't need to be cooked. Something about living through storms makes everyone hungry. I'm thinking a buffet in the lobby. What do you think?"

It was hard for me to think about anything after touching the ring. It seemed to me like I should look for its owner—she was in trouble.

But there was so much to do to take care of almost a hundred people—I couldn't just abandon Nancy, Marissa and the other two women I'd asked to be here.

While I put out cups and plates, and located forks and knives for the buffet, I hoped that what I'd felt wasn't as bad as it had seemed.

Sometimes my gift exaggerated things—made the emotions or events tied to them seem bigger or more important than they were. Sometimes the things I saw were unclear. They made sense only later, after I'd found out what had really happened. But deciphering my visions that way was confusing.

The fear I'd felt from the ring still made me shiver. The images chased around in my head as I smiled and asked people if they wanted a wheat or white roll. I believed someone might need help—but where or how, or even when, was hard to say.

That thought made me begin watching the faces as they went by the serving table heaping food on plates and filling cups with tea or coffee. Was anyone missing?

There were too many people. I tried to get a head count, but everyone was wandering around, sitting in spots on the stairs and in the lobby eating their food. How could I find out if anyone was missing without drawing too much attention to the fact?

I finally came up with an idea and got some paper and a clipboard from behind the check-in desk. I asked everyone to write down their names and home contact numbers.

"We might need to contact you later for insurance purposes," I explained in what I hoped was a rational way. I didn't want to cause a panic.

Apparently my request made sense—or people just didn't want to argue about it. They scribbled their names and numbers on the paper. I kept looking around, trying to see if I could spot anyone who should've been there and wasn't.

"What's up?" Marissa asked when I got to her.

I didn't tell her about the ring I'd found in the ballroom. She was new to Duck—it would require too much explanation. "I'm worried someone might have wandered off. Just trying to keep up with everyone."

"Great! And we just got them calmed down with food." She sighed. "Well, let me give you a hand. It will look more natural if we both do it."

I had about fifty people on my list. Marissa was getting the names of the people in the lobby. I walked across the foyer toward the bar and looked back.

A shaft of moonlight came through the undamaged picture window and fell across the carpeted floor in the lobby, creating a haze of dust motes spinning through the air. The motes seemed to move together—as though creating an image.

I couldn't make out what it was, and an instant later it was gone. I shook my head to clear it and went on to the bar. Maybe the storm had done something to me. I kept thinking that someone was watching me—even in the deserted ballroom. Maybe all those storm ions were fooling around with my normal energy.

I talked with the fifteen people eating in the bar area, got their names and numbers. Everyone asked when they could leave. I didn't have an answer for them.

One of the younger men—I recognized him but couldn't recall his name—was insistent about it. He put his information on the paper and demanded to know when he could leave. I gave him my stock answer. He got more upset than the rest of the guests.

"It's stupid to keep us here," he said. "We can find our own ways home. We're not prisoners."

I started to answer and dropped the clipboard. He handed it back to me when he caught it. Our hands held for a moment. I felt that same strange sensation I experienced whenever I looked into someone's mind to help them find something they'd lost.

And I realized this man and I had something in common—we'd lost the same person—Sandi Foxx.

Chapter 5

"Someone's missing from the group," I told him, hoping the blunt admission would make him forthcoming with his information.

He was probably in his twenties, with a dark, full head of hair and a ruddy complexion. His brown eyes shifted away from mine, and his hands moved restlessly in and out of his pockets. "I don't know what you mean. Who's missing?"

"I think you know." I studied his face. "You came here with Sandi Foxx, didn't you? Where is she?"

"I don't know. We got separated when they moved everybody in here."

"You work with her?"

"Yeah. I'm her personal assistant."

I didn't have to be psychic to hear some guilt in his voice and the emphasis on "personal." He was probably *too* personal with Sandi—maybe the man she was talking about breaking up with.

"Is this her ring?" I asked him, showing him the ruby.

"Yes. Where did you find it?"

"Probably where she lost it." I didn't know what else to say to him. Obviously he was hiding something. Was it more than the two of them sneaking away together for this conference?

She was lost, at least in his mind. My gift for finding missing things worked only when the lost item was in the forefront of the "seeker's" thoughts. I had to have physical contact with that person to get an image from them.

I looked at his name on the list. "Matthew Wright. You came with Sandi but now you can't find her. Is that right?"

"That's right. I thought she'd be in here with the rest of us, but I haven't seen her. I tried to go back in the ballroom, but the doors were locked. I don't know where she is."

"She's not in the ballroom. All I found there was her ring." I looked up the stairs—no elevator without electricity. The generator produced only enough power for the lights and refrigeration. I realized we might have to search the inn for Sandi.

I wasn't as concerned with upsetting people now that it appeared my instincts about someone being in trouble were right. I didn't know if I should trust Matthew—but I wasn't in a position to restrain him in any way.

I decided I'd keep him close at hand in case it became apparent that he'd hurt Sandi in some way. I hoped my vision about her looking up and seeing a gun was not part of why she was missing. But if something had happened to her, Matthew was an obvious suspect.

"Excuse me!" I raised my voice in each room where parts of the group were gathered. "I'm looking for Sandi Foxx—mayor of Manteo. Has anyone seen her?"

People looked around like they always do, as though the person in question might be standing right next to them and they hadn't noticed. Heads shook and stories were offered of when they'd seen her last. Everyone agreed that they hadn't seen her since we'd left the ballroom during the storm.

Matthew stood at my side and shifted the expensive watch on his wrist, wiggled his feet, bit his lip and cracked his knuckles. He seemed guilty of something. The more people talked about her, the more nervous he got. He was a wreck.

Once we'd all agreed that no one had seen her, I enlisted the aid of several people I knew I could trust. Marissa got the master keys for the rooms after I assured her that Kevin wouldn't fire her for helping me. She helped me lay out a room-by-room map of where everyone was staying.

"This is Sandi's room," she said. "It's on the third floor."

"What about his room?" I pointed to Matthew.

"He's staying down the hall from her."

It seemed likely to me that Sandi somehow got away from the group to look for her ring when the rest of us left the ballroom. When I presented that theory to Matthew, he broke down. "We went upstairs for a while. She thought it was funny being up there—doing it—you know? While everyone else was downstairs scared of the storm."

"Wasn't she scared of the storm?" I asked him. "Weren't *you* scared?"

"I was terrified." He glanced away, clearly scared now. "I didn't want to go up there, but she insisted."

And of course, he didn't mind helping her out. He didn't have to explain any more than that. She probably just didn't come right back down after they were finished—and when she did come down, she went to find her ring.

I scrutinized Matthew with his wild hair and narrow face—what did Sandi see in him worth losing her job and her family? He was young, that was true. Maybe in his early to late twenties. Sandi was in her early forties. Maybe that was his charm.

He was lucky Sandi's husband—a very large ex-marine

from Charleston—wasn't here to help look for her. I didn't want to know how nervous Matthew would be in that case.

Nancy, Marissa and I walked up the dark stairs to the third floor—Matthew closely in tow where I could keep an eye on him. There were only small emergency lights to guide the way. We were kind of bunched together as we felt our way down the long hall.

I glanced out of the window on the third-floor landing. The dark, angry sea was detailed by moonlight as it slapped at the shore. Despite the bright moonlight, I wished it was morning. I wished someone besides me was leading this effort to look for Sandi too. But I was stuck with the night and the responsibility, at least for a while.

Matthew led us to Sandi's room, but there was no answer when I knocked. Marissa unlocked the door—which said something to me about Sandi and Matthew's relationship. He didn't have a key.

Impatiently, I pushed into the large room, but there was no sign of Sandi. The bed was tumbled, pillows and blankets everywhere. Matthew hung his head when I looked at him. Marissa took a step back from him as though she was afraid of being too near.

Clothes were strewn around as though the storm had swept through the room. Sandi's pocketbook with her driver's license, credit cards and pictures of her family was still on her bedside table. She couldn't be far away.

"Could she be in *your* room?" Nancy asked Matthew in a none-too-delicate tone.

"I suppose so," he said. "She was in here when I left to go downstairs. I don't know why she'd be in my room. It's really small. She forgot to book it for me until right at the last minute."

"Let's take a look," I suggested. "Maybe she wanted to surprise you."

"Believe me—this trip has been one *big* surprise," he

commented in a bitter voice as he led the way down the hall. He opened the door as we got there. The room was empty.

"You weren't kidding about this being small," Nancy said. "I don't know if I could fit on that bed."

"It's meant for a child," Marissa explained. "It's all we had left. I'm sorry. Mayor Foxx said it would be fine."

"She would," Matthew said. He glared at Marissa.

I could imagine Sandi hadn't planned for him to spend much time here. I looked around the room anyway. It was as neat as Sandi's was messy.

"She isn't here," he said in an obvious way. "I don't know where she is."

"But you seem to be the last person who saw her." I didn't add *"alive,"* but I tried to sound as intimidating as Chief Michaels would have in this situation. As I finished surveying the room, I noticed something on top of the tiny dresser—the other part of the broken key chain.

I felt the anger and frustration again—stronger this time—when I picked it up. But while the key belonged to Matthew, the energy left in the key chain was from Sandi. She'd thrown the key ring at him and the dolphin fob had shattered against the hitching post.

"I don't see what that has to do with anything," he said, twisting his watch.

"You were breaking up with her, weren't you?" It was just a guess, but an educated one. Why else would Sandi be that angry and frustrated with him?

I could see from the look on his face that I was right. I put the key chain in my pocket. I might need it later.

"She was so demanding," he said. "You just don't know what it was like. I told her I'd do this conference with her but I was leaving when we got back. She thought coming here together would make some big difference."

"Demanding?" I asked. "What do you mean?"

"She wanted to get married, okay?" He shook his head,

his dark hair flopping around on his forehead. "I told her I wasn't ready. She promised to help me get a good job with the government. Instead, I ended up being her lover and errand boy."

"She was going to leave her kids and that gorgeous hunk of husband for *you*?" Nancy asked exactly what I was thinking.

"That's what she told me," he answered. "I don't know why. I didn't encourage her. I never thought it was that serious. I have plans of my own."

I could hear Gramps saying this was motive. But I held that back—we didn't know yet where Sandi was or if anything had really happened to her.

"So Sandi was up here and you came downstairs." I tried to get back to finding our missing mayor.

"She said she wanted to clean up first, you know?" He shrugged. "I thought she came down after me and I just didn't see her. There were a lot of people down there. She said something about looking for the ring she lost. She might still be looking for it."

"All right." I tried to decide what to do next. "I think we should go back downstairs for a minute. Matthew, you're going to stay down there with a few of my friends. Don't get any cute ideas about trying to leave."

"I can't anyway," he snarled. "She lost my car key."

"That must be the one you turned in, Dae," Marissa added in an excited voice.

Thanks for the help, I thought, but said, "We'll deal with that later."

"Never mind all that," Nancy said, grabbing Matthew's arm in what appeared to be a painful grip. "I'll take the little boy toy downstairs and let some of the guys keep an eye on him. He's not going anywhere until we find Mayor Foxx. You guys start searching the rooms up here. That must be the plan, right?"

I almost said, *Yes, ma'am*, but I didn't want to undermine her authority. Besides, Nancy could be pretty tough when she chose to be. "That works. Thanks."

"Look, I didn't do anything wrong." Matthew defended himself. "She wanted me. She just wanted me too much. She threatened not to give me a good job reference if I tried to leave. I was angry. We settled it later. You can ask her when we find her. Then I'm going to sue the whole town of Duck for false accusations."

"No one is accusing you of anything—yet." I dismissed him and turned to Marissa. "I guess we'll have to go room by room. There doesn't seem to be enough damage from the storm that she could be hurt somewhere up here. But she might've had a little too much to drink."

"Maybe we should call the police, Dae," Marissa said, her gaze fixed on Matthew. "They'll know what to do."

"I don't want to call them away from this emergency to find Sandi," I replied. "There are only thirty rooms in the inn. We can look through them, and if we don't see her, then we'll call someone. Okay?"

"The mayor can take over for the chief if necessary, you know. It's in the town charter," Nancy said. "I'll take him downstairs and come back up to help."

After Nancy went downstairs with Matthew, Marissa and I began to work our way down the third-floor hall. She opened every door while I came behind her and checked under every bed, in every bathroom, closet, and any other place an adult woman could fall asleep.

There was no sign of Sandi. I began feeling some tension in my neck and shoulders that had nothing to do with looking under beds. What if something really bad had happened to her? I hoped I was doing the right thing not calling the police.

We moved to the second floor and did the same thing. Sandi wasn't in any of those rooms either. But we did find a few more wayward gulls who'd taken refuge from the storm. They'd flown in through the broken windows and weren't in any hurry to leave. We used towels and bedclothes to try and scare them back outside. They squawked at us—finally giving up and vanishing into the night.

I stood by the window (at least where the window used to be) and watched the last one fly away. The moon was bright in the clear black sky. I hoped all of this would be over by morning. Cleaning up after a storm I could deal with—trying to make what could be life-and-death decisions about another human being was another story.

"Kevin's gonna have a mess to clean up," Marissa observed, waiting for me at the end of the second-story hall. "There's a hole in the ceiling."

I looked up where she pointed and saw the spot, about the size of a hatbox, right above our heads. "How did we miss that when we were upstairs?"

"I don't know," Nancy said as she joined us. "Maybe we missed Mayor Foxx too. We're not professional rescue workers."

"What now?" Marissa asked.

"I guess we search the rooms on the ground floor." I was really beginning to worry. I didn't want to call the chief in from storm detail—no telling what all had happened out there that needed his attention. And truthfully, the police wouldn't even look for Sandi yet if she was reported missing.

On the other hand, what Matthew had said and the way he was acting were very suspicious. He might not have done anything, but his attitude made me feel less than charitable toward him. What if I waited and something worse happened?

Chapter 6

The problem was solved for me when Duck Police Officer Scott Randall greeted us at the bottom of the stairs. He'd been injured the week before, and his broken arm was keeping him from being much help on the roads picking up trash from the storm. He'd been assigned to checking on Duck citizens.

I'd never been so glad to see someone I was barely acquainted with!

"The chief said I should head over here and make sure everything is okay," he said in his quiet, almost shy way.

I liked Scott. He wasn't from Duck, but, like Kevin, he'd settled in so completely, it felt like he'd been here forever. I wanted to hug him at that moment but didn't want him to take it the wrong way. He was a very serious, reserved young man.

"Thanks for coming." I drew him into the kitchen and shooed some children out who were raiding the refrigerator. "How are things out there?"

He shook his head. "About the worst I've seen. The roads are impassable—all kinds of debris covering them. A few houses lost their roofs, a few more are flooded. There's not much electricity anywhere on the island. To make matters worse, the bridges are closed."

That sounded worse than I'd anticipated. "What happened to the bridges? They should've been able to withstand some feeder bands."

"Yes, ma'am. I understand the high winds impacted the bridges. Department of Transportation wants to make sure they're safe—once they can get down here. They said to expect them to be closed for the next twenty-four to forty-eight hours."

That was a worry in itself. No bridges meant no supplies for stores. With no power, food in freezers and refrigerators would go bad pretty quickly. That could also mean water shortages if the pumps weren't working.

The only good thing was that it was October and the thousands of visitors who'd been here over the summer were now safely back in their own homes.

"Was there something you wanted me to do here?" Scott asked. "If not, I'm heading back out to do what I can."

I could tell from the sound of his voice that he wanted to be back out on the streets. But we had our own crisis here—I explained everything that had happened—at least what we knew for sure. Gramps always taught me to repeat the facts and not the fears, as he called it. I kept myself from jumping to conclusions and waited to see what Scott had to say when I was finished.

He finally nodded. "You've done the right thing, Mayor. I'll take over from here. Where did you say the man is who was with Mayor Foxx?"

We found Matthew being detained by Mayors Barker Whiteside and David Manning. They'd taken the liberty of raiding Kevin's bar and were halfway through a bottle of his best scotch.

When Scott questioned Matthew again, the young man repeated everything he'd told us upstairs. But this time he was a little less antagonistic. Maybe the police uniform made a difference—or maybe he was beginning to understand that this was serious.

After hearing what Matthew had to say, Scott thanked the two mayors for keeping track of him and asked them if they would continue to do so. Barker and David were happy to continue sitting there with Matthew between them.

"So the only places you haven't searched for Mayor Foxx are down here on the first floor, is that correct, Mayor O'Donnell?"

"That's right," I said without my customary admonishment to have him call me Dae. This wasn't the time or the place. "I found Sandi's ring in the ballroom. Shall we start there?"

I left Nancy with the others, but Marissa came with us. We searched all the closets, cupboards and pantries, even the walk-in freezers. We checked in the laundry room and in Kevin's downstairs suite. But there was no sign of Sandi.

"She could've just left on her own," Marissa said. "That man she came with made it plain he didn't want to be with her. Maybe when they were done upstairs, she just left."

"What time do you think that would've been, Miss Endy?" Scott asked her.

Marissa shrugged her shoulders and looked at me. "I don't know. I think they took us out of the ballroom about nine thirty. I'm not sure how long we were in the lobby."

"The first time I looked at the clock, it was around midnight." I tried to help fill in the gaps.

"If Mayor Foxx went upstairs with Mr. Wright at nine thirty or around there, then came downstairs an hour or so later, the storm was pretty fierce right then. It didn't really let up until about two A.M." He looked at both of us to verify that.

"I don't know," I admitted. "I lost track of everything while we were all sitting around."

"So we really don't know," Marissa said again. "She could be back home for all we know. Maybe we should give it a rest until we can contact someone in Manteo."

"That's a good idea," Scott said. "I have a friend with a ham radio. He should be able to get through to the police in Manteo. They could check on Mayor Foxx and find out if she made it back okay."

"There's only one problem with that theory," I said. "Sandi came in Matthew's car. I can't imagine her hot wiring a car or hitchhiking to get home."

"I've hitched rides before when I was desperate to get home," Marissa said. "Mayor Foxx might've been desperate after that confrontation with her boyfriend. If she put her whole heart on the line for him and he rejected her, she would've walked home if she had to."

I couldn't argue that logic. No matter what I felt from the ruby ring, there was no way to know what happened until we found Sandi.

Chapter 7

Of course, that meant waiting around to hear something after Scott left to ask his friend to call Manteo. I knew it could take hours—if we were lucky enough to get through to someone. And this wouldn't be as much of a priority for the ham radio operators trying to help coordinate medical efforts for people who were injured.

The mayors and their families and associates were bored and restless. They wanted to know what was going on outside the inn. They wanted to talk to their families and find out if their houses were still standing.

I didn't blame them. I wanted to know about my house too. And no matter how much debris was in the roads, I could've walked home easily. But someone had to keep everything together, and this was my town. I wanted everyone stranded here to remember that even though this experience had been bad, the people of Duck handled the situation in a calm, efficient manner.

The first thing I did was create a cleanup brigade for the

areas where people were eating and sitting around waiting for news. I got another group into the kitchen to wash
some dishes and get ready for a breakfast of some kind in
the next few hours. It was almost four thirty A.M. I knew the
late-night snack everyone had shared would be wearing off
soon.

I made a list of all the possible breakfast foods Kevin
had on hand. I couldn't believe how much food he had
stored. With these provisions, he could probably feed everyone at the hotel for at least the next few days. Of course, the
town would have to help him financially. It would be the
least we could do for eating all of his food.

I had games arranged for the older children who were
still awake. There was always something on hand for
Kevin's guests. It wasn't too long before there was a large,
noisy game of Monopoly going on around the big table in
the lobby. Adults picked up some cards, and a few played
checkers.

I knew everyone was waiting for daylight—like I was.
We all wanted a chance to really see the damage, and hopefully the power would be restored by then. We were all
anxious to hear the news about our homes and the towns
around us. Television, radio and the Internet were still silent when we needed them the most. Civilization could be
stripped away very quickly.

I remembered my good friend, Max Caudle, who knew
everything about Duck history. He always said it was a
miracle that anyone decided to stay here long enough to
build homes and lives. Even things that seemed stable could
be swept away by the sea and the wind. Yet, here we were—
descendants of those people who lived here four hundred
years ago.

It was cheating, I know, but I changed back into my shirt
and jeans. Everyone else was stuck in their slightly damp
evening wear, since Scott said they shouldn't go back upstairs. My clothes were dry, and I was planning on doing

some heavy cooking shortly. It seemed like I deserved this little accommodation.

My new dress was bedraggled and had a few pulled places along the hem where I'd walked through the water in the ballroom. There was also every possibility that the white stain on one side was bird poop. The birds I'd shooed out the windows had apparently gotten their revenge. I put the dress in a plastic bag and planned to visit the dry cleaners when they opened up again—whenever that was.

I took off my wet shoes—they were ruined, no help there. The shoes I'd worn over from Shayla's were soaking too. The tennis shoes I'd left here last week when I was helping Kevin move some furniture were dry. They felt good on my cold feet.

The bridal suite was untouched by any of the events of the long night. How quickly things could change! When I'd left here last night, I was worried about my speech. Now I was worried about feeding an army and finding out if the people I cared about were all right.

Something caught my eye as I glanced up after transferring the key chain to the pocket of my jeans. It seemed to be a mote of light, but from where? The only light source was my flashlight (no emergency lighting here), and it was pointed in the opposite direction.

I watched the light drift across the room—like the spirit balls, but much smaller. This was only a pinpoint, like a twinkle from a diamond ring in the sun.

The light turned and began to come toward me. I swallowed hard and glanced away—

If I looked back maybe it would be gone.

No such luck.

I couldn't move, couldn't think, swallow or breathe for a moment as I watched it come closer. My gaze was glued to it—I fought to do something. I didn't know if I wanted to be there when it finally reached me.

Then I did something I never thought I'd do in these circumstances—circumstances I'd waited my whole life for—I ran out of the room and slammed the door behind me.

I forgot the flashlight. I didn't care. I didn't stop running until I reached the kitchen where everyone was busy working.

"Is everything okay, Dae?" Marissa asked, her hands full of clean dishes.

"Fine," I answered quickly. "Everything is fine."

I couldn't believe that I had gotten cold feet. Since my mother died, seeing ghosts had become almost an obsession for me. Or I guess seeing *her* ghost had anyway. I didn't know if I wanted to see every ghost on the island. But I realized one might come with the other.

It had been a long night. I made excuses for my cowardice as I took out several pans to start making breakfast. I was exhausted and stressed about finding Sandi. If I'd been my normal self, I would've waited to see what that light brought to me. I hadn't run out of the room when Shayla and I saw the spirit balls after the séance.

Of course, I hadn't been alone in a dark room either. That probably made a difference.

I put butter in two frying pans and began cracking eggs into a bowl. Scrambled eggs and toast would have to do for the crowd I'd be feeding. I could also start some grits and oatmeal in case we needed more than that or someone was allergic to eggs.

I put on some coffee and took all the juice out of the refrigerator. After this meal, there wouldn't be much fresh food left, but there was plenty of canned and frozen food to fall back on. I couldn't even begin to guess when we'd be able to leave the inn.

"We're done with the dishes," Marissa said, wiping her hands on a towel. "I wish there were paper plates to use for breakfast. I've always hated washing dishes. Do you need some help over here?"

"Maybe you could look around and find a breadlike substance for toast." I stirred oatmeal into boiling water. "I'm sorry I got you into this. I really appreciate your help."

"It's starting to get light outside." She glanced out of the window at the back of the kitchen. "I'd really like to call my grandfather and make sure he's okay. He's not good at remembering to take his meds. I know everyone would like to go home so we can see what's going on."

"I know what you mean. But I think we should stay put until we get the all-clear. Officer Randall said it's bad out there."

"I know." She sighed. "But how bad? I know I haven't lived here all of my life, but I can take it. I can walk around a car in the road."

"You know it's not just debris. There are power lines on the ground, ruptured mains of one kind or another. Dangerous stuff. That's why they try to keep people off the streets after a big storm."

"I know." She absently stirred the grits that was beginning to bubble in the pot. "I know."

When the meal was finally put together—buffet style, like earlier—everyone hurried to eat. Watery sunlight was calling us all outside, and no one would be happy staying in playing games now.

Many of the men wanted to volunteer their assistance in the cleanup. The women too, for that matter, although most of them were more concerned with what had happened to their families and homes. After that, they'd be ready to help out the town. I couldn't blame them and I knew I couldn't stop them.

Everyone wolfed down their eggs and grits. Once the food was gone, the front doors were thrown open and everyone rushed outside into the cool morning air.

It was like walking out into a massive, open-air flea market where anything and everything was available—except you might have to climb up a tree for your kitchen table or get some help flipping your car upright. I was certain all of this couldn't have come from Duck. Surely some of the items had blown here from Corolla, Southern Shores and Kill Devil Hills.

Once everyone got over the first glimpse of what the storm had done, anyone who had a car at the inn rushed to see if it was drivable. I cautioned them that they couldn't drive down the streets. I wasn't surprised that no one listened.

I found my little golf cart. It was about two hundred yards away from the hitching post where I'd left it. There was a recliner in it that pretty much made it worthless, since there was no way to reach the controls.

For once, I abdicated my position as mayor. I couldn't force all those mayors and their families to stay—I wouldn't want to anyway. I heard some of their cars starting and knew they would take their chances on the roads, trying to get back home. I'd probably walk home once I got the inn straightened up. It was human nature to want to protect our own.

I heard a whining sound coming from the back of the inn. Worried about the generator giving out or running out of gas, I walked around the structure, picking my way through clothes, furniture and other storm-tossed rubble.

I'd spent enough time here that I knew there were two sheds in the back. One of them, obviously the one left standing, was the shed that housed the generator.

I checked the generator—it was fine. Probably just not used to running for so long. There was plenty of gas in it. Kevin's freezers were good for a while longer. Maybe he wouldn't lose everything.

The other shed was just a place to store tools. Kevin kept his lawnmower and other outside maintenance equipment there. The storm had flattened it—boards and shingles sticking up everywhere.

I was about to go back inside and begin the cleanup when I saw something protruding from one side of the demolished shed. I walked a little closer, At first, I wasn't sure what it was on the soggy ground near the collapsed building. But as I looked down at it, I realized there was still a foot in that pink shoe and it was attached to a leg. I dropped down on the saturated ground, trying to catch my breath.

It seemed I'd finally found Sandi.

Chapter 8

I couldn't bring myself to move. I finally thought—
she might still be alive. There was that time a few years
back when Mr. Fitzroy was trapped under his house after a
storm. He was ninety years old, but he'd survived.

I knew it was a long shot with the whole shed blown
down on top of her, but I couldn't ignore the chance that I
could save Sandi.

"Dae?" Nancy called from the kitchen door. "What are
you doing out here?"

"I found Sandi," I called back as I began throwing the
boards that covered her. "Help me, Nancy! She might still
be alive!"

"Don't be daft!" I heard someone say in a very un-
Nancy-like voice.

I looked around, but no one else was near. Nancy was
still trying to make her way past all the wood and other
items that had blown here to the shed where I was working.
It must have been the crashing waves hitting the sand as the

water churned and spit only a few hundred yards away. Or the raucous call of the gulls above me.

"The lass be long past your earthly ministrations," the voice continued. *"Best not bother."*

Okay. This was too weird. But then the entire night had been one long weird fest. "Who's there?" I demanded. "You'd better get back inside with your parents instead of out here playing this stupid game!" I decided it had to be one of the kids staying at the hotel. No adult would be so callous.

"Is she alive?" Nancy asked when she finally reached me.

"I don't know," I answered. "Did you see anyone else when you came out here?"

"I think everyone else left the inn. I guess they'll come back for their stuff once they think about it. There might be a few left lingering at the bar. They'll be lucky if they can walk out here on their own after they've been drinking all night."

"Did you *hear* anything?" I asked as we moved the lumber away from Sandi.

"The ocean," she replied. "Dae, we have to call someone."

"I know. Any ideas? There are no phones—no radios."

Officer Randall was obviously born with perfect timing. He came around the side of the Blue Whale and picked up speed when he saw us by the remains of the shed. "I'm calling EMS," he said after we'd explained to him about Sandi. "I hope they can send someone right away. Things are really backed up."

With Scott's help, we were able to reach Sandi in no time. I knew when I saw her blue-tinged face and white lips that there was no help that could reach her. Scott checked for a pulse, then shook his head.

"I'm sorry, Mayor O'Donnell. I managed to get in touch with her husband in Manteo. He's on his way up here anyway."

"I hate these storms that come up so fast," Nancy said,

her hands shaking. "Why can't they give us better warning? You'd think after all these years there'd be a better way."

I looked at the generator shed only a few feet from the collapsed shed that had killed Sandi. It was in good shape, not even a board missing. It was amazing how the fury of the storm could pick and choose what it was going to take.

Kevin had heard the call as well and got back to the hotel a little after EMS workers officially declared Sandi dead. They were putting her body on a stretcher as he ran back to where we were standing. "Can you tell what happened?" he asked the paramedics.

"The storm must've collapsed the shed," one EMT said. "There's a lot of tissue damage from the boards and nails. We'll have to wait for word from the medical examiner. But that's the way I see it."

"What was she doing?" He looked at me and Scott. "Did anyone know she was out here?"

Scott shrugged. "I don't know. I got here after Mayor O'Donnell realized she was missing."

I quickly explained the night's events to Kevin, but I had to agree that Sandi being out here in the shed didn't make any sense—unless my vision of the gun meant someone had forced her out here so the gunshot wouldn't be heard.

After the EMS team had left and Scott was busy typing his report into the computer in the police car, I took Kevin aside and told him about the items I'd found at the inn.

He listened calmly, as he usually did. "So you think this man who was working with her did this?"

"I don't know. I don't see him out here collapsing a shed on top of her. But I did see a gun."

"Has anyone searched him for a gun?"

"We searched his room. At that time, I wasn't even sure that what I'd seen in my vision was something that had happened recently. I didn't want to say anything to Scott about it."

"Matthew could've killed her and put her body in the

shed. The storm might have done the rest of the work for him. It was dark when we were in the lobby. He could've moved her and no one would've known."

We were still standing outside the inn, looking at the angry gray ocean as it tried to settle down after the storm. The generator hummed in the shed that was still standing. I thought about the strange voice I'd heard while I was trying to uncover Sandi's body. I decided not to mention it. It was kind of crazy anyway and nothing to do with what had happened.

"It was so dark out here when I came out to turn on the generator," Kevin said. "I never even noticed the garden shed was down."

"I guess the ME should be able to tell what happened if they do an autopsy, right?" I asked him.

"Yes. Scott said her husband is on his way here. Do you want to tell him what you know about what happened?"

"But not about her affair with her assistant, right? Because I'm not telling Sandi's husband that his dead wife was cheating on him—even though he probably knows already."

"I only asked because you know them. And maybe that would motivate him to demand an autopsy. With everything that happened last night, it would be easy to overlook evidence. I'm sure the medical examiner's office will have their hands full anyway."

I really didn't want to be the one to tell a grieving husband that his wife was dead, possibly murdered by her lover. I wished someone else could get that job. But Kevin was right. Gramps always said bad news was best gotten from friends instead of law enforcement.

Kevin and I went inside to take a look at the damage the storm had done to the inn. Scott's police car was gone from the front, but Barker and David were still holding on to Matthew. The two mayors weren't so drunk that they didn't hurriedly hide the scotch bottles they'd emptied during the night when they saw Kevin.

"I'm surprised you're still here," I said to them. "Weren't you worried about your homes and families?"

Both the older men shrugged. "Not so much," David said. "My wife is in Florida with the grandkids this week."

"And my wife is busy working on the divorce papers with her lawyer in Raleigh," Barker explained with a sigh. "If the storm wrecked the house, maybe Loraine won't want it. I hate living in hotel rooms."

Matthew stood up. "I'm getting out of here. You have no right to hold me. I don't know where Sandi is, but she's not my responsibility either."

"Kevin, this is Sandi's assistant," I explained. "Probably the last person to see her alive."

"Alive?" Matthew stared at me. "What are you saying? You finally found her?"

"Yes," Kevin answered. "EMS took her a few minutes ago. Her husband is on his way. He doesn't know she's dead yet. I think you should stay."

"No way! He's not the forgiving type. Sandi said so. And don't try to make it sound like I had anything to do with killing Sandi."

"Who said anyone killed her?" I asked him.

"I assumed you wouldn't try to keep me here if you thought it was an accident."

"We can all talk about that when Chief Michaels gets here," I said. "Until then, I think you should stay here as a guest."

"You can't make me," Matthew charged.

"Yes she can," Nancy reminded him as she walked by. "I told you, in the absence of the police chief, the mayor can assume his authority. If she says you stay, you stay. Anyone want some iced tea?"

Matthew sat down again. He stared out of the window in the bar. He seemed to finally realize that this wasn't something that would go away quickly.

I wondered, looking at him, if he was the kind of person

who could've killed Sandi and tried to cover it up by putting her body in the shed. There was no way to know for sure, but he didn't seem the type to me.

Of course my mind jumped ahead to other questions. Why didn't he walk the extra few hundred yards to the edge of the ocean and dump her in? That was always an easy way to explain any mysterious deaths that happened this close to the water.

But there had to be other variables too—she looked awfully heavy for his meager frame to carry very far. Maybe he got as far as he could. Maybe he was scared to get that close to the ocean during the storm. I felt sure there was no way anyone could have known that shed would collapse over her.

I knew from years of listening to Gramps talk when he was sheriff that these things didn't always make sense—until all the pieces fit together. It would probably be the same way with Sandi's death. We wouldn't know for sure what had happened—but we'd find out eventually.

"You think he's okay there with the mayors?" Kevin asked me as we walked into the kitchen. "Otherwise, I can lock him up in the root cellar out back."

"He's been there all night. I think Barker and David can handle him." I was glad to see the kitchen was in order—though lacking most of the fresh food that had been there when Kevin left.

From there, we headed to the flooded ballroom. The look on Kevin's face when we walked in was heartbreaking. Knowing how hard he'd worked on the old inn made me feel even worse. I watched him slog through the water and debris to stare out of the big, broken window.

"What a mess," he said. "I'm glad I have good insurance."

I took a deep breath, not realizing until that moment that I had been worried he might not want to clean up and start over. Not everyone did. Some people came to live in Duck and didn't make it past the first storm. Kevin had staying

power. He was a keeper. That made me smile despite everything that had happened.

I helped him put boards across some of the windows
upstairs. There weren't any pieces of wood big enough to
put across the window in the ballroom. We put a few tarps
over it until repairs could be made. At least the damage
wouldn't get any worse.

I really didn't want to be at the inn when Sandi's husband got there. But I felt like I owed it to her. I was the
one who noticed she was gone—and had found her body.
I hoped that obligation didn't include telling him about
Matthew. It seemed like too much for a person to hear at
one time.

By lunchtime, the inn was cleaned up and all the holes
were patched, at least temporarily. With no supplies coming from the mainland, we were going to have to make do
for a few days. I knew from past experience that it would
be a rough time for everyone, but we'd get through. We
always did.

Some of the mayors came back to the inn, since they
couldn't make it through to their homes and there was nowhere else to go. Motels were full up with refugees. We'd
heard stories about houses with roofs missing, cars upside
down in the middle of Duck Road and electric poles down
across the island.

The Blue Whale had become a refuge for stranded travelers and local residents whose homes were badly damaged.
They kept coming and Kevin found places for them. At
lunch, we put together a meal for over two hundred people,
many of them strangers. It was one of Duck's finest hours.

We were joking around in the kitchen when Shawn Foxx
arrived with his two little girls. I knew him right away even
though it had been a few years since I'd last seen him.

"I heard my wife is missing," he said. "I hope you have
some news for me."

Chapter 9

Althea, who was used to dealing with small children at the library, took the two little girls into the next room, promising them ice cream. Everyone else cleared out of the kitchen, leaving Kevin and me to talk to Sandi's husband.

I wanted to tell Kevin that he could leave too. This wasn't his responsibility. But I knew when he pulled up a chair for Shawn and then sat down opposite him that he wasn't leaving. I was glad to have him there. I'd been mayor of Duck for two years, but I'd never had to tell anyone that their wife was dead. I wouldn't be involved now except for that feeling inside that I should be the one to break the news.

"I don't know if you remember me, Shawn," I began. "I'm Dae O'Donnell. Sandi and I went to a few conferences together."

"Sure. I remember you. What's this all about, Dae?"

There was no easy way to tell the story. I told him that I'd noticed Sandi was missing during the night and that we'd found her this morning. "I'm so sorry."

He took it well. The only sign that he was upset was a tightening around his eyes and mouth. Of course he'd been a marine for many years. He probably wouldn't break down and cry in front of us.

"What happened?" he asked, glancing at Kevin. "What was she doing outside during the storm anyway?"

Kevin introduced himself and shook Shawn's hand. "We're trying to figure that out. Everyone else was in the lobby, since we felt that was the safest place. We don't know how she got outside."

Shawn's gaze flickered over us. "What are you saying? You mean someone might've *taken* her outside? What aren't you telling me? Exactly how did my wife die?"

At this point I thought it was a good idea to be a public official. "We don't really know yet. EMS took her to the hospital. I'm sure they'll do a full autopsy. All we know right now is that Sandi died during the night and we found her outside in a shed. Again, I'm so sorry. If there's anything we can do—"

"Can I see her?" he asked.

"I'm sure you can, but they moved her to the hospital. I'm sorry."

"What about her assistant?" Shawn asked. "She didn't come here alone. Maybe her assistant knows something about what happened. Where is she?"

I didn't know what to say. Sandi must've told him her assistant was a woman. This was going to get awkward very quickly. "Her assistant is in the bar, actually. We thought it would be best if he waited here until travel was better."

"*He?*" Shawn's blue eyes narrowed into slits. "What's his name?"

"Matthew Wright," I said, hoping that didn't mean anything to him.

Shawn brought his beefy fist down on the tabletop. "I

knew it! I told her—I warned her—to stay away from him. I warned him too." He got to his feet and his chair tipped over. "Where is he? That skinny little runt has a lesson to learn."

Kevin stood up too. He wasn't as big as Shawn Foxx. I hoped there wasn't going to be a problem between them. "Not here, Foxx. Not now. You've got two little girls in there who just lost their mommy. You can rip Wright a new one later."

Shawn's eyes lost that killer look, and he picked up the chair. "Sorry. I knew something was going on between them. She told me it was over. Not like this was the first time for Sandi. I don't know what it was—she was never happy just being with me and the girls. Wright just happened to be the one *this* time."

I took a deep breath and was glad I didn't have to tell him that his dead wife had been unfaithful. It was bad enough telling him he had a dead wife.

"You and the girls are welcome to stay," Kevin said. "You must've had a hard time getting here from Manteo. I know the roads are a mess."

They started talking about the storm, and it turned out both of them were volunteer firefighters. I got up and got them both a cup of coffee, glad the tension had eased.

Marissa was peeking around the corner as I walked by. "Is everything okay? I hope that big guy isn't going to hurt Kevin."

"I think it's fine now. It was just a shock."

"I guess it would be a shock to find out the person you loved was cheating on you."

I didn't say anything, refusing to add to the local grapevine. There were bound to be rumors and speculation about everything that had gone on before and after the storm. The best thing was to leave them alone and not add to the problem. Gossip wouldn't help find out what had happened to Sandi.

I looked in the bar after that—Matthew was still there,

his head resting against Barker's shoulder while both men took a nap. I left them alone and looked for other things to do.

I had just started helping Althea with Sandi's daughters in the lobby when the front door opened and Mrs. Euly Stanley bounded into the inn. She was an older lady with a shock of curly gray hair that almost overwhelmed her fragile face. Mrs. Stanley was a great patron of the Duck Historical Museum.

"Dae, we need help at the museum next door. There's been some damage, and I think we better get it taken care of in case it rains again. Mildred and I are the only ones over there. Thank God we live close by. Think you could spare a few men for us?"

Althea seemed to have everything in hand with the two little girls. Marissa waved me on when I told her I was going to the museum for a few minutes. I was glad for the chance to get out of the Blue Whale for a while—even if it was on cleanup detail.

The Duck Historical Museum was right next door to the Blue Whale Inn. It held all the treasures of our sometimes checkered past, from pirates to the present day. Before leaving, I rounded up some volunteers from among the hotel guests who were looking for anything to pass the time. A few bored mayors' assistants came with us, along with a few Duck residents who'd been put out of their homes by the storm.

The museum was one of my favorite places. Not that it mattered much in this case. I just wanted to get away from what had become an impossible atmosphere next door. Something ached inside of me when I thought of Sandi dying alone out in the storm.

Maybe we hadn't been the closest of friends, but no one should have to die that way. Looking into the faces of her two little girls, I felt heartsick. What a terrible thing for them. At least I'd been an adult when my mother died.

It would be simpler—safer—to think that the strong winds had collapsed the shed on her. And maybe that was exactly what had happened—once she got outside.

But Sandi hadn't lost her ring outside. She'd lost it while she was still in the ballroom. The fear I'd felt from the ring—Sandi had experienced that fear—while she was inside, relatively safe from the storm.

Maybe I was too emotional about it, I thought as I walked around the museum with Mrs. Stanley, surveying the damage. Maybe I wasn't seeing clearly. The whole evening had been strange, even for me.

But why had Sandi been outside in the shed while the storm was raging over Duck? Sandi wasn't exactly a back-to-nature kind of person. I didn't have to know her well to know that about her. She'd probably been terrified out there.

Rationally, I supposed she could've run out of the back door after being with Matthew upstairs. Maybe she was looking for a place to be by herself. It was possible she got outside before she'd realized how bad the storm was. Maybe she'd gone into the shed to get away from wind and rain. People had died from collapsed housing many times. There was no real mystery to it.

I closed my eyes and rested my forehead against the bronze bust of one of our Duck forefathers. I was exhausted. The events of the previous night kept whirling around my head, like the storm had never left. I knew there was no point in going over it again and again. If Sandi was killed by Matthew, the medical examiner would pick up on it. We'd know soon enough.

In the meantime, I helped scoop water out of one of the rooms that housed a collection of clothes worn by generations of Duck families. There were dresses and suits—even baby clothes, some laid out on chairs and others on mannequins. I swept sand that had come in from a broken window on the ground floor. A few of the men were hammering wood slats—from pallets or whatever else they could find—over the broken windows to keep the weather out.

The museum was housed in one of the oldest buildings in Duck—the home of Wild Johnny Simpson. It had been donated for the purpose of holding the ever-growing collection of artifacts that was the museum. People of Duck loved their history, and they were proud of it.

I walked through the rooms filled with paintings, photos, pirate maps, and old letters, seeing all those things I had heard stories about growing up here. I loved the tales of the old Bankers, the pirates and the scallywags. I mourned the hundreds of ships that had gone down in the Graveyard of the Atlantic. They were all a part of me.

I had that strange, fluttering feeling again as I walked by an old mirror. It was a little corroded on the sides, but the gilt edging was still beautiful. The tag said it had once belonged to Bridget Patrick, a Banker woman who raised twenty-three children here after her husband's death.

Floating along the edge of my vision was that strange pinpoint of light again. Seeing it raised the hairs on the back of my neck, and I thought about the strange voice I'd heard when I found Sandi's body.

I hastened to remind myself that the voice must have come from the wild, crashing Atlantic and the call of the misplaced seagulls. But only part of me believed that.

I needed to see Shayla and talk to her about the things I'd seen. I wasn't sure exactly what spirit balls were, but one seemed to have followed me from the séance. And I had a feeling it wasn't my mother.

Chapter 10

I said my good-byes to Mrs. Stanley quickly so I could get back out into the sunlight and fresh air. Usually the stale air of the museum suited me perfectly—but not today. I had my gifts and they had nothing to do with seeing ghosts or spirit balls. True, I had invited my mother's spirit to be with me. That didn't mean I wanted some strange spectral presence to come by for tea.

I couldn't say why I didn't think the pinpoint of light was my mother—just a feeling. If that strange voice at the shed was any indication, it most definitely was *not* my mother or anyone else I knew.

As I walked out of the museum, I passed one of the treasures we'd managed to find through the years—a portrait of the pirate Rafe Masterson.

He was the last pirate hanged in Duck. He was said to have cursed the area after being tricked into the custody of the local people he'd pillaged and raided. Three hundred years later, people who were born here still saw his malevolent designs in any unfortunate occurrences. Fires that seemed to start on their own, sometimes even storms, were blamed on him and his curse.

I'd seen this portrait dozens of times, but I never really noticed how lifelike his dark eyes were. They seemed to be looking out at the world around him. His pencil-thin mustache above full lips had obviously been added for drama. He wore a black tricorn hat and a red coat, with heavy black boots on his feet. The cutlass at his side looked deadly.

It was said he was one of the most evil pirates to sail in the area—killing people for sport, stripping merchant ships bare and lighting them on fire—sometimes with the travelers still aboard.

His eyes looked cold and evil as I stared into them. I got an odd feeling that he was judging me too, even thought I saw his lips quirk slightly. I took a step back.

"Easy there, Mayor!" Mark Samson, owner of the Rib Shack, caught me as I walked into him. "Old Rafe give you a scare, did he?"

He laughed, of course. So did I, but I also continued my progress out the door and into the backyard. The storm had spooked me—the storm and the séance—not to mention finding Sandi's dead body. I felt weird because the last twenty-four hours had been very weird.

Mark had followed me outside. "You know, they say old Rafe had settled down before they trapped him and hanged him. They say he had a wife and a family and that he had given up being a pirate."

"Maybe so," I said, not wanting to be rude but needing to get away. "But he must not have changed too much or they wouldn't have been able to trap him. Thanks for your help. See you later."

But there didn't seem to be any way to get out of the situation. I needed a shower and a nap—maybe a good, stiff mocha or something stronger. Everything made me jumpy. Nothing felt normal.

I was glad to see Chief Michaels's patrol car in the drive outside the Blue Whale. I walked a little faster, knowing he would have some resolution to our problems. The whole thing with Matthew weighed heavily on me. I wanted someone else to make a judgment on the strange circumstances and take control of the situation.

And he'd done exactly that. As I walked in, Officer Tim Mabry was walking out with Matthew in handcuffs. Tim nodded to me but didn't speak. When there were handcuffs involved, he was always focused. He didn't have an opportunity to use them that often. I was glad Chief Michaels wanted to keep an eye on Sandi's assistant.

He wanted to talk to me too. "If you don't mind, Mayor," he said. "I'd like to hear what you have to say."

"There's no one in the kitchen," Kevin told him.

"That sounds fine. Thanks. After you, ma'am." The chief held the door for me.

I hoped, as I repeated my account of the previous night's events, that this time would be the last I'd have to say it. I also hoped the retelling would somehow make me feel better—less guilty for not noticing sooner that Sandi was gone. I felt like it was my job as the hostess of the group to make sure none of my guests were injured or killed.

Chief Michaels nodded as I spoke. He wrote what I said in his little notebook.

I'd known him all of my life. He was good friends with Gramps, who was the former sheriff. They'd worked together for many years. Gramps had recommended Chief Michaels for the job of Duck police chief. But unlike Gramps, who'd always been casual and laid-back, Chief Michaels was like an old drill sergeant with his graying flattop and perfectly pressed uniform. Even having been out after the storm doing cleanup, he wasn't dirty. His usually shiny black patent leather shoes *were* a little scuffed and sandy. Maybe he'd gone home and changed before he came here.

"I hear you telling me the everyday things," he said. "Now what about the not-so-normal things? I know you, Dae. Anything unusual—anything you picked up with your gift?"

Chief Michaels, like so many other residents of Duck, took my gifts for granted, most of the time. Once in a while, I went beyond the edge of what his good sense told him was possible. But his Banker roots made him pay attention to the unusual.

Since I still had custody of the ruby ring and the broken key chain, I laid them both on the table between us. Marissa gave the chief the key I'd found earlier that was for Matthew's car.

"This is Sandi's ring and Matthew's key chain." I explained what I knew about them—what I felt from them and how they had played a part in finding Sandi's body.

He nodded. "I see. So you have the impression that this young man—her *assistant*—might be responsible for what happened to her."

"I don't know. Maybe. He felt angry enough, and her fear was strong enough. But I can't explain why she was outside."

"Of course not, ma'am. And I'm not asking you to. Just your impressions. The rest we'll have to leave to the medical examiner. I have a rush on Mayor Foxx's autopsy results. Until we know something—in the next forty-eight hours, I hope—I'm holding Mr. Wright in custody. I don't want him wandering away in case the death turns out not to be accidental."

"I see."

"What about Mayor Foxx's husband? Do you know anything about him?"

"Not really. I picked up a few things from talking to Sandi the last couple years. There were a few times we bumped into each other. Otherwise, I don't know him. Why? Do you think he was involved?"

"I don't know yet." He put on some latex gloves and sealed the ring, the key and key chain into an evidence bag. "I suppose you weren't able to see where the gun in your vision ended up?"

"No. I'm afraid not. But I don't see how Shawn could be involved in Sandi's death. What about the storm? He was all the way in Manteo."

"Let's just say it wouldn't be the most extreme thing I've heard of a man doing who suspected his wife was having an affair." Chief Michaels put on his uniform hat. "Thank you for your help, Mayor. By the way, I saw your grandfather a few hours back. He said your house made it through without much damage. Just thought you might want to know."

"Thanks for telling me, Chief. I'm sorry about all of this—you had enough to handle with the storm and all."

"Not your fault. You can't help what people do. Ask your grandpa. He'll tell you the same."

I nodded, knowing it was true but still feeling I could've done something that would've kept Sandi from dying. I was relieved that the investigation was now in his hands. Holding Matthew against his will and being responsible for what could be evidence of Sandi's murder had been a burden. Now I could just cope with the leftovers of the storm.

Tim was getting a list of everyone who had been at the Blue Whale the night before from Marissa. They were acting a little flirty together—which was good, since otherwise Tim tended to think of me as his true love.

We'd shared our first kiss when we were in high school, and many people thought we'd end up together. But I never had those kinds of feelings for him as an adult. He only *thought* he felt that way about me—when he wasn't seeing someone else. I seemed to be his port in the storm when he was single.

"Nothing too ragged, I hope." Kevin put his arm around me, taking my thoughts away from my first boyfriend.

"Not at all. It was a relief to hand it all over to the chief. I don't think I'd be very good at law enforcement. Too much responsibility."

"What about being mayor?" He smiled. "I've seen you worry enough about trash thrown out of a car on Duck Road to go out at midnight and pick it up."

"That's different," I told him. "Being in the FBI must have been a lot worse. You had to think about the whole country. No wonder you retired early."

He laughed. "There's no doubt it takes a toll on you. Now that everything is cleared up here, you want to walk down and see how Missing Pieces is doing?"

I cringed thinking about it. My little thrift shop was right on the Currituck Sound—on a boardwalk, no less. I'd done repairs to it and claimed damages dozens of times on my treasures that were stored there. This storm had been bad enough that I knew what to expect.

"Aren't there potatoes to peel or something? I'd rather do almost anything else."

"Come on. You've patched everyone else's roofs and windows, let's go take care of yours before it gets dark. Chief Michaels tells me there's a curfew in force until the power comes back on for the streetlights."

"What about dinner?" I procrastinated. "Shouldn't we cook something?"

"There's plenty of time for that later. I'll get some tools."

While I waited for Kevin to return with tools, Shawn Foxx was getting ready to leave with his little girls. Talking to them was probably even further down on the list of things I wanted to do today. I couldn't stand the idea of facing those two pairs of blue eyes wet with tears for their mother.

"Thanks for everything, Dae." Shawn shook my hand. "I know Sandi considered you a friend. We're heading back home to get things straightened up there."

His two little girls smiled at me, and I could tell their father hadn't told them the result of their trip here. They didn't know yet. Maybe he couldn't bear to tell them either. I hoped he had someone who could be there for them.

"I'm so sorry about everything. I wish it could be different."

He shrugged. "Life isn't always what we expect. We have to make the best of it." He smiled at his daughters. "Thank the nice lady for your snacks and for her help."

Both girls had a sweet lisp as they thanked me. They followed their father out of the front door. It was all I could do not to break down into a sobbing heap on the floor. I didn't blame him for not telling them about Sandi yet. A quiet place at home was a better spot for that explanation. I didn't envy him the task.

I confided my feelings to Kevin as we went down toward Duck Road, walking around and under everything that had been deposited there during the night.

"I wish I'd realized what was happening before it was too late."

"That's a high level of responsibility even for you, Mayor. Sandi made her choices, which may or may not have played a part in her death. You didn't have anything to do with it."

"I hope not." I saw my neighbor's distinctive garden trellis in one of the trees as we walked by. I made a note to tell her in case she was wondering where it went.

Of course, it would've taken a huge spreadsheet to keep track of everything that had blown away during the storm. Just on the corner where we turned, there were two picnic table umbrellas hanging from trees. Beside them were green velvet drapes and a matching chair. We walked around a bed frame, complete with mattress. And there was a toilet. Cars were on their sides, pushed into places they didn't belong. It would take months to get everything back to normal.

But at least most of the road on one side was clear for

emergency vehicles and for people whose cars weren't upside down in their living rooms. I hoped those people were helping others who needed it. I promised myself I would be one of them tomorrow after getting my house and shop in order today.

"This is a mess," Kevin said. "But farther down toward Kitty Hawk and Kill Devil Hills, they got hit a lot worse. Duck is in good condition compared to that."

I was pleasantly surprised to find the Duck Shoppes on the Boardwalk were almost untouched. A few signs had been blown away or fallen down, but my shop was exactly as I'd left it the day before.

There was no water in Missing Pieces when I opened the door—even the window that fronted the sound was in one piece. I looked around at my treasures that I'd collected over the past few years and sighed. Everything was safe. I wished I could just sit on my burgundy brocade sofa and drink a cup of tea. It would be wonderful to feel as though everything was back to normal.

But Kevin was at the door, remarking that Wild Stallions, the bar and grill at the other end of the boardwalk, wasn't so lucky. Their sign had ended up in their front door. "I'm going to walk down there and give them a hand," he said. "You can stay here and take a break for a while. You've been going all night."

I knew he meant well, but he'd been going all night too—like most of the people around us. I didn't want to take a break yet. I did, but I wasn't going to. Cody and Reece Baucum, the brothers who owned Wild Stallions, were my friends too. They needed help to get the large sign out of the doorway so they could secure the space in case it started raining again. Once it got dark, nothing would get done until tomorrow.

It took about an hour for us to get the sign out on the boardwalk and close up the doorway. Kevin hadn't needed his tools at Missing Pieces, but they came in handy here.

We also helped August Grandin at the Duck General Store as he tried to get a large flowerpot back up again. All of the big flowerpots on the boardwalk had been tossed on their sides, dirt and flowers spilling everywhere. I scooped up the flowers and pushed them back in the soil after August and Kevin had set the pots right again.

By that time, my good friend Trudy Devereaux, who owned the Curves and Curls Beauty Spa next door to Missing Pieces, was out examining her shop. We hugged and talked for a while about the storm. She already knew about Sandi's death. Even without phones and power, the Duck grapevine worked overtime.

"It must've been terrible," Trudy said as Kevin worked to get her water-warped door open. It had swelled too large for the frame. "You knew Sandi Foxx from before, right? I thought I remembered you talking about her."

I nodded, not wanting to give too much away before the medical examiner and Chief Michaels had a chance to do their jobs. "I had to talk to her husband about it. I'm just glad I didn't have to explain to her little girls."

"She had *kids*?" There were tears in Trudy's eyes. She'd always had a soft heart—saving beetles and spiders from children at school who wanted to squish them. "That's even worse. I'm sorry you had to be involved, Dae."

Kevin gave her door a solid push, and it finally popped open. The shop seemed fine. We all walked through it to be sure.

Trudy thanked Kevin for his help as she checked her always-perfect platinum blond hair and makeup, and then asked, "So what are they going to do with her? She's not still at the Blue Whale, is she?"

"No," Kevin answered. "The medical examiner has her body."

Her blue eyes widened. "You mean they think someone *killed* her? It wasn't the storm?"

Kevin was used to talking with a different crowd when

it came to things like this. All of Duck would be talking about Sandi's murder by tomorrow morning.

"It's not like that." I tried to contain the damage. "She died outside during the storm, but all suspicious deaths go to the medical examiner. They have to check these things out."

"What in the world was she doing outside during the storm?" Shayla asked as she joined us, no doubt on her way to her own shop—Mrs. Roberts, Spiritual Advisor—on the other side of Missing Pieces. "That was a bad storm for someone to be standing in."

"Dae found her body," Trudy answered. "It was terrible."

Shayla stepped back and looked at me from head to toe. "That must be why your aura looks all smudgy. You need some rest—and stay away from dead bodies."

"If you two wouldn't mind"—I grabbed Shayla's arm— "I have to talk to her about something."

Trudy sniffed and waved us away. "I've only been your best friend since kindergarten, Dae O'Donnell. If you have something you can't talk about in front of me, that's fine. Kevin and I will go for a stroll down the boardwalk. It's not a problem."

Kevin didn't look as convinced of that notion. "I want to hear more about the spirit balls."

"There were *spirit balls*, and you weren't going to tell me about them?" Trudy was outraged. "What's a spirit ball?"

"Never mind," I said. "Let's all sit down in Missing Pieces and I'll explain what's been happening."

"Good." Shayla started out the door. "Then we can go down to my place and make sure it isn't leaking. I see Kevin is prepared to work, so let's get this over with."

Back at Missing Pieces, I put on some tea and everyone sat down on the burgundy brocade sofa, my favorite piece of furniture even though it was too big for the shop. I constantly had to work around it to find room for my treasures.

I took a chair on the side, trying not to envy the three of

them sitting in my favorite place, and explained about the séance to Trudy while the water boiled.

"That's amazing!" Trudy said. "Do you really think your mom was trying to talk to you?"

"I don't," I admitted. "Other things happened after I got to the Blue Whale." I filled them all in on the point of light that had come at me and the other odd phenomena that had occurred. "I don't know who's following me, but I don't think it's my mother."

We all had a cup of Earl Grey tea and contemplated my recent otherworldly experiences.

"Maybe it was the storm," Trudy said. "Maybe all those extra storm ions they're always talking about created some kind of spectral field during the séance."

Shayla shook her head. "That sounds good, but I knew last night something was up. I could feel it before and again during the storm. Spirit balls aren't a normal presence, even during a séance. It takes a powerful spirit to put all its energy into producing a visible, moving light. I think we might've called up another spirit—maybe one related to you, Dae."

"You could've mentioned that last night," I suggested.

"You were in such a hurry to get to the conference," Shayla fired back. "And now look what's happened—that poor woman is dead."

"I don't think Mayor Foxx's death was related to spirit balls following Dae from the séance," Kevin said.

"But you don't know for sure, do you?" Shayla asked. "You may be an expert on police things, Mr. Ex-FBI Man, but leave the spiritual things to me. That's *my* expertise. I'm fourth generation at this. *And* I might be related to Marie Laveau."

"That's no reason to get nasty," Trudy said. "Kevin was just stating his opinion. That's still legal here, I think."

Shayla *humphed* and sat back to drink her tea. Trudy was quiet, drinking tea with a smug smile on her pretty face for putting Shayla in her place.

"Whatever happened, it's affected me," I said. "I can feel that something isn't right. And I keep seeing things in mirrors."

"What kinds of things?" Shayla asked.

"I can't explain it. It's like something is there, but I can't quite make it out. Like when you see things out of the corner of your eye."

"Sounds like you've got a haunt following you." Shayla put down her empty tea cup and stood up. "Stand over there and let me clear your aura. That should help. Then get some rest and don't eat any meat. My gran used to say haunts can smell that and find you again."

I stood toward the back of the shop, and Shayla stared at me for a few minutes before mumbling some words and walking around and around me. She threw back her head and wiggled her arms around like snakes.

Then she patted her thick black hair and smoothed her black silk shirt. "That should take care of it. Not quite your normal green-blue Dae aura. But close enough. And at least it's clear now."

"What was that?" Trudy asked.

"I was working on Dae's aura," Shayla explained. "It wasn't looking too healthy. Yours could do with a tune-up too, missy. I'll do it for free right now."

"No thanks." Trudy stepped back, almost behind Kevin. "My aura is fine just the way it is. I'm going to call my appointments for today and see if I can reschedule for when power comes back on. I'll see all of you later."

"What was the bee in her bonnet?" Shayla asked when she was gone. "That woman has some serious superstition going on, you know? Okay, now that we're done with that, can we go take a look at my shop? Kevin, honey, you bring that hammer right on next door. I'm sure we're going to need it."

"But there wasn't anything wrong with Missing Pieces or Trudy's shop," I said. "I'm sure your place is fine too."

Shayla turned up her nose. "Then you don't know anything. My instincts tell me I've got some damage. I'm willing to put money down if you are."

But I never bet against Shayla's instincts. They were usually right. She took Kevin's arm and they walked out the door together. It only bothered me a little—they'd dated briefly before Kevin and I got together. It didn't mean anything. Shayla liked to remind me in small, annoying ways that he'd been hers first.

I glanced in the small mirror near the door as I was walking out behind them. I looked in it carefully and didn't see anything unusual. All that reflected back at me was what was supposed to be there. With a smile, I left Missing Pieces and locked the door.

There was a creak on the boardwalk behind me and a strange rattling sound from the locked door to the shop. The temperature outside was mild and damp after the storm. A gust of wind blew across the boardwalk and made me shiver.

I heard laughter—solid, male-sounding laughter—and turned back quickly, but no one was there. I hurried into Shayla's shop to find her and Kevin. Something was still not right. A haunt, she'd called it. Was I being haunted by a strange spirit that had been called up instead of my mother?

Chapter 11

There was only a little damage done to Shayla's shop—nothing major, but she smiled and let us know that she was right about it. She hovered while Kevin did a few repairs to one of her windows and a warped spot on her door. He told her a professional should come and replace the door later.

I was just glad to be there with them. I thought a crowd might discourage a ghost from making itself known. So far, at least, all my supernatural encounters had occurred while I was alone.

Maybe Shayla's aura-clearing ritual would help later. I definitely wasn't eating any meat for a while. Despite my long-held desire to see a ghost, I was more than ready to get rid of this one.

It was starting to get dark by the time we finished tidying up Shayla's shop. The sun was setting—which meant Kevin and I needed to get back. I was dreading the coming night.

"Do you need any help over there?" Shayla asked. "I've

been a hostess at a restaurant before. I could do something along those lines."

"All we really need is a dishwasher," I said. "The job's yours if you want it."

She made a face. "I don't think I want to do that. It's not that I can't—it's just something I hate doing. I guess I'll wander back home and try to find out what's haunting you, Dae."

"Don't you mean who?" I asked.

"Not always. There are entities that have nothing to do with human beings. I hope one of them didn't latch on to you." She shivered. "They can be pretty nasty."

"Thanks for telling me that *now*!"

"Don't worry. Whoever or whatever decided to follow you—I'll get rid of them. And that's not to say getting the mud out of your aura won't work. It'll be fine."

With a little wave of her mocha-colored hand, she swept down the boardwalk toward the parking lot.

"Don't let her get to you." Kevin put his arm around my shoulder. "She's just playing with you."

I felt as if I should be the one saying that to him. I'd known Shayla longer and I realized she liked to play games. "Thanks. I'm feeling a little like a mouse to her cat right now."

He laughed as we walked more slowly behind Shayla toward the parking lot. "I think you're probably just jumpy from everything that's happened. Get a good night's sleep tonight and you'll be fine tomorrow. If you want, I can dance around and chant a little, like Shayla."

"That's okay." I stared down from the boardwalk into the parking lot where several EMS vehicles were gathered. "I wonder what's going on down there."

"Let's find out."

All of the emergency workers were from Duck. Their exhaustion showed on their smudged faces. A few of them—Phil De Angelo from the Coffee House and Bookstore, Luke

Helms, a retired attorney who'd recently moved here, and Barney Thompson from the Sand Dollar Jewelry Store—nodded to me. Cailey Fargo, the fire chief, was outlining some kind of rescue plan they were all about to embark on.

"Need some help?" Kevin asked when Cailey was finished.

"Yeah, I'd say so." Cailey smiled and thanked him. "I hope everything is okay over at the Blue Whale. It must be since Dae's here."

Kevin gave her a brief account of Sandi's death. She nodded and told him the problem they were facing on Duck Road. "Some man is trapped in his van. A transformer fell on top of the vehicle. We're scrambling for manpower as it is. I grabbed these fellas out of their homes to help me with this."

"I'll be glad to do what I can," Kevin said.

"Me too," I added with a bright smile. "I don't know a lot about emergency work, but I can drive or fetch equipment."

"You're hired!" Cailey slapped me on the shoulder. "Let's get going. It's gonna be dark real soon. I managed to get a generator and one flood light so we can work, but that's about it."

I drove one of the smaller vehicles with Cailey beside me. Kevin rode with Phil and Barney in the lead. Everyone else followed behind us. Cailey was working the radio trying to find a paramedic in case the man in the van was injured.

The crash site was easy to spot, even in the deepening twilight with no streetlights. The van had smashed into the power pole, and the transformer was sending showers of sparks across it and into the street. We all found places to park along the road and walked to where an EMS worker from Corolla was already on the scene

"Have you been able to communicate with the driver at all, Dwight?" Cailey asked.

"Not yet," he told her. "We can't get close. We need

someone to cut the lines to the transformer so we can move it off the vehicle."

Cailey surveyed the transformer. "Did you try the power company?"

"A dozen times," Dwight said. "Their emergency lines went down about two hours ago. We're on our own out here, Chief."

Cailey looked around at her dirty, exhausted crew. "I don't know what to say, boys. We're not supposed to touch that equipment without someone here from the power company. Any suggestions?"

"Have you got the tools to cut it?" Barney asked. "I'll step over there and take it out."

"We have the tools, but we need someone with the expertise," Cailey answered. "I've never worked as a lineman, Barney. Have you?"

"We can't let the man die in the vehicle," Luke said. "There must be some way to do it."

"I have an idea," Kevin said. "Is there a rescue pole in one of the trucks?"

"Never go out without one," Barney said. "We're kind of surrounded by water you know."

"What do you have in mind, Kevin?" Cailey asked.

Kevin explained that there was a cutoff lever at the top of the pole. "The power company has a tool to shut it down from the ground. I think we could modify the rescue pole to do the same thing."

"Sounds good," Cailey said after a brief hesitation. "If the power company doesn't like it, they can give me a call. What do you need, Kevin?"

It sounded simple until I realized Kevin was going to be the one climbing up on top of one of the EMS trucks and using the makeshift pole.

"Have you ever done anything like this before?" I asked while they got the pole ready.

"The FBI trains agents to think on their feet and come up with alternative scenarios," he explained.

"In other words—no?"

"In other words—but it will work."

I watched nervously as Kevin climbed up on the vehicle, sparks from the downed transformer flying around us like thousands of fireflies. Barney handed him the pole when he was in place, and Cailey held the floodlight on the pole so he could see what he was doing.

"Don't walk too far that way," Phil said, joking. "We can't rescue you too."

There was some pathetic, exhausted, good-humored bantering for a minute or two, then everyone was quiet as we all watched Kevin try to hit the cutoff switch.

I held my breath as he tried to maneuver the long pole into place without losing his balance on the vehicle. A few times, I started to reach up and steady him—Cailey pulled my arm back.

It was dark by then. Even the floodlight seemed useless against the night. I couldn't see Kevin's face without getting too close to the transformer. All I could do was pray that everything would be okay.

"Praying never did no one any good, girl," a voice I was beginning to recognize told me. *"Next time, tell the lad not to be such a hero."*

Chapter 12

"I don't know who you are," I whispered, "but leave me alone. Go back wherever you came from."

I wasn't sure whether that was the proper response to a ghost—if a ghost was what was bothering me. It probably wouldn't work as an exorcism. But it came from the heart.

"*Aw, don't be that a'way, girl,*" the voice continued, mocking me. "*He's a good lad, no doubt. Not too bright, eh? Maybe you should look around a little more. You could do better.*"

I spun around and stared into the face of Dwight, the EMS worker from Corolla. There was no one else in sight.

Of course not. It was a ghost. Or something.

"Are you okay, Mayor O'Donnell?" Dwight asked.

"I'm fine—sorry if I—"

"He got it!" Cailey yelled. "Good work, Kevin. You're not too bad for an outsider."

"Thanks," Kevin replied. I could hear the smile in his voice though I couldn't see his face. "Just how long is somebody considered an outsider here?"

That brought a few chuckles from everyone.

"Probably until you die," Cailey assured him.

"Yeah," Phil said. "I've been here ten years. Still an outsider."

The transformer was sparking less and less. Long wires hanging down from the pole were cut away from it. It took four men to lift the transformer away from the van. No one knew what to do with it—there was no truck to transport it. Eventually they put it into a drainage ditch on the side of the road near the pole. Cailey said she would call the power company and tell them where to find it.

Barney Thompson had to use the jaws of life to get the door open so they could reach the man in the vehicle. They shone the floodlight in the opening as Dwight, the only licensed paramedic in the group, came to check out the driver.

"He's the only one in there," Phil said after looking through the back of the van. "But he either robbed a liquor store or he was having one hell of a party. There must be at least a dozen cases of whiskey in the back."

I heard Cailey swear under her breath. "Great! Is he okay?"

"Looks like a bump on the head," Dwight said. "Could be a concussion, but he's conscious. We should take him in anyway—just to be sure."

My hands were tingling as I moved closer to the vehicle. I usually have that kind of reaction when I've located a fantastic treasure for Missing Pieces. Lately, it's been happening a little more often. It struck me that I might know the driver we'd just rescued.

"Who is it?" I asked.

"Don't know," Phil said. "I don't recognize him."

"Can you tell us your name, sir?" Cailey asked the driver. "Where are you from?"

A shaken, breathless voice replied, "My name is Danny Evans. I live in Duck. Get me out of here, huh?"

Danny Evans—the tingling became a buzzing in my ears. *My father.*

Chapter 13

No one there knew that I was related to Danny Evans—except me. I'd only recently learned who my father was and that he was alive. My mother, even Gramps, had always told me he was dead. It was only by chance that I found out otherwise.

"Bring in the stretcher," Dwight yelled back to the others.

"We'd better do a sobriety test on him," Cailey said.

"Hey! Just because I work at a bar doesn't mean I'm drunk," Danny protested.

"I guess that explains the whiskey." Phil laughed.

"It does since someone already broke into the bar and stole a couple cases. My boss expects me to protect his investment until this is over," Danny explained.

"It's just for your own good, sir," Cailey told him. "The drugs they give you at the hospital might work against any alcohol in your system. Best to know ahead."

"I haven't been drinking," Danny said again. "I don't

drink. Not anymore at least. I've been sober six years, five months and seven days. I'm just good at being a bartender."

"We'll have to test you anyway, sir," Cailey repeated. "Sorry."

He was an alcoholic. I knew from the way he'd said exactly how long he'd been sober. My father was an alcoholic.

I'd followed him around a few times since finding out about him and where he worked. I didn't want him to know about me. I wouldn't introduce myself, although I ordered a drink from him once at his bar, the Sailor's Dream.

Gramps told me that Danny hadn't wanted me, or my mother. He'd never checked to see what I was like as I was growing up. There was never a card or a phone call. I figured he wouldn't want me now either.

But every new piece of information I learned about him was like a treasure from Missing Pieces. I'd tuck it away to look at later as I tried to understand him. What had my mother seen in him? How was I like him?

I mentally filed this latest discovery that he was an alcoholic. I'd retrieve it when I had time to scrutinize it properly.

Gramps didn't know I'd looked Danny up and had come in contact with him. Having kept him a secret for more than thirty years, he wouldn't have been too happy about my interest. I didn't tell Kevin either, even though he'd offered to help me find Danny. I just wasn't sure he wouldn't tell Gramps.

And there was something exciting and satisfying about not sharing the treasure I'd found with anyone else. Maybe it only meant something to me, but my mother must have loved this man. I didn't know what had happened between them that had made her lie to me about him. I might never know. But I wanted to figure it out.

I watched as Cailey and Dwight helped my father out of the van. They placed him on the stretcher and took him to the ambulance. I knew they wouldn't make him do a field sobriety test to tell if he was impaired. They'd do a blood test on the way to the hospital. I hoped for his sake that what he'd told them was true.

Next in line was getting the van off the road. While traffic was minimal, no one wanted to get a call later that night about another accident involving the vehicle. Kevin and I waited with Luke for the tow truck while Cailey, Barney and Phil went on to the next emergency caused by the storm. It was going to be a long night for everyone.

We sat around in the emergency vehicle, talking about our experiences during the storm. I had the best story—hands down. No one else was actually involved in a possible homicide.

It wasn't much to brag about, of course. I didn't have my usual relish for telling what was bound to be a tale that would go down in Duck history. Despite Luke urging me for more details, I was finished quickly, then listened to Luke and Kevin talk about their experiences working with other emergency crews.

The tow-truck driver—all the way from Sanderling— wasn't in a mood to talk either. He kind of grunted as Kevin and Luke explained that the van needed to go to the Duck Police impound lot. Our usual Duck tow-truck driver wasn't able to come because part of his house was on his truck. They finally made the Sanderling driver understand the request, and he hitched the van to the back of the tow truck.

While they were talking, I noticed something on the wet street right outside the van door. The floodlight was gone with Cailey, but this glinted in the bright headlights shining across Duck Road from the tow truck and the emergency vehicle.

I walked over and picked it up. It felt cool in my hand. It was a smooth, flat rock that had been made into a necklace. The gold chain that ran through it wasn't new. As I held it, a flash of emotion went through me.

They were playing around at the beach when they saw the stone. She picked it up and held it for him to touch. The sun was hot on their hands as they held the stone between them. He kissed her and she laughed, splashing water at him before she ran away. He put the stone into his pocket as he followed her.

I took a deep breath and steadied myself with my hand on the side of the emergency vehicle. The man in the image I'd gotten from the stone was a much younger version of Danny. The woman was my mother.

He'd kept this stone for more than thirty years. It went everywhere with him. It was the only thing besides memories that he had of her. Danny Evans had loved my mother—still loved her.

My hands were shaking as I put the necklace into my pocket. What had happened to them? Gramps said Danny had kicked my mother out when he found out she was pregnant. But the emotions from the stone didn't feel like something that anyone would give up so easily.

It was no use asking Gramps again. He'd told me his side of the tale. There was only one side left besides that of my silent-as-the-grave mother—Danny's. He was the only one who could tell me why he'd abandoned us.

And though I'd promised myself I would never tell him who I was, I knew I would have to ask him my questions. I needed those answers. Though I'd grown up without ever really thinking about the father my mother and Gramps had told me was dead, he was now an important part of my life. I had to know what had happened between him and my mother.

Chapter 14

"Everything okay, Dae?" Kevin asked after Luke had dropped us off at the Blue Whale.

"Sure. Why do you ask?"

"You're too quiet. I know you're thinking about something. Are you still blaming yourself for Sandi's death?"

It was a convenient excuse, and I snatched it like a hungry turtle with a fish. "I know I shouldn't," I lamented falsely. "It's just been a long day."

"I think all of this qualifies as more than one day," he told me, wrapping his arms around me. "We all need some sleep."

I closed my eyes and silently apologized to him for lying. I hated to do it, but I couldn't tell him what was really on my mind. "Definitely. When are you going back out again?"

"My shift starts at five A.M.," he told me. "I hope things are better out there by then."

But we both knew they wouldn't be all that much better. There was only so much emergency services could do to clean up in the dark.

"Well, I hope we have power in the morning so I can take a shower," I said. "If not here, maybe at my house. How is it possible that the power is on in some places but not in others?"

"I think you know the answer to that," Gramps said as we reached the verandah where he sat in the dark. "You're the mayor. You know how these things work. I was beginning to get worried about you two."

I told him about the crashed van—leaving out that the driver was Danny—and how Missing Pieces had suffered no great damage from the storm.

"I've been back here a few hours," he replied. "That bunch in there is going to eat you out of house and home, Kevin. I hope you've got something left for breakfast."

"I hope so too," Kevin said.

"There's no way even a big group like that could eat all the food he has stashed away," I explained to Gramps, glad that we were all on the dark porch so he couldn't read my face. It was harder to lie to Gramps than to Kevin. Not that Gramps suspected anything from our brief account of the rescue on Duck Road. I had to keep my conscience out of this. By the time I faced him in the daylight, I'd better be ready to handle what I needed to tell him.

We went inside together—the emergency lights not really enough to qualify as lighting up the rooms. About fifty people were staying for the night, according to Marissa. Most of them had gone up to their rooms already. Sandi's room and Matthew's room had been sealed off as possible crime scenes.

"There's still plenty of space," Marissa told Kevin briskly. "I think we have enough food and water to get by another couple of days if we have to. I'm not sure about toilet paper.

I've looked everywhere but I can't find any more. Do you want me to look in the root cellar?"

"No. That's okay. I'll check down there in the morning. We'll have to get by until then. Thank goodness it's night-time so everyone should be asleep."

Gramps sat down in an easy chair. "Not me. I can't go to sleep without the TV. Ask Dae. It's like warm milk for me."

Kevin patted his shoulder. "Sorry, Horace. I thought the freezers were more important than TV. Maybe I was wrong."

All of the camaraderie—people singing softly at the old piano in the lobby, playing cards on the stairs and drinking in the bar—should have made me feel better about facing the night. It didn't.

That ghostly presence was still on my mind. It accompanied the thoughts about my mother and father. There were too many questions. My mind was exhausted but full to bursting, like some sandbag dam trying to hold back the flood. I knew I wouldn't sleep.

I reminded myself again of how often I'd wished to see a ghost. Since I was a child and had heard the supernatural stories of the Outer Banks, I'd imagined what it would be like. I'd thought about it every way possible—except this one.

If the spirit following me was my mother, that would be different. But this presence sounded like some sleazy sailor who wanted to voice his opinion on everything. And that was assuming it was a human. Shayla's comments on that had left me even more apprehensive. How could this be?

I'd managed to stick my nose into plenty of things where it didn't belong. Maybe one of those was trying to contact my mother. Gramps always said I didn't know when to leave well enough alone.

At least I didn't have to worry about being alone with the ghostly presence. There were people tucked into every corner of the inn. I stretched out in a king-size bed—

accompanied by Nancy and Marissa. Both of them had stayed on at the inn to help out. There were several others on chairs and cushions around the room. I could hardly reach the bed without stepping on someone.

Marissa sighed as we lay there, unable to sleep. "I know I should go home tomorrow, but I'm dreading it. You didn't hear or see anything around or about my place, did you, Dae?"

"No. I'm sorry. Kevin and I were at the Duck Shoppes before we went to help Cailey with that accident. But you're facing the sound—Gramps said our place was in good shape. Maybe yours is too."

Nancy sighed too. "I'm not facing the sound. I hope I have something left to go home to."

I was sure many others felt the same. Staying here at the Blue Whale for one more night put those realizations on hold until morning. But we would all have to face reality tomorrow.

I think, despite not believing it was possible, that I fell asleep. I woke up and looked at my watch—it was almost two thirty A.M. I'd been asleep for at least four hours!

I felt a little better, a little more clearheaded. I knew what I had to do—at least in regard to my father.

The ghostly presence? I lay quietly for about twenty minutes, waiting to see or hear something. There was nothing. Maybe my "ghost" had been nothing more than exhaustion and stress. Maybe I could even attribute what I'd seen to the weather, like the warning ghosts that everyone talked about. It might not have anything to do with the séance.

Sandi? Her death was a tragedy, and I wished I could've helped her. But I had to let it go. There was nothing I could do. Unfortunately, terrible things happen. I knew that better than most people, having grown up in the home of the Dare County Sheriff. Gramps had always been careful not to involve me too much, but I'd still heard bad things about our neighbors. I knew even Duck had problems.

Renewed by my four hours of sleep and a confidence born of believing I knew what to do next about each of my problems, I was suddenly hungry. My stomach was growling loudly. Nancy groaned next to me and turned over. I was embarrassed to think I might wake her with my internal noises. Marissa was gone—maybe she was restless too.

Carefully, I inched out of bed and across the old hardwood floor. It squeaked and complained under my weight in places—but that was the only unusual noise I heard. The sleeping crowd around me sighed and muttered but didn't wake up.

I crept down the hall to the kitchen, hoping there was something light to eat in the fridge. I didn't want a full meal, just something to tide me over until morning. I knew Nancy and Marissa would thank me for quieting my stomach.

I found some leftover pancakes from breakfast and ate them at the table in the kitchen that Kevin and I usually shared when I visited.

The old inn that had seen many disasters like this storm—and worse—seemed to sleep around me too. It sheltered all of us who weren't very eager to face the next day and what it might bring. I sipped the last of the fresh milk and sat back in the chair, replete, and felt ready to go home and do whatever else needed to be done.

I let myself glance carefully around the dark kitchen, keeping an eye open for any spirit balls that might be lingering, Nothing. No weird sensations of static electricity, no oppressive, frightening feelings of someone just behind me.

Those scary sightings of spirit balls and hearing someone speaking to me that wasn't there had probably been triggered by the storm, I decided. A big storm has some odd precursors to it. A doctor once explained that to me when I told him about my storm knee that could predict the weather.

The ghostly presence was nothing more than my old storm knee acting up. I indulged in a banana, put my plate and glass in the sink and headed back to my room for a few more hours of sleep.

I saw a flashlight beam headed toward the bar area and wondered who was up drinking at this time of the morning. Kevin had shooed all of the drinkers out of there last night with a warning about touching any more unopened bottles. There'd been some grumbling, but the bar patrons had cleared out. I suspected one of the drinkers had probably come back for a late-night snack slightly different than mine.

But when I got to the bar, the room was empty, quiet. I was sure I'd seen a flashlight headed this way. Maybe whoever was holding it had changed their mind and gone back to bed. Which was where I was headed. I yawned and turned to leave.

It was then that I heard the chuckle. There was no other word for it—it was a chuckle. It seemed to come from behind the bar. I approached the long wood slab carefully, thinking the late-night drinker was hiding there. Probably David or Barker.

But as I reached the bar, a light that had nothing to do with any modern-day convenience like a flashlight bloomed in a strange iridescent way. I watched as the light coalesced into a form. And the form was chuckling.

"If this be yer rum, ye be cheated, girl."

So much for believing my ghostly friend wasn't real.

Chapter 15

The ghost, if that's what it was, stood about six feet tall, had thick, shaggy black hair and a mustache. He wore a red coat and a tricorn hat.

Without really thinking, I remarked, "I know you! You're Rafe Masterson, the pirate."

He lifted a bottle, shaking out the lace at his wrist. "It's about time. I thought I would have to introduce myself. You all but walked into me at that blasted archive of foolishness you call a museum. Why the blazes have you kept all that bilge?"

"If we hadn't, I wouldn't know who you are," I reminded him. "I've seen your portrait a hundred times. You look exactly the same."

"Ye see what ye wish." He shrugged and poured rum into the glass on the bar. "I promise you, I don't look at all like this fantasy you've created. A man doesn't age well in the grave."

I almost laughed. It struck me as funny that I was talking

to a pirate ghost. Especially the ghost of this pirate—the scourge of Duck, the man whose curse still lived with us. The dread Rafe Masterson.

He drank the rum he'd poured and smacked his lips. "Almost like drinking mother's milk. Why the blazes do ye water it down? In my day, men would string up a tavern keeper who served slop like this."

"It's not watered down," I explained. "This is probably just different—more refined than what you're used to."

"Well, I don't plan to be here long enough to learn the ins and outs of this godforsaken time." He set the glass down on the bar with a decided thud. "What the hell do you want of me, girl? Why have you bothered my sleep?"

"Me?" I did laugh now. "You've been following me around. Why are *you* here?"

"Why? Because you called me. Why else would I be here?"

"I didn't call you—I was calling my mother. Maybe you can leave now and get her for me." Talking to a ghost wasn't as hard as I'd expected. Or maybe I was dreaming. I couldn't tell.

"Yer mum, huh? She must be related. That must mean you're related, girl. What's your name?"

"My name is Dae O'Donnell. I'm mayor of Duck, and I assure you, my mother wasn't related to you."

"O'Donnell, eh?" He stroked his chin and peered off into the dark. "I knew an O'Donnell—Lewes O'Donnell. As fine a pirate as I ever sailed with. But no relation. What's your grandmother's maiden name?"

I thought back. "Her name was Eleanore Bellamy."

"Bellamy! Why didn't you say so? That was me mum's name before she married that scoundrel Robert Masterson. He left us to fend for ourselves when I was four. We be kin, my dear. No wonder you raised me—fooling around with the dark arts. You'd better be careful or you'll feel the noose around your neck, or worse. They say the fire is a bad way to go. Not that hanging is any fun."

I didn't believe him—didn't want to believe him. We weren't related. There were probably dozens of Bellamys. It was ridiculous. Gramps wasn't related to a pirate either. "I didn't raise you from the dead, Mr. Pirate Masterson." I stumbled over my words. "And if I did it was a mistake. Please go back to your grave or wherever now."

"So yer mum is dead, eh?" He continued as though he hadn't heard me. "Murdered, was she? That's why you're trying to raise her?"

"No." I choked a little on the explanation. "She drove off a bridge and died in the water, they say. Her body was never found."

He nodded. "And you had unspoken things between you. I see."

"Then you see why you can't help me," I said. "Go back home now. Leave me alone."

"Dae?" Kevin's voice got my attention and I looked away from the bar. "Can't sleep?"

"No," I said. "I slept. Then I was hungry. I saw a light on in here." I looked back at the bar and the pirate—possibly my pirate ancestor—was gone. I noticed the glass and the bottle of rum were still there.

"Did you chase someone out of here?" Kevin looked around at the empty bar and bottle.

"Maybe. I don't know." I shook my head. "I'm going back to bed for a while. Sorry I woke you."

"You didn't." He smiled and put his arms around me. "I was having really vivid dreams about being a pirate. Crazy, huh?"

"Maybe not so crazy. The way we talk about them around here, they almost seem real."

I couldn't bring myself to tell him that I'd chatted with Rafe Masterson while he drank Kevin's rum. I wasn't sure

I believed it myself. Maybe I was just hard to convince. It was going to take more than a middle-of-the-night conversation when I was half awake to make me believe.

I went back to bed but sleep eluded me. I was up and cleaning an hour later when the first of the guests came down for coffee. Soon after, all the restless souls were eating breakfast and listening to Scott Randall explain which roads were closed and how people could best get back to their homes.

It sounded like the roads and the town itself were in much better shape than they'd been yesterday, which made everyone happy. It was easier once you'd seen all the damage for yourself and could make a plan for what needed to be done. Gramps and I had faced storm damage many times, as had everyone else who lived in Duck.

Several local insurance agents came by to talk with their clients privately. A few relatives stopped in to pick up their husbands, wives or other family members who'd been trapped at the inn since the storm.

"I guess we should be heading home," Gramps said after filling up on oatmeal. "I know there's some damage to the house. Sooner we get started on it, the sooner it'll get done."

I agreed but thought it was only fair to stay and help Kevin clean up. The guests were leaving a mess behind— every room in the inn was dirty.

But Kevin disagreed with me. "I have my usual cleaning crew coming in today. We'll handle it. I'm going to try and drive over to Hank's Hardware to order glass for the upstairs windows. Let me give you two a ride home, since the golf cart was trashed."

I had to admit I was ready to go. I was eager to get home and see how the house had fared. And I had a few private questions I wanted to ask Gramps. I hoped the words would come for those questions. It wasn't easy to talk to him about my mother.

Kevin's cleaning crew was arriving as we left. Marissa waved to us as she told them what to do. Duck maintenance crew members were out too, cleaning up the streets as we made the trip home.

Gramps and I lived only a few minutes away from the Blue Whale (along with everything else in Duck), but it took about twenty minutes to get there. There was still so much debris in the road, Kevin had to drive very slowly and continually go around tree branches and manmade items that blocked our passage.

"I heard the cell phone towers might be working today," Kevin said as I got out of the truck. "Let me know how things are going, if you have service. Or I can come in now and we can look at the damage."

I hugged him. "Go home. Take care of your own damage. Gramps and I have been at this a lot longer than you. I'll call you later if I can."

"Okay. I'll talk to you later."

I watched him leave, wondering if I should've told him about the pirate ghost—in case Rafe was haunting the Blue Whale now. Who knew if ghosts could travel from one spot to another? He might be drinking rum in Kevin's bar for the next hundred years.

Gramps and I walked around the outside of the house that had been in our family for several generations. The clapboard siding had splintered in a few spots where something had been blown against it, and two windows had been smashed, but otherwise, nothing major was wrong. We closed up the windows with plastic right away. We'd have to replace them later.

"Not too bad," Gramps said when we got inside. "We were pretty much spared."

"I guess this house is in a good spot." I looked around at the place I'd always called home. "Whoever built this place knew what they were doing."

"That would be your great-great-grandfather, Lewes O'Donnell," Gramps said with a smile. "He was a merchant who traded with the ships that docked here."

I couldn't believe it! Rafe had said that Lewes O'Donnell was a pirate. Basically when anyone from Duck talked about their ancestors trading with English or Spanish ships, at the very least they salvaged goods from their wreckage. In the worst cases, they caused it. "Was he a pirate by any chance?"

Gramps shrugged. "Could be. But he died in his bed at the ripe old age of ninety-two. If he started out as a pirate, he was never caught. Anything is possible, Dae. Not many people who are from here have a family history that doesn't include pirates or scavengers."

As our house was in fairly good order, we went next door and checked on our neighbors. Their homes had been hit a little harder. We swept sand, mopped water and put up tarps in places that needed repair. It would take a few days to get the insurance adjusters in to appraise the damage. In the meantime, everyone would have to make do.

When we were finished, we had lunch together. Most people didn't have generators. When something happened and they were on the verge of losing the food in their refrigerators and freezers, they hauled out grills and smokers to cook as much food as could be saved. I had no doubt that there would be large crowds at supper, inside and outside the house. Not everyone put in enough seafood to feed an army like Gramps did. But at these times, it was a good thing.

The weather was nice. I decided to walk down to Missing Pieces for a while. I wasn't really expecting any customers. There weren't many out-of-town visitors in October, and most local people would be occupied with their own storm cleanup.

But I never minded being at the shop, even without customers. It was Gramps's idea for me to open a shop to sell the things I collected. He said the house couldn't hold any more and I could make some money. As usual, he was right.

The only thing I'd known him to be wrong about was not telling me about my father. When I'd first found out, he'd said it was my mother's story to tell. But with her dead, that left him in the hot seat. It was hard hearing from a stranger, the infamous Bunk Whitley, of all people, that a big part of my life had been a lie perpetrated by the two people I trusted and loved most. Old Bunk was supposed to be dead. People had a way of coming back sometimes.

I knew it would be hard for him to explain why he'd lied. Gramps was basically an honest, decent person. He had a stronger sense of right and wrong than most people—which had made him a good sheriff.

He was protecting me, I realized that. But I was an adult. I didn't need protection from the truth. No matter what kind of man my father was, I could handle it. From what I'd seen and the research I'd secretly done, Danny Evans wasn't cut from the same cloth as Gramps. He'd made a lot of mistakes in his life. But it had been a while since he'd been in trouble—about as long as he'd been sober. Surely everyone deserved a few chances.

Martha Segall was waiting outside Missing Pieces on the weathered boardwalk when I arrived. She was the town nuisance—although she'd been called worse by the town council. She attended every town meeting and was an alternate on the planning and zoning board. She'd run for town council when Duck first incorporated, but frankly, no one liked her well enough to vote for her. So she just came to every meeting and complained.

"About time you got here," she said when she saw me. "I've got this package I want to send to my son in Dallas. When do you think it will get there?"

I had become the UPS packager for Duck recently—I didn't make a lot of money from it, but every bit helped. I opened the shop and set down my bag before I answered.

"I don't think UPS will pick up or deliver until the repairs have been made to the bridges."

"And when will that be? And before you say you don't know, let me remind you that you are also the mayor and up for reelection next year, missy. So answer carefully."

I thought about it. There was no clever response. "I know I'm the mayor, Martha, and I know I'm up for reelection. But what I don't know is how much damage was done to the bridges or how long it will take to repair them. We can walk down to town hall and see what Nancy knows about it, if you want."

"All right. Maybe then you'll know what to tell the next person who asks." She took a small notebook out of the pocket of her rain jacket and wrote in it. "That's right. I keep track of these things. And it's a sad state of affairs when the town clerk knows more about what's going on than the mayor. Mad Dog Wilson might just get my vote for mayor next year."

I smiled and closed the door to Missing Pieces. I'd rather have tea and look at all my treasures than spend time with Martha, but I was the mayor and that was part of my job.

Town hall was only a few doors down on the boardwalk. It was filled with Duck citizens complaining and yelling at Nancy, who was trying to answer their questions. The phones were working again—and they were ringing off the hook. It was like a scene from one of those badly made disaster movies I'd loved so much as a teenager.

And as much as I loved my fellow Duck citizens, this was no way to get the answers they needed. I tried to calm everyone down, to no avail. Finally, I grabbed my gavel from Nancy's desk and pounded hard with it until everyone was quiet.

"I know this is hard for all of you," I said to the crowd, "but it's hard on us too. Now I want all of you to make a line, single file, and come to the desk one at a time with your questions and problems. We'll do the best we can to get answers for you. I know most of you—Martha, Vergie and Andy—you've lived here all your life like I have. We get through these things together but not by going crazy."

"Thanks," Nancy whispered as the crowd grumbled but made a line that stretched out the door. "I was about to take out my pistol and shoot a few of them."

"Why didn't you call me?" I asked as I took a seat and got ready to talk to people.

"I did—I called you and everyone else on the council. I guess none of your cell phones are working yet. Home phones are still offline too. We're just blessed up here to have working phones to add to the chaos."

I apologized. I had no way of knowing about the chaos here. While Nancy manned the phone, I wrote down names and questions as each person had their turn. Basically, the Harris Teeter, the only grocery store in Duck, was running out of food and none was expected for at least another day. I told Martha again that I wasn't sure when UPS would pick up, but I would keep her package until I heard from them.

Andy Martin, who ran the ice cream and Slushee store, was understandably upset because there was no power. "My ice cream is ice goo, and my Slushee machine won't work without electricity. Isn't there some way to get some? I know the hospital has power and some of the houses in Duck have power. Why don't I?"

"You might want to consider buying a generator, Andy," I said. "Since your business depends on your freezer, it's a good idea. For now, I'd suggest you clean up and close down for a few days. We must be almost at the end of your season anyway."

He nodded. "I close for the winter and these last few days are important to me. I don't understand why the power comes on for some people and not everyone."

"My best advice on this is to talk it over with the power

company. You know there's only so much we can do from town hall. I'm sorry about your ice cream, and I hope you have insurance to cover it."

He nodded and put his cap on, then left the line.

Almost all the questions, the bulk of which focused on water leaks, power outages, and beach erosion, went the same way. People asked, and I offered suggestions but had no definitive answers.

Little Hailey Baucum, the daughter of Reece Baucum, claimed to have seen a ghost ship. "I saw it last night, Mayor Dae. It was real old looking, and there was no one on it."

Reece, who'd been there to complain about a broken water main, grinned. "You know how kids are."

"Sounds like the *Andalusia*," said Vergie, Duck's postmaster. "You know how people see her from time to time. Especially after a bad storm."

I knew. The *Andalusia* was a Spanish treasure ship that had foundered off the coast of Duck around 1720. Several sailors had made it to the coast to tell of the huge treasure that went down with the ship. Though hundreds of people had searched for it, no one had ever found the gold and jewels that were on it.

Through the generations, Duck citizens, and even some vacationing visitors, had called or written about seeing the ship off the coast. The *Andalusia* was our resident ghost ship. We all knew the story.

"There was a moon last night," Nancy reminded me while she was on hold with the North Carolina Department of Transportation asking for a time reference for the bridge repairs.

Hailey nodded her head with the vigor of an eight-year-old. "I got a telescope for my birthday last month, so I got a really good look. It was the ghost ship for sure. The moonlight was shining on it, so I could see no one was there. But it was sailing anyway. The sails were like big spiderwebs. No way they could catch any breeze like that."

"Well, don't worry. A lot of people have seen the *Andalusia*, but the ghosts never come to Duck," I assured her. "They seem to stay on the ship, and they never bother anyone. We have a book here that we write down every time someone sees her. The sightings go back to the 1800s. You're in good company."

I felt a chill sweep through the room as I finished speaking. My own personal ghost appeared at the back of the line of people waiting to see me. "Why are ye filling the child's mind with such drivel?" Rafe demanded. "There are no ghosts on that ship. Those poor souls lie at the bottom like so many others."

I couldn't answer him, since I was fairly sure no one else could see or hear him. I smiled at Hailey and gave her a sucker. Nothing like a ghost to put ghostly events into perspective.

As soon as possible, I was going to find Shayla and see if there wasn't some way to lay this ghost to rest.

Chapter 16

"There are serious problems needing yer attention." Rafe waited impatiently, the heel of his booted foot stamping on the hardwood floor. As the line of residents moved forward, so did he—until he was standing at the desk, his hands on the pistols he wore at either side of his hips.

Funny how I'd never noticed those pistols in the portrait or during our encounter in the bar. Maybe it had been an oversight on my part. Or maybe he'd added them from his ghostly wardrobe.

I also had never realized from his portrait what a large man he was—wide hips and shoulders, long legs and arms. Probably scared people long before they saw his cutlass unsheathed.

"I need a word with ye," he said, glaring at Nancy. "Ditch the woman."

"Thanks for your help, Dae," Nancy said. "Is it me or is it getting colder in here?"

"You're welcome. I'm sorry I wasn't here sooner. I'm

going over to Missing Pieces for a while if you need me again."

"Okay, sweetie." She hugged me. "Be careful out there. One of the maintenance men went to the hospital with a concussion this morning after a trash can fell on him."

"I know I shouldn't ask—how'd he get under a trash can?"

"It was on the roof of the community center. Crazy, right?" She laughed but not in a mean way—Nancy doesn't have a mean bone in her body. But both of us had seen some weird things while taking care of Duck for the past two years.

"Simpering, blubbering female," Rafe grumbled as I walked out of town hall with him at my side.

"She is not," I corrected him when we were out of ear-shot. "Not that you'd know the difference."

"And why do you say that?"

"Because you've probably never known anyone like Nancy." I waved to Trudy as she worked on Mrs. Marsh's hair at her salon, still without power. "Women are different now. I don't expect you to understand that, since you're a pirate and all."

"Are you saying I'm daft or addlepated? Mind your words, girl!"

"Or what? You'll jump back into your picture frame?"

He laughed—a loud, arrogant kind of laughter like you'd expect from a big pirate. "Oh, I can do much more than *that*. You see that window over there? The one ye were so happy yesterday that it had escaped the storm?"

Before I could respond, he took a deep breath and blew hard on the glass. It didn't break but it splintered into a thousand lines.

"I can't believe you did that!" I stormed at him. "Now I'll have to get it replaced. What was the thinking behind that?"

"Eh? I don't understand what you mean. My own kin— not able to speak the King's English."

I didn't bother with a reply. For one thing, August Grandin walked by with a nod of his head, his Meerschaum pipe in his teeth. The smoke blew in my face as he passed—a sweet smell of fruit-scented tobacco.

"Now that's a man." Rafe followed August toward the Duck General Store. I took the opportunity to hide in Missing Pieces. It would be nice if he couldn't find me. But it didn't seem to work that way.

If I had to have a ghost attached to me, why wasn't it one of our stalwart Duck female role models?

I closed the door behind me and took a deep breath, relieved to be alone.

"I didn't mean to scare you," a familiar voice said. "I wanted to thank you for your help yesterday."

I wasn't alone after all. My father had finally come calling.

Chapter 17

"Your name is Dae O'Donnell, right?" he asked with a little smile playing across his lips. He needed a shave, and there were scratches on his cheeks and forehead. "Mayor of Duck!"

"Yes." I wondered if he still recognized the name. "Shouldn't you be at the hospital?"

"Nah. They released me when they found out I didn't have health insurance. Besides, they needed the bed."

"Well, maybe you should be at home then. I could drive you, if you need a ride." My heart was hammering in my chest. Why was I so nervous? After all, he was my father, though he didn't know it.

"Trying to get rid of me?" He got up from the burgundy brocade sofa and came closer. "I bet your mom and your grandpa have been telling you all kinds of bad stuff about me."

I could honestly say neither one of them had mentioned

him—at least not until I asked. "No. Not really. Would you like some tea?"

"Nothing stronger?"

"No. Sorry. I have some strong tea—that's about it."

"That's okay." He stopped at the counter that I'd put between him and me. "You know, I recognized you yesterday at the accident. You come into the Sailor's Dream once in a while and order rum and Coke, right?"

"Yep. That's me." I wished I could think of something fascinating to say to him. But glib conversation was difficult for me with him.

"That's why I asked about you. You look just like your mom. How is she, by the way? Happy with Mr. Right?" He looked up at me with a cunning knowing in his blue eyes. "I guess since your name is O'Donnell, Mr. Right either never came along or left real sudden."

I didn't know how to answer that. I hadn't anticipated having a conversation with him like this. He thought he knew who I was—the mayor of Duck and his old flame's daughter. But he hadn't guessed that I was his daughter. I felt awkward and even more nervous. "I'd like some tea." I bustled to the cabinet and took out the Sterno and folding stove I kept for emergencies. After lighting it, I put some water in the kettle and put it on the stove. "Are you sure I can't get some for you?"

"No, thanks. I'm not that thirsty." He started walking around looking at my treasures. He picked up the flintlock pistol that had belonged to pirate Stede Bonnett, a summer find at the Charleston Market.

It had engraved silver mounts, gold leaf, silver wire inlays and a carved stock. The French barrel had a carved relief of St. George slaying the dragon. It wasn't fully functional. There was no fly in the tumbler and no bridle in the lock. That meant it wouldn't fire properly. It was a special piece—one that would net enough to tide me over for a long winter—but only to the right person.

"So you own this place?" He kept talking. Maybe he was nervous too. "And you're the mayor and you work as a firefighter or something?"

The dealer who sold the pistol to me thought it was junk—but then he couldn't touch it and find out where it came from like I could. I'd struggled for a while, wondering if that was cheating, until I thought about all the fake treasures I'd paid too much for. Treasure hunting was up and down.

"I was just helping out," I told him. "I'm not an official volunteer or anything."

"This is a nice place." He came back and sat down. "You're kind of young to own something like this, aren't you? Does your mom help out?"

"My mom is dead." There—it was out. The teakettle whistled, and I poured the hot water over the blackberry tea bag in the cup. "She's been dead a long time."

"Sorry. I didn't know."

"How could you? Why would you?"

He shrugged. "I guess she didn't mention me then. We dated for a while. It was a long time ago. We were both just kids. Did she marry someone?"

"No." Despite my earlier resolution to confront him, I wasn't sure how far I wanted this conversation to go. It was crossing over into part of my life that I wasn't comfortable sharing with him yet. I didn't even want to think what Gramps would say if he knew Danny Evans was having a casual conversation with me about Mom in Missing Pieces.

"I'm sorry." He backed down. "I don't know you well enough to ask you this kind of stuff, I guess. You're just a lot like Jean. She was easy to talk to."

"Sure." I added some honey to the tea but didn't sit down to drink it.

"Anyway." He got to his feet and hooked his fingers in the pockets of his well-worn jeans. "I just came by to say thanks. And, I admit I was a little curious about you. I'll see you around, Dae. Next time, the rum and Coke is on me."

I realized after he was gone that I'd been holding my breath, hoping he wouldn't guess the truth. The connection was there—he couldn't see it yet. How was I going to feel about it when he could?

I took my tea and sank gratefully down on my sofa—only to jump up an instant later, emptying my cup as I sat on my ghost pirate's lap.

He winked and grinned at me, gold tooth showing on the right side of his mouth. "Aw, we ain't that close related, dearie. The ladies favored me when I was alive. No reason we couldn't have a little fun, even though you're a mite scrawny for my taste."

"Don't even go there!" I warned, not sure what I could do to prevent it, since I couldn't stop him from being there at all. "Never mind. We're going next door. Shayla has to know some way to get rid of you."

"Look, girl, there's a very easy answer to you getting rid of me. You're the last of my line—far as I can tell. I need yer help with the kind of thing only a relation can do. You do that, and I'm gone. *Poof!* Not like I want to be half alive, half in the grave in this foul time. The air stinks like bilge water, and the women have no rounding to them. What's there to make a man feel welcome here?"

The shop door flew open and Shayla stalked inside without bothering to close the door behind her. "I knew it! I *knew* I sensed a presence here somewhere. Dae, what have you taken up with? Haven't I warned you about messing around with things you don't understand?"

Chapter 18

"Me?" I put down my teacup. "What are you talk-ing about? He was in one of those spirit balls that came from the séance. In case you didn't notice—he's not my mother."

Shayla frowned, brows knitting over her dramatically made-up dark eyes. "I don't know how that's possible. I was *very* specific. Not just any spirit could come through like that."

"He says we're related through my mother's side of the family."

"Well, of course! That makes perfect sense."

"I'm glad you think so. But you haven't heard the best of it yet. Shayla Lily, spiritual advisor—meet Rafe Masterson, hanged pirate who cursed Duck."

"That's an old wives' tale," Rafe objected.

"A pirate?" Shayla giggled and pranced around like a teenager. "How exciting!"

"Shayla—"

"Pleasure to meet you, beautiful lady." Rafe sketched an

elegant bow to her. "Is that a taste of the old spirits, from the islands, I feel about you? I had a friend—a very *good* friend—from Barbados who knew the spirits well. She was sweet and dark as good rum, like you, wench. A lovely prize for the taking."

I was getting impatient with this mutual admiration society. "All of this is very nice, but can we get rid of him or not?"

"He's amazing," Shayla said. "I don't know why you wouldn't want to keep him. He could help you identify old stuff that you find."

"He's not a puppy," I reminded her, even though I was glad she was able to see and hear him too. "And I don't want him hanging around."

Shayla walked around him with her eyes closed and presumably her mojo working. "I'm not sure," she said finally. "We can try. But blood ties are strong."

"Now wait a minute," Rafe interrupted. "I have a valid reason for being here. This isn't a lark for me, ladies. I need a relation to help me clear my name."

"Clear your name?" I laughed. "Clear it of what? Everyone knows you did terrible things. You were hanged as a pirate because of them."

"I was," he agreed. "But I wasn't a pirate when that unfortunate event took place. And I had papers of pardon from the governor himself."

I thought about what Mark Samson had said about Rafe. Maybe he was right. But having a large pirate ghost tag along with me everywhere I went wasn't exactly my idea of a good time. There had to be another way.

"Let's say you're telling the truth," I said. "How about you go back to your grave and I look into it for you."

"Why would I take yer word for what you'll do when you are so eager to get rid of me? I wasn't born yesterday."

"Because otherwise Shayla will make you go away for good and you might never get your name cleared." Although what difference that would make after all these years was beyond me. "At least if I promise to investigate the history of your death, you have a shot."

He stroked his chin. "I don't think so. Not that I want to be here, but this is important to me. And your friend here doesn't seem too sure she can get rid of me at all. Besides, I can help you find who murdered the woman at the old house. Ye need me too, girl."

"We don't know yet if she was murdered at all," I told him. "But thanks for the offer."

"I know," he assured me. "I can smell it a league away."

"I thought you said that was an accident, Dae?" Shayla asked.

"It probably *was* an accident. She shouldn't have been out there during the storm."

"An accident," Rafe scoffed. "If it was an accident, then I don't know gold from dross."

"Okay. Who killed her?" I asked the pirate ghost.

"That I don't know—but I could be helpful in the search for the devil who done the deed," he said with great confidence. "It's the smell of blood. T'would be all over him."

I thought about his offer. Maybe he knew something the rest of us didn't. He was a ghost, and ghosts were supposed to know things—see things we couldn't from the other side. And Shayla seemed really uncertain about getting rid of him.

And I supposed I could look into the matter of his history, since Mark had already said much the same thing. The usual Duck history must be missing some facts if suddenly Rafe Masterson was the wronged party in his hanging.

I still didn't believe he was really related to me. But it could prove interesting finding out for sure and possibly rewriting part of that Duck history.

"All right," I agreed finally. "I'll help you, and you can help me. But we need some ground rules."

"I don't take to rules well," he growled, dark eyes fierce.

"That's your choice." I smiled at Shayla. "Any time you want to get rid of him—"

"All right! All right! You made your case." He paced about one inch above the floor. "Ye drive a hard bargain, girl, and that's no lie. What do you want of me?"

"You stay out of my private life—no standing around while I'm sleeping or hanging out in the bathroom for any reason with me. You have to keep your distance. And no starting up conversations or making demands while I'm with people who might think I'm crazy talking to you."

He agreed. "Done and done. You must be my own flesh and blood to be so hard on a man. That must be why ye aren't wed at such an old age. No man wants you, I warrant."

I ignored the backhanded compliment. "Deal?"

He spit on his hand and reached it toward me. "Deal—and no going back on it."

Lucky for me he wasn't real enough to have spit that I could touch. "Good. You can start by leaving right now and going wherever it is you go when you disappear."

He frowned and kind of growled at me again, but he disappeared.

"He's gone," Shayla said. "Wow! What a spirit! You're so lucky to have him as an ancestor."

"Thanks." I cleaned up my tea spill. "No telling what I just agreed to."

"Admit it—you're excited. You love all that old dusty stuff. Look at what you collect here. I know you want to prove your ancestor was wrongly put to death. It's your kind of thing."

"You really think he's related to me and not just saying that so I'll help him?"

"I think it's the only thing that could have brought him and held him here. Blood is very powerful. It's hard for any spirit to get a foothold in our world much less be able to speak to the living. It's the bond between you that gives him strength. Look how he can follow you around from place to place. That's very unusual. He's definitely your ancestor. Don't you have a family tree or something?"

I remembered hearing something about my grandmother having started work on family records. I wasn't sure if that was for the O'Donnell or the Bellamy family. I'd have to ask Gramps about it.

"It's weird thinking I have an ancestor that was a pirate," I admitted. "I always think of my predecessors as being hardy Duck folk—Bankers who survived by their wits and backbones and who held on to their homes with their fingertips when the storms came."

She shrugged. "You never know, do you? We don't get to decide where we come from. I've never been able to shake the feeling that Marie Laveau is watching me. Who knows? Maybe I'll get lucky and she'll have some urgent need to be avenged."

Only Shayla would think being haunted by a pirate ghost was a good thing. I asked her to look up information about getting rid of Rafe in case our agreement didn't work out. I could tell she thought I was crazy not taking full advantage of this opportunity, but I was worried about the potential consequences of having a ghost in my life.

Shayla went back to her shop, and I got out the duster to go over my treasures. I considered what she'd said about Rafe helping me identify things I'd found from his time. I didn't need his help anyway. And it wasn't worth having a pirate looking over my shoulder.

How would I know if he was there—even now? What about when I dressed, showered, spent time alone with Kevin? I didn't want to constantly feel his presence or be the butt of his pirate jokes all my life. He was very good at making fun of me already.

I realized as I finished dusting that something was missing. I couldn't tell at first what it was. It seemed that something was out of place. Then it came to me.

A small, gold makeup case, its crest set with red and

green stones. It had been on the counter when I was speaking to my father. Had he picked it up because it looked valuable? I hated the idea that he'd steal from me.

He was going to be disappointed if money was his motive. The eighteenth-century piece was valuable—but only to the right collector. It had graced the vanity of Lady Suzanne Forester, a wealthy beauty who briefly lived in the Carolinas with her uncle, Lord William Forester.

But the stones weren't real. The gold was good, but—

I stopped in midthought, hating that I was accusing him in my mind. Gramps had told me so much about him being a shady character—and I knew something about his checkered past from my own research.

But that wasn't me. I tried never to judge a person without first knowing them.

I knew Shayla didn't pick it up. I was fairly sure Rafe couldn't pick it up. But maybe the case had fallen. I'd had it on the counter for a customer who would've already purchased it, except for the storm.

I was on my hands and knees looking for the case, fueling my guilt about accusing my father, when Kevin stopped by. He looked exhausted, filthy from working with the cleanup crew in the street.

"I'm on my way home for a shower and some sleep," he said. "Just wanted to stop by and let you know that the medical examiner is calling Mayor Foxx's death a murder."

I got to my feet—thinking about what Rafe had said. "If the shed collapsing didn't kill her, what did?"

"The small-caliber bullet shot at close range into her heart. The ME said whoever did it was standing almost on top of her when it happened."

"That's terrible." Even though I'd seen a gun in my vision and felt Sandi's fear, I'd really hoped this wouldn't end up as a murder.

"Yeah. Another death at the Blue Whale." His smile was

tight and not amused. "You think it's something following me around?"

I didn't answer—though the similarities of our circumstances struck me. I knew the Blue Whale had a dubious past. This was bad news on so many different levels. I hated to think of Sandi's two little girls going through a murder trial.

But it was the soft pirate *I-told-you-so* laughter I heard from close behind me that made me shiver.

Chapter 19

I left Missing Pieces with Kevin—I didn't want to be alone. My favorite places were suddenly too empty, too likely to be visited by a ghostly pirate. We were going to have to have a word or two about that. I should've added "No laughter in the background of conversations" to my list of demands.

Kevin and I talked about the things he'd seen while he was working and the progress the cleanup crews were making. He said he could tell the difference later in the day. There was less debris in the roads and more along the sides.

Traffic was beginning to flow more freely—we had to wait for cars to pass to get across Duck Road. I wasn't sure where everyone was going, since most of the stores were closed and there was no way off the island. But the drivers seemed intent on being out and pursuing their own agendas.

I wanted to tell Kevin about my ghostly pirate ancestor, but really—how do you say something like that? Even though Kevin was rational about my gift, I didn't want to find out yet how far I could push his belief in the paranormal. I was having a hard time believing Rafe Masterson's appearance myself.

We walked back to the Blue Whale, reaching the crushed mermaid fountain (minus the car) as Tim Mabry circled around the drive in his police car.

"Brickman." Tim nodded at Kevin as he got out of the car. "Dae, I'm afraid I have some bad news."

Tim was a born storyteller. He'd weave even the most mundane aspects of his everyday life into an hour-long tale. I wasn't in the mood for it. "We know about the murder," I said, showing less tolerance than usual.

"Damn! How'd you find out?" he demanded. "I've only known for a few minutes."

"I was there when the ME called Chief Michaels," Kevin answered. "Sorry."

Tim hitched up his uniform on his six-foot-six, one-hundred-eighty-pound frame. He ran his hand across his blond flattop and wrinkled his nose the way he'd done it since we were kids. "I might still be one step ahead of you, Brickman."

"Okay." Kevin paused. "What's the other bad news?"

"Chief says everyone is coming back to the Blue Whale—everyone who was here when Mayor Foxx was killed, that is. They have twenty-four hours to get back here and answer questions about where they were and how they felt about the deceased."

"The bridges must be fixed," I muttered.

"Not yet—but you didn't know that, right? They say the bridges will be open and the ferries will be running tomorrow morning. That's why the chief is giving all the suspects twenty-four hours to get here."

"The crime scene is a mess," Kevin said. "What's the point?"

"In case you haven't noticed"—Tim looked at me while he was being clever—"we're not the FBI. We only have a few officers to conduct a murder investigation. We can't be running around after all those people. Chief says they need to come to us or risk having a bench warrant put out on them."

"Great," Kevin replied. "This just gets better and better. I hope the chief has thought about who's feeding these people while they're here."

"I'm sure you'll be compensated for everything," I said. "I'm sorry you have to go through this."

"What about Matthew Wright?" Kevin asked. "I thought everyone was looking at him for this—if it turned out to be foul play."

"He'll be here." Tim put his hand on his gun holster. "If he knows what's good for him."

"I thought he was in custody," I added. "Weren't you holding him for a while?"

"We could only legally hold him for forty-eight hours, Dae. You know that! Or did you lose track of time?"

"It hasn't been forty-eight hours," I argued.

"He convinced a judge that his time at the Blue Whale should be considered. We let him go—but he'll be here."

Kevin shrugged. "I'm going to take a shower and get some sleep before the new arrivals get here. I'm sure everything will look better then."

"Would you like me to make you something to eat?" I offered.

"No, thanks. We were well fed today. Everyone is cooking all their food on their grills and giving the food away before it spoils. Betty Vasquez makes a mean bowl of chili in her cooker."

"Okay. I'll talk to you later then." I glanced around, not sure where to go to find enough company to keep Rafe Masterson at bay.

"You don't have to leave." Kevin kissed me and smiled.

"You can hang around here. You don't even have to clean up or anything."

"No, I should go home and see if Gramps needs any help. Give me a call when you get up—if your cell phone is working."

He looked at me for a minute longer. Sometimes I felt as though he was the one with the gift. He always seemed to know when something was wrong.

But I was determined to let him rest in peace (no pun intended) while I tried to decide if I should tell him about my ghostly visitor.

"Dae—" Tim began when the door had closed behind Kevin and we were alone.

"Don't start," I warned, walking away, hoping Gramps was home.

"What? I was only going to tell you that I'd be glad to drive you home. The mayor of Duck shouldn't have to walk everywhere she goes."

"Thanks," I said grudgingly. "I'd rather walk."

"What happened between us?" he asked, going where I wished he wouldn't go.

"We grew up, Tim. We weren't meant to be together."

"But you and Brickman are?"

"I don't know. I only know that you and I aren't ever going to be romantically involved. You know that too. That's why you keep trying other people. We just have to move on."

"My mom still believes we'll end up together," he said.

I waved as I walked briskly away. There was no use talking to him when he got this way—usually between girlfriends. I was always "the one" when he wasn't dating someone else. It was kind of depressing.

So was thinking about Sandi being shot behind the Blue Whale while the rest of us cowered inside, afraid of the storm. I wished I could say I was surprised by the news, but I'd felt it in my bones before Kevin confirmed it.

The killer must have forced her outside—maybe Matthew, maybe someone else. It was probably to use the storm to shield the sound of the pistol. He or she lucked out with the shed collapsing on Sandi and conveniently covering up the crime.

I wished for the millionth time that my visions were more precise. It would've been more helpful to have seen the killer's face than to have seen the gun. Surely Sandi had enemies—everyone in political office did. But there was a big difference between Martha Segall writing down my faults as mayor in her little book and someone dragging Sandi outside the Blue Whale and shooting her.

It seemed so obvious that Matthew Wright was guilty of shooting Sandi. He was there with her—they were lovers who were quarreling over their relationship. He had motive, means (possibly) and opportunity.

But I knew the obvious answer wasn't always the right answer. How many times had I seen Gramps convinced that he knew what was going on in a case only to find out he had to go in another direction. Chief Michaels would have to prove Matthew had a .22-caliber pistol and find some way to put him in back of the Blue Whale with her when she died. That probably wasn't going to be easy.

Halfway home, I decided to turn around and go back to take a look at the collapsed shed and the area around it again. It might not officially be a crime scene yet—they'd just received the medical examiner's report.

If the police had already roped it off, I'd cross that stream when I got there. Everything I'd heard so far had been secondhand reports. How was I supposed to know that I shouldn't go back there? That was my story and I was sticking to it.

But there might be something left behind that I could pick up on and give the chief a hand. Not that he'd be happy about it, but I knew he'd take any help he could get. The shed had been such a mess, and finding Sandi dead out there had been a shock. I was bound to have overlooked some potential clues.

I wasn't born a crime solver. Somehow it had happened to me, kind of like being the mayor. One day, Gramps said I should run. I hadn't planned for it. I had to learn on the fly—just as I was learning to do more than find lost jewelry.

I saw Town Councilman Mad Dog Wilson on the road coming toward me from the Blue Whale. No doubt he'd been looking over the crime scene. I almost turned back, but he waved and I knew he'd seen me. Too late to escape.

I knew he was going to be trouble. He was looking for any ammunition to use against me in the upcoming election. Sandi's murder, tragic though it was, wouldn't be off the table for him. We'd never exactly been friends—he was much older than me. But lately we'd become adversaries.

"Mayor." He nodded and paused, leaning heavily on his oak walking stick.

Gramps said Randall "Mad Dog" Wilson was a fearless stock car driver in his youth—until a terrible wreck had almost killed him. Hence the nickname—Mad Dog—and the cane.

"Councilman."

"This is some bad business," he said. "Bad news for Duck."

"Yes it is." I could have pretended that he was talking about the storm, but what was the point? Better to get it over with. "I hope we can clear it up quickly and put it behind us."

"I hope so too. You know, I don't have any choice but to point out how much civil unrest there has been during your term as mayor when I write my blog this week. The people expect the truth."

I groaned inwardly but kept my cheerful mayor's smile on my face. Mad Dog's blog—*Duck Notes*—had become infamous since he announced his decision to run for mayor. He sent email alerts to everyone in town—and a few media people too—whenever he posted an update. Mostly the media ignored him, but I had heard people in town talking about the blog.

"You have to do what you think is right," I told him. "But I'm wondering how much it will hurt the town to publicize the murder. This could stay quiet, Councilman, at least for now. I know you want to use this tragedy in the campaign, but it could end up hurting you too."

He smiled in a sad, avuncular way. "Dae, it has never been my intention to hurt you in any way by the things I've said and done. I've known you since you were a baby. You've grown into a wonderful, caring young woman. I'm proud that you were the first mayor of Duck. I just think we need some new blood in the position—a firmer, perhaps masculine, hand on the reins."

This was Mad Dog at his worst—pretending we were friends, almost relations. All the time he was talking, I knew he didn't mean a word of it. He'd spoken out several times after my election, once demanding that the town take another vote. The problem was that no one had run against me, not even him. He was busy running for town council at the time.

"I appreciate that," I said, playing the game. "But please consider that your words could cause more headaches than they'd be worth to you. I know we both want what's best for Duck. Nice talking with you."

"Going to see your boyfriend?" He baited me even as I walked away from him. "Mr. Brickman could be a liability to your campaign, you know. There are many people here in Duck who might not like the idea of their mayor prancing around town with her boyfriend."

I ignored him. I knew from the past that we could argue all day and never reach any kind of agreement. There was no point in wasting my time with him. He was going to do whatever he wanted anyway.

I started around the side of the Blue Whale, careful to be observant as I went. I was looking for anything out of the ordinary—something that not even the most experienced police officer would think was a clue—something that would call only to me.

Of course there were countless footprints and the track from the stretcher they'd used to take Sandi away. Kevin was right about the scene being compromised. I still wanted to give it another look.

Shawn Foxx apparently had the same idea. He looked up as I walked closer. "Is this where she died?"

"Yes. Maybe. I'm not really sure."

"But this is where you found her?"

"Yes." I could answer that at least. I felt terrible for him, but I didn't know what to say that might give him closure. "I'm sorry I don't know more."

He stood up and looked out at the sea. "I always knew something like this would happen to her. I begged her not to keep meeting those other men on the side. What did she think would happen?"

"I don't know. Would you like to go inside and sit down?"

"No." He glared at me and clenched his fists. "How could she do this to me and the girls? Why didn't she ever think about them?"

I certainly didn't have an answer to that question. I'd asked it many times myself. I didn't understand the attraction of infidelity, but I never thought Sandi would end up dead because of it. "The police will find out who did this, Shawn. You just need to take care of yourself and the girls."

"You know what, Dae? It doesn't matter. I don't even care anymore."

I watched him stride around the side of the inn.

Rafe appeared—who could stop him? He was furious

about the things Mad Dog had said to me. "I can't believe ye let that scurvy dog speak to you in that tone—and you the Lord High Mayor of this town!"

I couldn't complain. He'd kept to the rules about leaving me alone when I was with other people. "That doesn't mean all that much anymore," I told him. "I guess it meant something in your day?"

"A man like that would be clapped in irons," he replied. "Depending on the mercy of the mayor, he could find himself flogged too."

I smiled, concentrating on the area around the shed. "We don't do much flogging nowadays."

"More's the pity from what I've seen!"

"You were in the shop when Kevin told me about Sandi being murdered."

"Aye. That doesn't break our treaty, girl. You said not to speak to you—I did not speak."

"I think I said not to hang around," I corrected.

"A pleasant thing to say to a man whose corpse still bears marks from the hangman's noose!"

I refused to feel guilty for the gaffe. "How did you know that Sandi was murdered? I mean before Kevin told us. Is that a ghost thing?"

"I don't know what ye mean by 'a ghost thing,'" he said. "Unless you're speaking of common deduction. I heard all the same things you heard. It was simple to conclude she met up with foul play. Did you really think she was just standing out here and let the storm kill her?"

"Not everything is that cut and dry," I explained, feeling kind of stupid. I reasoned that he probably had more experience with murder than I did. And I wanted to believe that she'd died accidentally.

"If you say so. What are you looking for out here?"

"A clue—something that will help tell us who killed Sandi."

"Such as what?"

"I don't know. I'll know it when I see it."

I tried to concentrate, but instead, I looked at Rafe. He stood beside me with his fists on his wide hips—large, booted feet never touching the wet ground. He had a perpetual scowl. Deep frown lines ran between his eyes in his darkly tanned skin. His lips pulled down at the corners—they would forever. Various scars across his cheek, near his eye, and a long one near his ear, gave the impression that he was not a friendly man. Curiously, there was no sign of the noose, as he'd said.

"What happened when you were caught and hanged?" I asked, trying to cut to the heart of his problem. I didn't need a ghost in my life any longer than necessary.

"Caught?" He laughed in an egotistical manner. "I was never *caught*, girl. I gave up the pirate life for a comely young lass who proceeded to bear babes every time we scratched that itch. I made some deals, tried to become an honest merchant. But the magistrate kept at my heels like a rabid spaniel. He wouldn't rest until he had me in the noose. Finally he made up a crime and convicted me of it. The result of which ye see before you—a murdered man."

I didn't mention that he'd lived more than three hundred years ago and would have been dead by now, no matter what. "How do you think I can clear your name at this late date?"

"The magistrate kept a journal. I have it on good account that he wrote all of his crimes in it. If we were to find it, my name would be cleared."

"Can you ask him where it is?" I wasn't sure where to look for something like that. I'd never heard of a magistrate in this area. "He must be dead too."

"No doubt. But we aren't all out here bobbing around like sailors after a wreck. I found you because you called. Yer friend was right—blood is the only thing that can call a spirit. You'll have to find an ancestor of the magistrate and ask about his journal."

"That sounds easy," I muttered, looking carefully through the pieces of wood hastily thrown aside as we'd tried to pull Sandi from the wreckage. "You should be out of my life in about ten years."

Chapter 20

I moved everything—even ripped my hand open on a nail. I crawled along the ground. There was nothing out of the ordinary.

I sat on the wet ground for a while, looking out at the now placid gray ocean. I let my mind wander along those gentle waves, but no brilliant revelations came to me. In a way, it was too bad that I couldn't communicate with Sandi's ghost. She could tell me what had happened. That would be easy.

My ghost told me stories about plundering rich merchant ships, drinking and spending time with prostitutes. Hardly conducive to helping with my search for a clue.

The wind was still running wild along the island. Nancy was right. The storm seemed to have brought in the cooler fall temperatures. I shivered, wet and dirty, deciding to go home. There was nothing else I could do here.

Rafe went with me like a friendly puppy—a puppy wearing pistols and a saber—still talking about his pirate exploits. He might have settled down at the end of his life, but it was obvious which life he preferred.

I kept hoping I'd run into someone coming out of the Blue Whale or walking up the street. No such luck. I didn't want to violate our agreement—especially since I was going home to shower and change clothes. I wanted him gone for those events. I could imagine him comparing me to his pirate girlfriends. I didn't think it would matter that we were related.

There was traffic on Duck Road, but it was slow even for this point after the season. Several people waved and yelled their greetings to me, but none of them walked over to save me from Rafe.

I noticed someone near the Duck Shoppes trash bin. It was in a sheltered area to the side of the ground floor. The out-of-the-way location was supposed to keep the area hidden from tourists and other visitors. We had some problems with people sleeping here, mostly over the summer. Tourists would come to Duck without making a reservation, expecting they'd be able to find a hotel room. As a result, some of them ended up on the street.

But there were also hardship cases—people who lost their money and credit cards, whose cars broke down or had other misfortunes. They needed help to get back home, maybe a few dollars or a place to stay for the night.

I walked over to the trash bin and peeked behind it, ready to smile and offer whatever help I could. The man I'd seen from the street looked up, fear in his familiar face.

"Danny?"

"Dae?" he said, surprised and clearly uncomfortable. "What are you doing here?"

I could have asked him the same thing, but his purpose was obvious. "You don't have any place to stay."

He shrugged. "My house is flooded. The bar is closed for repairs. I don't even have the van to sleep in, you know?"

"No friends—relatives?"

"Not anymore. Not for a long time." He grinned. "You give up drinking and your old life and all your friends are like rats getting off the sinking ship. I've never had family out here. They're all in Virginia. I left Duck after your mother and I broke up, came back just a couple of years ago. I didn't have a reason to stay in Virginia anymore."

I felt sorry for him. But I couldn't offer him the spare room in our house as I would another Duck resident. If Gramps even knew we were speaking, he'd hit the roof.

"Come with me," I said. "You can stay in the shop until the house, bar or van is fixed. It's not much, but it's dry and warm. Do you need money for food or clothes?"

He dug his hands into his dirty jeans. "I can't take that kind of help from you. You don't know me. You don't know if you can trust me."

"Maybe not. But I have an instinct about these things. It's never let me down."

I refused to think about that niggling doubt—he'd taken the makeup case from the counter. I couldn't live that way. Besides, he was my father. If I didn't help him when he needed it, who could I help?

"Yeah, well, your instinct isn't so good, Dae." He took his hand out of his pocket and in it was the gold makeup case. "I'm sorry. I won't make excuses about being desperate. Old habits die hard."

I took it from him with a smile. "You *were* desperate. I can't even imagine not having anyone I could depend on. Besides, you gave it back to me."

"It won't happen again," he promised. "I was thinking how I could give it back to you without you knowing about it. This is it for me. I have a different life now."

"A different life is good," I told him. "But if you need money, I'd rather give it to you upfront."

"I could use a few bucks," he admitted. "The owner of

the Sailor's Dream evacuated before the storm with my paycheck. I'm broke, and I haven't eaten since I got out of the hospital."

I fished forty dollars out of my purse and put the gold makeup case in its place. "I'd invite you home—"

"But Sheriff O'Donnell has a long memory?" He shook his head. "You don't have to tell me about it. That's why your mom and I broke up, you know, all those years ago. He found out who I was and told me I wasn't good enough for Jean. He threatened to put me in jail—make my life hell. I laughed at him. My life had been one long hell until I met your mother. But I guess he got to Jean. I never saw her again."

I was surprised by the story but didn't let on. Maybe it was the truth—or at least his version of it. Gramps hadn't said anything like that to me. He'd said Danny kicked my mother out after learning she was pregnant with me.

And while Gramps had lied to me my whole life about my father being dead, I couldn't completely distrust him either. I didn't know Danny well, but he'd obviously had a troubled life. I didn't want to start making him a hero when he obviously wasn't.

But I was interested to know which way the truth lay on this path.

"Come on. Let's get you settled into Missing Pieces," I said after handing over the forty dollars. "There's another curfew tonight. I don't think either one of us wants to be out after dark."

We walked up the stairs to the shops on the boardwalk in the evening stillness. He turned to me before we got to Missing Pieces. "Why are you doing all this, Dae? I know you're the mayor and everything, but I don't see you out rescuing every lost soul in Duck. Why me?"

I smiled as I opened the door to the shop. "I try to help as many souls as I can every day." *Literally—since there's a pirate ghost standing at my shoulder, no doubt.* "I think that's part of my job as mayor. There aren't a lot of people in Duck. We have to stick together."

He smiled and put his arms around me. "You're so much like your mother. She wanted to save the world too. I'm sorry she's dead. I always thought I'd see her one more time."

I felt tears welling in my eyes and blinked them back before they could roll down my cheeks. "I'm sorry she's not here too." I changed the subject to something less emotional, pointing out the hot plate—if the power came back on during the night—the Sterno if it didn't. I showed him where the extra key was over the door and where to find the spare blanket and pillow. I always kept one in back in case I decided to spend the night.

"That should do it," I said, fastening a smile on my face and holding on to it despite the dangerous emotional undertow this man represented for me. "If you need to get in touch with me, here's my cell phone number."

"I'd say thank you, but it wouldn't really cover it. I've never met anyone like you and your mother, who always see the best in everyone. I hope I can do something for you sometime when you need it."

Again, I was ready to cry. I hugged him, then got out of there before I started blubbering and told him I was his daughter. It wasn't the right time yet. I didn't know when the right time would be, but it wasn't now.

"I'll see you tomorrow," he called out the door while I ran down the boardwalk as if Davy Jones himself were after me.

As I was running down the stairs into the parking lot, Rafe joined me again. "What a sniveling worm of a man that is! I can't believe ye let him stay in your shop knowing the blackguard stole from you! What kind of man does that?"

"You're a pirate. Or at least you were. Figure it out." Once I reached Duck Road, I slowed my frantic pace. It was getting dark, but I figured Tim could stop me and tell me the curfew was in force if he wanted to. I wasn't running all the way home. I needed a little time to take a few deep breaths and think about what Danny had said about him and my mother.

"Aye, at least I never pretended to be anything else," Rafe continued. "That boyo is just waiting for the right moment to steal you blind. I can't believe any relation of mine would be fooled by all that mucky sentiment."

"And maybe you're not as smart as you think," I yelled back at him. "That man is my father."

"Maybe so—but don't trust him. He's a scallywag, mark my words."

I kept walking down the deserted road. There were no streetlights, no lights from stores or houses. Only the glow of candles and lanterns, from living room and kitchen windows, showed anything was out in the dark at all.

"Have you given any thought to who the ancestor of the magistrate could be?" he asked before we reached the house.

"I've been a little busy," I replied. "And it's going to take some research. Have you given any thought to who killed Sandi Foxx?"

He grunted at me and scratched his head. "Keeping up with you has been a job, girl. I haven't worked so hard since I started my career at sea as a boson's mate."

"Then I guess we both have work to do."

Chapter 21

I went inside where Gramps was waiting with supper at the candlelit table in the kitchen. "I've been wondering where you were," he said, serving up stew that had been in the freezer. "There's a curfew, you know. The mayor isn't above the law and needs to set an example."

"I know."

"You've been at Missing Pieces, haven't you? You always lose track of time when you're there."

"Yep." I wished I could say more. It was a strain holding back the things I really wanted to ask him. But I needed time to sort through everything and figure out what to say to him.

"I suppose you heard that the ME has ruled Mayor Foxx's death a murder," he continued.

"Yeah. That's going to be a mess."

"It'll be bad for Kevin, since it means all those people coming back again on his dime."

I stopped pushing the stew around on my plate. "What do you mean?"

"I mean the county won't want to pay for them to be at the Blue Whale, and it will likely take a while for Ronnie to question all of them. Big group."

"Maybe the town can help. Kevin is too good-hearted to complain about it. I'm sure it will seem like another civic duty to him. But that's not fair."

"Good luck getting that past the town council."

"We have an emergency fund," I reminded him. "This seems like an emergency to me."

"That will be depleted after the storm," he said. "Besides, how will it look for the mayor to advocate giving money to her boyfriend?"

"You sound like Mad Dog." I told him about what the mayor wannabe had said.

"He's right." Gramps shrugged. "You have to start thinking about your reputation if you're going to run for reelection. You can't just run around doing what you please and expect the people of Duck to look the other way."

I wasn't sure where all of this was coming from. Yes, Gramps had been sheriff for many years. Yes, he was a stickler for the rules. But now he was just being inflexible and judgmental. I didn't like his tone—especially since it pertained to me.

"I'm not any different now than I was two years ago when the people of Duck voted me into office," I reminded him. "I don't see the problem."

"The problem is Kevin. I like him, but the two of you should cool your heels on this relationship some. At least until after the election next year. You keeping clothes over there—showing up at all hours—this is a family community, Dae. People aren't going to want their mayor to be carrying on this way."

"Are you saying this because Sandi was having an affair?" I glared at him, all thought of eating leftover stew out of my mind. "Because it's not the same thing. Kevin isn't married. Neither am I. It's not like he's sneaking out of my house in the middle of the night with his clothes off."

"There's no reason to take that tone with me, young lady." Gramps cleared his throat and pointed his spoon at me. "If you want to be mayor and serve your community, it takes some sacrifice. It took some sacrifice to be sheriff all those years. It didn't just happen. My family had to be above reproach. The community looks to its leaders to be examples of the best."

I got to my feet and in a hot moment, I shouted, "Like you wouldn't let my mother be with the man she loved? Is that the kind of sacrifice you expect me to make?"

"What are you saying, Dae O'Donnell?" he demanded, equally angry. "You know your mother's boyfriend—your father—threw her out into the street."

"Do I? Or was that another lie made up for me, like my father being dead? I've heard different, Gramps. I've heard that you ran my father out of Mom's life because he wasn't good enough to be Sheriff Horace O'Donnell's son-in-law."

His shoulders heaved beneath the blue plaid shirt he wore. "I don't know who told you that—was it Mad Dog? He doesn't know what he's talking about—always meddling in other people's affairs."

I didn't tell him it wasn't Mad Dog who talked to me about my mother. I had cooled down a little and realized what I'd said. I didn't want Gramps to know about Danny yet. "I'm not hungry. I'll be up in my room."

"Dae?" He called after me. "Whatever I've done, I've done to protect you and your mother. Your father was a good-for-nothing, drunken layabout. He'd been in and out of jail since he was seventeen. There was no future for you and your mother with him."

I turned back. "Did you make that decision for her? Did my father really kick her out? Did he even know she was pregnant?"

Gramps's hand shook as he wiped his mouth on his napkin. "Yes—he threw her out and left town—after I paid him one thousand dollars and threatened to serve the outstanding warrants against him. You can't judge me on that, sweetheart. I did what was best—what I had to do."

"I know. Good night, Gramps," I said before I left him in the kitchen.

Chapter 22

There was a secret stairway from my room to the widow's walk on the roof of the house. I liked spending time up there, looking out over Duck and the sound. On clear days, I could see the Atlantic on the other side of the island.

The widow's walk was a common feature on local houses, especially the older ones. Women had waited and watched for their men's ships to come home. Sometimes, women threw themselves from the walk when they learned those ships were never coming back.

It was strange being out there in the dark with no lights dotting the town around me. I could see lights farther down the coast toward Kitty Hawk. The lighthouses along the island were all still working, their powerful beams warning ships at sea of the danger presented by the Graveyard of the Atlantic.

"You were hard on the old man." Rafe leaned against the wrought-iron rail beside me. "I expected better from a soft heart like yours."

"He lied to me. He told me my father was dead."

"No wonder! I'd lie about that sniveling worm too. What man takes pity from a woman like your father done? No wonder the old man ran him off. I would've ran him through."

"You don't understand. Go away."

"Maybe you don't understand, girl. That boyo ye be helping will never bring you anything but grief. I know the type—hell, I *was* the type for many a year. The old man was protecting you and your ma. I'm siding with him in this."

"I don't remember asking you."

"Well, if ye don't want my advice, get to looking for the magistrate's ancestor and let's put an end to this."

"I don't have any idea how to find the magistrate's ancestor. I don't know anyone by that title. I think this is just a waste of time. You should go back where you came from. I don't think I can help you."

Rafe nodded at the duck weather vane, and it spun around in the dead quiet of the evening. "That's enough of your bellyaching, my girl. You're blood, and you're making me regret whoever the wench was who begat your line. Think on it, and I'll look around for some evidence of your own problem. I'm not going anywhere until you've cleared my name."

He disappeared, and I sat down to look up at the stars in the dark sky. They were much brighter without lights around me.

I thought about Rafe being my ancestor—he'd looked at the same October sky I was looking at more than three hundred years ago. I wanted to help him, in a way, because of that link. I wished the circumstances were different. There was so much going on in my life. I needed time to think—alone—and without ghostly pirate interference.

It did occur to me as I tried to untangle everything about my mother and father and Sandi's murder that I could possibly access information about the magistrate from the

Duck Historical Museum Web site. I'd been a member forever but had hardly ever used the knowledge compiled by countless Duck residents down through the years.

I tried not to think about Rafe or about my family's past. Or about Sandi. But the more I pushed these thoughts away, the more they came back to me. Like Rafe himself. Maybe there was an easy answer to proving his innocence and I wasn't taking advantage of it. I knew I couldn't easily unravel the tangled events that had happened between my mother and father thirty-six years ago. I knew I couldn't do much to help find Sandi's killer. But maybe I *could* get rid of my ghostly visitor.

I went downstairs to get on the computer, before remembering there was no power and no Internet. It looked like it was back to the old way for me.

I located an old book Gramps had given me when I was a teenager. It was titled *Pirates of the Outer Banks*. The pages were well worn from my leafing through it.

There was enough information about the infamous scourge of our area to tantalize but not really to answer questions. There was a grisly wood carving of Rafe hanging from a tree. There were illustrations of his ship and drawings of him. There were paragraphs describing the terrible things he'd done.

But there was no magistrate mentioned. The book referred only to "the law" or "the people," never to any specific person or officeholder in charge of administering that law. Whoever the magistrate was, he'd had the power to have Rafe arrested and hanged. There weren't a lot of people like that in those days. The Outer Banks was a lawless area—the governor of Virginia had to send troops to kill Blackbeard.

I wrote down a few names to check out the next day when I could go to the museum. I had to find Mark to see what he knew. His words at the museum about Rafe's death were tantalizing, but I needed more information.

I tried calling Rafe a few times but got no response. I wanted him to hear the names I'd found in the book and see if any of them sounded familiar. Of course, since I wanted him to come, he didn't show up.

After midnight, I closed the book and tried not to think about anything else. I needed some sleep. Tomorrow would look better if I was well rested. I finally drifted off and found myself on an old ship that was flying the Jolly Roger. I was dressed in pants and a loose shirt. My boots were full of sand and had slits up the sides. I couldn't see my face to know whether I looked like myself or some poor mate who was unfortunate enough to be on a pirate ship.

"*Look alive there, boy.*" *Rafe answered my question.* "*I'll not have any of my crew lollygagging on deck while we look for a place to hide my treasure.*"

"*Aye, sir!*" *my dream persona said, saluting smartly.* "*How will we know where the treasure will be safe, Cap'n?*"

"*I'll know when we get there. Enough questions. Get to work trimming those sails.*"

I wasn't sure exactly what to do. The sails I'd been raised around were nothing like these billowing monsters. Gramps had a boat—the Eleanore, *named for my grandmother—but it had a motor. He never trusted sails.*

But while I didn't know what to do, the boy whose body I was currently inhabiting did. He climbed the mast like a monkey until he was high above the deck.

"*Sails, Cap'n!*" *he called out.* "*British frigates!*"

He looked across the gray water toward the horizon. Two ships were heading toward us, sails unfurled. Their colors proclaimed them as British. He yelled down another warning. It wouldn't do to hide treasure when they had to get away from the authorities.

But Rafe wouldn't be deterred, telling the men his ship was lighter and faster and could outrun the frigates. They'd have plenty of time to escape. "*You there—load the chest into a longboat. We'll row to the island. The rest of them can get away and come back for us."*

Two burly men, the cabin boy (me) and Rafe left the pirate ship with the treasure chest stashed in the stern of the longboat.

The rest of the men stayed on the ship, making preparations to get out of the cove where they would be trapped if the frigates caught them there. The sails were unfurled. We could hear the voices of the sailors yelling orders as they struggled to turn and head out to sea.

But long before they could reach the freedom of the open waters, the British ships were on them. The battle was fierce but short as the ships traded cannon fire. In the end, the single pirate ship was no match for the British ships. The sky seemed to be on fire—smoke filling the air as the pirate ship broke apart and sank into the Atlantic.

"Get to work, ye scurvy bilge rats," Rafe said gruffly, everyone jumping at the sound of his voice. "What's past is past. Start digging. Let's be done with it and get out of this godforsaken place."

The sailors nodded and put their backs into shoveling sand at the base of a rocky outcropping near the water's edge. The chest was deep and wide. It took them hours to get a hole deep enough for it using the flimsy tools they had.

When the chest was completely covered in sand, Rafe paced off the location from an odd-looking rock that resembled a duck head (a sign of the town that would be here someday?).

He made marks on the handle of his pistol to remember the number of paces to the place where the chest was buried. Then he grunted—a satisfied sound—and without warning, shot both the crewmen who'd buried the chest. They lay bleeding to death on the shore, waves lapping at their feet.

The young cabin boy was terrified. He didn't know what to do. Should he run? Was there any way to escape Rafe?

"Drag 'em into the water and be quick about it," Rafe instructed him. "I don't want their bones giving away where the treasure is buried."

"You'll just kill me when I'm done," the spunky boy protested.

"I'll kill ye now if you don't," Rafe promised, waving his saber at him.

The boy knew the pistols were finished—they couldn't be used again until they were reloaded. He knew he was fast but had also seen a pirate trick of throwing a saber or knife a good distance into a runner's back.

He finally did as he was told, though the task was hard for his young arms. He strained and gritted his teeth, determined to do the job, and hoped the pirate would show him mercy. As dawn began to break over the horizon, he could see a bloody trail where he'd dragged the bodies into the water.

"What now, Cap'n?" the boy asked, praying for the first time in his life that he'd hear a different answer than the one he expected.

Rafe laughed. "Now I give you a chance to live, my fine boyo. You swim, don't you?"

He gestured with the saber toward the open sea. The boy began to walk into the cold water. "Don't turn around," Rafe instructed. "And don't be telling everyone about this if you make it to shore. I'll know if ye do and come after you. I'll slit you from throat to gullet."

The boy's anxious eyes searched the horizon, hoping for some sign that the British ships were still out there. But the chances were that they thought Rafe had gone down with his men. They wouldn't stay there to check the island. He was alone. There was nothing for it but to swim if he wanted to survive.

The water was up to his chin before he began moving his arms and legs through the waves. Maybe there was some *small chance that he could make it. If he did, he vowed to come back for the treasure—and kill Rafe Masterson.*

And I woke up, coughing and sputtering, my throat burning like I'd swallowed seawater.

I forced myself to take deep breaths until I felt more normal. It was morning. I got out of bed, thankful that my pirate ancestor was nowhere to be seen. It would take some time before I could look at him without remembering the terrible things I'd witnessed.

They were real events—at least they'd seemed real. I had the strongest feeling that the little cabin boy I'd spent time with last night had grown up and taken his revenge on Rafe. All I had to do was find some way to prove it.

I was thrilled to find out that we had hot water for a shower—the power must have come back on during the night. Every electrical gadget in my bedroom was blinking. I showered, got dressed and headed downstairs. I wanted to help Kevin today. He was going to need an extra hand.

Gramps was gone, leaving a note that asked me to keep an open mind until we could have a sensible conversation. I knew it would happen. We both loved each other. We'd find a way to make up. He'd forgiven me my youthful transgressions on numerous occasions. I wouldn't be able to stay mad at him forever.

He'd left pancakes in the microwave and coffee in the pot. The sun was shining brightly through the kitchen windows. Everything was looking up—including the pirate sitting at the kitchen table.

"It's about time," he said. "I thought ye were going to lay abed like some princess all day! We have work to do!"

Chapter 23

I yawned and heated up my pancakes, then drank some juice. "Speaking of work, I did some last night after you were gone. I called you but you didn't answer."

"I'm not some damn lapdog to be at your beck and call," he growled.

"Sorry. But I need to know the magistrate's name."

I found it difficult to talk to him after last night's dream. But I had to keep this in context if I wanted to get rid of him. What he'd done had happened more than three centuries ago. I wasn't so into history that it was like yesterday for me. Even if the dream was true—I had to move on.

"I don't know his name," he roared. "He was the magistrate who wrongly accused me and made me dance on the gibbet. What do I care about his name?"

"Pancakes?" I offered before I started eating.

He frowned. "Even a daft wench like yerself must know the dead don't eat."

"You've never seen a zombie movie, I take it." I poured

syrup on my plate. "I was just being polite. Did you find out anything last night about Sandi's murder?"

"Mayhap," he said in a coy manner, pulling at his mustache. "I'll trade for your information."

"I don't think you'd want to if you heard it."

"Tell me and I'll decide."

"You killed two sailors who buried your treasure chest on an island, and then you sent a young cabin boy to his death in the ocean."

His black brows knit together over his fierce eyes. "It's possible. What of it? What does it have to do with me being hanged?"

I shrugged. "Maybe nothing. I just wanted to know if my dream was real. It seemed real."

"That's right." He nodded. "The Bellamys were always being accused of witchcraft. What else did you dream?"

"That's it. Like I said, I don't know if it means anything or not."

"Blast your hide! And you want me to trade my valuable information for that piece of fluff?" He couldn't manage to pound his fist on the table—it never actually met the wood. But the salt and pepper shakers and napkins bounced up anyway.

"I guess that's up to you. I told you what I have. How do you know your information will be any more valuable to me? I mean, let's face it, half of what you're seeing and hearing has got to be confusing for you. You probably don't even realize what information you have."

His entire form rose up from the chair to hang above the table. He looked like an angry giant. He put his hands on his hips and glared down at me. "You push my patience to the limit, girl, even if you are blood kin. Ye don't realize who you're dealing with."

I ate some of the pancakes on my plate even though my hands were trembling. He was scary—I don't think anyone would disagree with that. But I knew if I showed him that I was afraid, he'd take advantage of me. I had to at least pretend I had the upper hand, even though I wasn't sure I did.

"You're so sensitive," I told him after another sip of juice. "I'm surprised you made it as a pirate at all. If I could hurt your feelings just by suggesting you might not know everything, what happened when someone actually challenged you to a fight?"

"I killed whoever challenged me!" His voice rattled the window pane behind me and made the floors creak upstairs.

I stood up and put my hands on my hips. "You might've been tough when you were alive—but you're not anymore. Stop trying to scare me into doing what you want. It won't work. Don't forget—we're blood kin and I think I may have some pirate in me. Be warned!"

He blasted out of the house, sending every electrical appliance crazy (more than they were already from the storm). The doors flew open, and the water turned on full force in the kitchen sink.

After turning off the water, I sat down at the table for a minute and tried to gather my wits. I had to talk with Shayla again. Despite our agreement, the ghost of Rafe Masterson and I were not compatible. I might have a nervous breakdown long before he could deliver any useful information to me or I could learn who the magistrate was who'd had him hanged.

Not wanting to be there if Rafe returned, I locked up the house and ran to Missing Pieces. I wasn't sure if my father would be there or not. I called his name when I opened the shop door. The pillow and blanket were still on the burgundy brocade sofa, but there was no sign of him. The front door had been locked, so maybe he'd gone out for breakfast.

I didn't want to get so attached that I began following him around. It wasn't easy, but I had to keep my distance. I noticed with a smile that everything seemed to be in its place—he hadn't stolen from me again. That was a good sign. Anyone could get desperate enough to do what he'd done.

I checked in with Nancy at town hall after locking up Missing Pieces again. Things had quieted down after the water and power were restored. There was an issue about garbage pickup—everyone needed to have trash removed and the trash company said they couldn't come back until next week.

I fielded that call and finally convinced the company to begin trash pickup again the next day. It helped that their contract was up December 1. A little leverage goes a long way. Speedy trash pickup was one blemish Mad Dog Wilson couldn't put on my mayor's scorecard.

"Thanks, sweetie," Nancy said. "Was it nice to have a hot shower this morning or what?"

"It was heaven. Is power on all over the island now?"

"There are a few places that were more heavily damaged—like Hatteras and Roanoke Island. The rest of us are in pretty good shape. And now we get garbage pickup too. You're a great mayor!"

"Be sure to tell Mad Dog that," I replied with a smile. "I'm headed over to the Blue Whale to see if I can help Kevin with anything. He had all those volunteers for the conference, but I think most of them will be working at their own homes and businesses today."

"Speaking of which," Nancy started, "I hope nothing was taken from the shop last night."

Did she know about my father staying there? It was always a possibility. The Duck grapevine was a powerful force.

"Everything looked fine this morning. Why?"

"Tim picked up some vagrant who'd gotten into your shop and was sleeping there. I'm just glad he found him before you checked in there this morning."

"Tim arrested someone in my shop?" I tried not to sound *too* surprised and concerned. My heart was pounding, wondering if everyone would find out that Danny Evans was my father. I reminded myself that the two events had nothing in common.

"Yep. You never know what people will do when they get desperate. I think Tim said they ran him over to the county jail this morning. Lucky thing for us that our Duck Police are on the ball!"

Chapter 24

I couldn't get in the garage to take out Gramps's old car and drive to Manteo. A tree had fallen from the neighbor's yard, blocking the door. With so much going on, I hadn't even noticed.

We rarely used the old garage, or the car for that matter. We usually walked or took the golf cart. Everything was close by in town, and the car was only for trips farther afield.

Like a trip to the county jail to bail out my father. I knew he wouldn't have anyone else to come for him, and he'd done nothing wrong. If it had been anyone else mistakenly locked up, I would've called a police car to go and get him.

But I couldn't do that in this case without a good explanation. I knew I couldn't ask Gramps for help, and I didn't want to involve Tim or any other friend for the same reason.

Kevin might be the one person I could turn to who wouldn't go crazy when I told him about Danny. I hoped I could convince him not to tell Gramps yet. I knew he wouldn't like keeping the secret but maybe just this one time.

I walked down to the Blue Whale—rehearsing what I'd planned to say like I was preparing to make a speech to the town council. I knew Kevin wouldn't be happy that I'd been seeing my father and hadn't said anything to him.

But other people I'd known all my life would be even more upset. All of them felt like they had a God-given right to know everything.

Two Duck police cars and three Dare County Sheriff cars were parked in the circle drive at the Blue Whale. At least twenty other cars—presumably belonging to the attendees of the botched mayor's conference who'd returned at Chief Michaels's insistence—surrounded them.

I noticed that the ruins of the crushed mermaid fountain were gone. I wondered what Kevin would choose to replace it. The mermaid fountain had been there since the Blue Whale first opened in the early 1900s. The museum had a picture on display of old Bunk Whitley standing in front by the fountain the day the inn opened.

Inside the inn, chaos reigned. I cringed at what Kevin must be going through and wasn't sure I should ask him to drive me to Manteo after all. The unhappy, sometimes angry guests seemed to be complaining loudly from every corner of every room.

"Dae!" Barker Whiteside greeted me from the bar. "Come sit down! You look like I feel."

I sat beside him on the bar stool. Marissa was getting drinks, finding pens and paper for guests to write on and doing whatever else was asked of her. She was clearly put out at having to do so much. "Can I get you something, Dae?" she asked.

"No, thanks. I came by to see if I could help you and Kevin get through this. I'm sorry it's making so much extra work for you."

She smiled though she still looked stressed. "I'm not complaining. At least I got to go home last night and check on my grandfather and the house. They were both fine. I think Grandpa slept through everything."

"I'm glad. Just tell me what I can do to help."

"Let me finish up here and we'll take a look around. You're a blessing, Dae."

"What are you writing?" I asked Barker when Marissa turned to get Cokes for two other visitors. Everyone in the bar area seemed to be intently writing something on Blue Whale stationery.

"The police asked us to write down exactly where we were and what we were doing when Sandi was killed." He put down his pen and took a sip of whatever he was drinking. "I can't believe someone had the nerve to kill her while all of us were right here. What kind of cojones did that take?"

"I agree. And what can everyone say now but that they were stuffed in the lobby during the worst of the storm and didn't really see anything?"

"Mayor?" Chief Michaels tapped me on the shoulder. "Could I have a word with you?"

We went down the hallway to the kitchen where Kevin was working with two assistants, making lunch for the group. He glanced at the chief in a questioning way and smiled at me. I made a mental note to approach the town council for money to cover this investigation. Despite what Gramps had said, there had to be a fair settlement for all this expense. It wasn't Kevin's fault that Sandi was killed here and the police chose to invite all the guests back again. I didn't think he should feel responsible for what happened.

"What was going on in there just now?" Chief Michaels asked me when we reached a side corner of the large kitchen, away from the cooking area.

I thought back. "I was talking to Mayor Whiteside."

"And what were you saying? If I hadn't been walking by and heard you, every guest that was here would use the alibi you just gave Barker! You're undermining the investigation. I know you want us to find who killed Mayor Foxx."

"I'm sorry. I didn't realize that's what I was doing."

I could tell the chief was under a lot of stress. He always was when he had to work with Sheriff Tuck Riley. Sheriff Riley had taken Gramps's place when he'd retired. While Gramps and Chief Michaels had a great working relationship, Sheriff Riley and Chief Michaels liked to play "who's the biggest fish."

"Mayor Dae O'Donnell!" Sheriff Riley joined us. He was a tall, stocky man with a full head of brown hair and brown eyes that narrowed when he looked at people, as though he was always trying to figure out what they were guilty of. "I was hoping to run into you while I was out this way. How are you? I hope your house made it through the storm in one piece. How's old Horace getting along? Still taking people out on his fishing boat? You know, I don't get enough time to fish nowadays. If I did, Horace would be the one I'd want to take me out."

Sheriff Riley always made pleasant conversation, and his smile was friendly. It was his eyes that I didn't trust. I'd heard too many bad things about him. He'd worked with Gramps but never as a high-ranking officer. Gramps hadn't trusted him.

"It's good to see you too, Sheriff," I said, giving him my hand and my big mayor's smile. "I'm sorry you had to come in on this."

"I admit I was surprised to hear there was a murder out here in little Duck. Once I knew, I had to come out. Ronnie doesn't have all the resources he needs to handle something like this by himself. We don't want to call in the SBI for every little thing, do we? We can handle this locally just fine."

"I'm glad to hear that."

"What's the powwow back here about? Trouble with the

soup?" Sheriff Riley laughed and nodded at Kevin. "Smells good, whatever it is, Brickman. Can't wait for lunch."

"I was just discussing the program with the mayor," Chief Michaels said, hitching up his pants. "I thought it would be good for her to know what's going on."

Sheriff Riley nodded. "Yep. That probably would be good—if she wasn't as much of a suspect as the other mayors here. Not that I mean any disrespect by that, Dae."

"No, of course not."

"Maybe it would be best for her to write down where she was in the hotel at the time Mayor Foxx was killed. And what she was doing, of course."

It was one thing for Chief Michaels to call me on the carpet for coaching suspects—it was another if I was going to be one of those suspects.

"You both realize that everyone was in the lobby at the time Sandi was killed, right?" I asked. "Everyone except Sandi and the killer. Obviously Sandi can't tell us what happened, and I doubt the killer is going to say he or she wasn't in the lobby with everyone else. Maybe you should ask everyone who they saw around them at the time. That might make more sense."

Sheriff Riley laughed. "That's a good idea. I wish I'd thought of that. Ronnie, let's ask that when we interview each person. And since Dae brought it up, let's ask her first. Who was around you in the lobby during the storm, Mayor?"

Chapter 25

I thought back to the storm raging around us. "Kevin was there and Nancy Boidyn, our town clerk. I saw Althea Hinson and Barbara. They were with me."

"Maybe we could cut through the chatter and get to the heart of it," Chief Michaels said abruptly. "Did you see Matthew Wright?"

"No. Not until later. But there were a lot of people here. I couldn't see everyone."

"Thank you, Mayor," Chief Michaels said, scribbling my words into his notebook. "That's really all we need to know."

I was dismissed after the chief reminded me not to "help" the other suspects. I wondered if Matthew Wright had arrived yet. He was bound to realize that he was the prime suspect. I was pretty sure the rest of the questioning was just to say they'd done it.

I went over to where Kevin was laying out dough for

yeast rolls. I knew he'd been listening to the whole thing. "What do you think?"

"I'd hate to be Matthew Wright."

His hands moved quickly and efficiently through the motions of making rolls of dough the right size then covering them with melted butter. He put the trays of rolls into the oven to rise and closed the door.

"Could I talk to you for a minute?" I asked. "I know you're busy—"

"Sure." He gave directions to his assistants after he washed his hands. "Let's go in the bridal suite. I don't think anyone's in there."

He was right—it had to be the only empty place at the inn. He sat down in one of the old-fashioned white chairs and waited for me to start. I paced a few times, realizing that this was probably the first place Rafe had haunted me—I just hadn't seen him.

Finally I said, "I need your help."

"You didn't murder Sandi Foxx, did you?"

"No! Of course not."

He relaxed in the chair. "Okay. What do you need?"

I couldn't look at him as I explained about my father. I told him how I'd found out where he worked and how I'd hung out there a few times. I told him about the wreck and about finding Danny by the trash bin and letting him stay in Missing Pieces.

I was relieved when it was over. I sat down in the matching old-fashioned white chair and waited for him to say something.

"I'm not surprised," he said. "You found out you have a father. You wouldn't be human if you didn't wonder about him. I'm not sure about letting him stay at the shop—"

I got up and started pacing again. "I didn't know what else to do. You have all this damage and Duck doesn't have a homeless shelter. I couldn't take him home and introduce him to Gramps—"

"That was my next question."

"No. I haven't told him." I explained what Danny had said about why he and my mother broke up. "I confronted Gramps with it. I think he lied to me again."

Kevin sat forward and took my hands, his gray-blue eyes worried. "You've only known your father for a short time, Dae. You've known Horace all your life. I'm sure whatever he did all those years ago felt justified at the time. What action do you take when you find out your daughter is pregnant and the father has been in and out of trouble his whole life? Multiply that answer times one hundred—that's for being sheriff."

"That's about what he said."

"So you let your father stay at Missing Pieces. Did he steal something?"

"No." I lied looking right into his eyes. "He got arrested."

I explained about Tim finding him in Missing Pieces and taking him to Manteo. "I have to get him out. He wasn't doing anything wrong. Tim misunderstood. But I couldn't get in the garage."

"You need a ride." He nodded. "I was wondering why you'd decided to come clean now. I should've known you needed something."

"It's not like that, Kevin. I didn't want to explain what I was doing to anyone. I needed to understand it myself."

"Do you understand it now?"

"Not really," I admitted with a smile. "You're right. I wouldn't have told you yet if I didn't need you. I'm sorry. If it makes you feel any better, no one else knows either."

"It doesn't make me feel any better that you've been hanging out at a sleazy bar alone, trying to decide if you should introduce yourself to your father. You could've gotten in trouble."

It suddenly occurred to me that he knew too much. "I never said it was a bar! You *knew*. Did you follow me or something? Is that once an FBI agent always an FBI agent? Did you say anything to Gramps?"

"I didn't tell your grandfather. I was worried about you, that's all. I knew you wouldn't be able to resist checking up on your father. I just wanted to be there if you needed help."

We stared at each other for a few seconds. I supposed I couldn't be too upset with him. Neither of us had actually lied to the other—it was more a sin of omission. Next time I'd have to remember to ask if he was following me.

"I'm sorry," I said. "I should've told you. Then you could've told me you were following me and we could've gone to the sleazy bar together."

"I'm sorry too. I should've told you sooner that I knew what you were up to." He smiled. "So? What's he like? Is Danny Evans every girl's dream father?"

"Hardly. He's not like anyone's father I've ever known. But he's probably never been anyone's real father either."

"You haven't told him, have you? He doesn't know he's your father."

"Not yet. But I plan to. He recognized my name, of course. And he remembers my mom. He said I look just like her. He knows I'm her daughter—but not his. I'm not ready to tell him yet."

"But you trusted him enough to let him stay at Missing Pieces. You know he's done everything from con games to breaking and entering. You may be letting the fact that he's your father overshadow who he really is."

"I know."

"For someone who seems so upfront about everything— you have a lot of layers."

"Yeah," I joked. "They used to call me Onion Head when I was a kid."

The remark didn't get the laugh I was hoping for. "Nothing happened, Kevin. It's not like he's a criminal or something—"

"You mean at least not right now?"

"I just need some time before I spring it on him that he has a daughter."

"What about your grandfather?"

"I need some time for him too. I don't know how he's going to take it when he finds out." I told him about Gramps giving my father money and threatening him to get him to leave.

"Okay. I can see it's a delicate matter. Let me change my clothes and we'll go."

"Thanks." I hugged him. "I knew I could count on you."

"Really? That's why you didn't tell me about it sooner?"

I sighed. It was going to be a long drive to Manteo.

Chapter 26

As we drove to the county jail, I was amazed all over again at all the damage the storm had done. No matter how many times I saw the aftermath, I was still struck by the awesome power of the wind and sea. A real hurricane would've been much worse—but the damage to homes and business property, not to mention house-size piles of rubble and garbage, was bad enough. I was just glad no one had been reported seriously injured or dead—besides Sandi, of course.

And that was a different story. I hoped the police would figure it out quickly. The longer people were left to wonder who the murderer was, the worse it would be for Duck. I hated to be part of the crowd wishing Matthew Wright had killed Sandi because he couldn't break up with her, but it would be better news for the residents of Duck if that were the case.

In the meantime, I had to focus on getting my father out of jail.

"I don't think they'll let you take him home because you give them a big smile," Kevin said as he parked his pickup in the Dare County municipal parking lot.

"I don't see why not," I argued. "He didn't do anything wrong. Tim misunderstood the situation."

"You probably should have brought Tim with you. As arresting officer—if he agreed with you, it would be much easier."

"You're probably right. But that would've meant telling Tim who he was. By tonight, everyone in Duck would know my father was sleeping at the shop. I was trying to avoid that."

"Let's see what we can do." He opened the door and took my hand as we walked across the parking lot. "Maybe you'll get lucky. It seems to me that your father has already run into a streak of luck by meeting you."

"I don't know if he'll feel that way, since he's lost everything. I don't really know what he's like, Kevin. But I know he was going to sleep behind the trash bin. No one should be down that low."

He kissed my forehead. "You're a very good person, Dae. I hope you won't let him take advantage of you."

"I'm sure *you* won't let him—you seem to follow me everywhere. Just stop him before that happens."

"I wish I could." He opened the glass door that was still sporting large masking tape X's to protect it from the storm.

The county jail was bustling with hundreds of people. They all seemed to be going in different directions. The woman at the front desk looked especially harried—there was a pencil stuck almost straight up in her dark hair and a long pen streak on one cheek.

"I can't do what you're asking," she told me. "But lucky for you, the assistant DA is here, and she can probably help you. Lord knows we need to get some of these people out of here. The state will shut us down if they find out how many inmates we have right now."

She pointed to a door down the hall on the right. Kevin and I continued our search there. I knocked on the door labeled "Conference Room," and when there was no answer, I opened it and went inside.

People were lined up wall to wall waiting to talk with a diminutive woman in a navy blue suit who was seated at a long table. There were so many briefcases—probably one for every lawyer present—they could've opened a luggage store.

People ranging from senior citizens to teenagers were trying to get their cases heard. Everything from breaking and entering (supposedly to get out of the storm) to stealing cars (to get away from the storm) was on the docket. No wonder they wanted to get a few people out of there.

I wasn't sure what the protocol was in cases like this, but when the assistant DA called, "Next!" Kevin pushed me forward. I stared at her for a moment, then told her the whole story about my father mistakenly being arrested in my shop.

I expected some questions, maybe paperwork, asking to talk to the arresting officer—everything except her saying, "So you aren't willing to press charges. Here you go." She handed me a file and I was dismissed from the group that surrounded her. "Take that to the sergeant at the admitting desk. He'll tell you where you can pick him up. Next!"

I was stunned and happy. I almost didn't know what to do. I'd been expecting such a major ordeal, and it was nothing. I grabbed Kevin's hand and we left the crowded room.

"I guess they have so many people in custody that they don't want to deal with anyone they don't have to." He shrugged. "You lucked out."

"I can't believe it," I agreed. "Let's find my father and get out of here."

We walked around until we found the right desk and gave the man behind it the file. He looked at it, shrugged and called to have Danny Evans brought up. He stamped the file, and we moved to one side so the people behind us could do their business.

Too bad the people behind us were police officers—Tim and Scott.

"Dae?" Tim looked surprised and puzzled. "Brickman? What are you doing here?"

Chapter 27

A hundred excuses came to mind. I was the mayor. I could be conducting all sorts of town business with the admitting office at the county jail. None of those excuses made any sense, so none of them made it to my lips.

Tim and Scott held a large, burly man dressed in overalls between them. He was covered in what appeared to be blood. There was a large cut on his head.

"Mr. Borden?" I looked a little closer and realized that I knew him. "Are you all right?"

"Sure thing, Mayor. It was nice of you to be here and see me off. You should'a seen the other fella." He chuckled. "He was a mess."

He smelled strongly of whiskey. I knew from past experience that Mr. Borden ended up here a time or two every year when he got a little carried away while drinking.

"Wilbur got into a fight with his next-door neighbor— again—this time about a tree that came down in his yard during the storm," Scott explained.

"I couldn't even get out of my driveway," Mr. Borden added. "How is that fair, Mayor? I asked him politely to move it, but he didn't. We got into an argument. He punched me—I punched him. He hit me with my own bottle of whiskey. I hit him back with a tree limb."

"And Mr. Arthur, your neighbor, is in the hospital," Tim reminded him.

Mr. Borden shrugged. "I didn't mean for it to go that far, Mayor. If you can help me out with this, I'll be sure to vote for you next year."

I appreciated the offer and could relate to having a tree in the way, but this wasn't a good way to handle it. "I'm sorry, Mr. Borden. I wish I could help. Maybe Mr. Arthur won't press charges against you."

"Are you two dropping off or what?" the sergeant behind the desk growled at Duck's finest.

"Don't move," Tim said to me. "I want to know what's going on after we get Mr. Borden processed. I think you at least owe me that much."

I wasn't sure why I owed him anything, but Tim had his own guidelines on these things. I didn't plan to wait around for the conversation—we could talk later in private.

But the side door buzzed open to admit Mr. Borden at the same time that the deputies released my father. They passed each other in the doorway.

"Hey! Wait a minute," Tim protested. "You can't just let this man go. I arrested him for breaking and entering last night at Missing Pieces." He looked back at me. "Dae, did you bail him out?"

"Not exactly." I wished I didn't have to deal with this right now.

"He doesn't look like he's escaping," Scott remarked. "Someone posted bail for him."

"Not exactly?" Tim asked. "Then what?"

Two deputies took custody of Mr. Borden, who went along peacefully, knowing the drill too well. I could hardly grab my father and make a run for the front door. I looked at Kevin, who shrugged but didn't say anything. I guessed this was my mess to clean up.

"I asked him to stay there," I explained. "Danny Evans, this is Officer Tim Mabry."

"We're acquainted." Danny nodded.

"And Officer Scott Randall," I continued while my brain searched frantically for a way to explain the situation without revealing our relationship. This definitely wasn't the place I wanted everything to come out.

"My house is flooded," Danny said. "I work at the Sailor's Dream—also flooded. My van is wrecked. Your mayor showed me some Christian kindness that I didn't know existed anymore. She let me stay at her shop instead of on the street. She bought me a meal and made me feel like I mattered to the world for a change. Then you two showed up."

He spoke with a passion that silenced Tim's outrage. Best of all, his explanation had nothing to do with him being my father. It seemed I was spared from explaining after all. I'd felt so guilty and conscious of my secret that I hadn't realized there was something else to say.

Tim turned to me and I nodded. "I didn't think about you noticing that someone else was in Missing Pieces."

He looked uncomfortable. "I always check up on you—the shop, I mean. It's part of my routine. Just to make sure everything is okay in town. You know?"

I smiled. It seemed Kevin wasn't my only guardian angel.

"I feel like a fool," Tim said. "I'm sorry, Mr. Evans. If the phones would've been working, my first course of action in these circumstances would've been to call the mayor and ask her what was going on. I hope you won't sue the town for wrongful prosecution."

Danny shook his hand. "I don't think I'd do that, since Dae came to get me out. But thanks for the apology, Officer."

After a long, awkward moment of silence, Kevin said, "Right. I guess we'll go now. See you guys later. Take care."

The three of us walked out to Kevin's pickup, leaving the two officers to file their reports and head back to Duck later. Once we were in the pickup and driving down the road, Kevin kept up a conversation with Danny, asking him about himself in subtle ways that I understood—he was trying to get more information about my father.

I interrupted a few times, but their conversation continued across me, since I was sitting in between them. Maybe it was just as well. I wasn't sure what to say at this point. Danny sounded like he thought I was near sainthood for getting him out of jail.

Of course, I was nothing of the sort. I'd done what any daughter would do for her father. Because he didn't know the truth, I felt awkward trying to explain. I was the mayor, but I didn't rush down to Manteo to bail out every Duck citizen who went to jail. Although I assured myself that I would've done the same for anyone I'd let stay at Missing Pieces.

I just wasn't sure who else that would be.

We drove to the Blue Whale again. I started to ask why we hadn't gone to Missing Pieces, but Kevin seemed determined to get back to his place and check out what was going on. I had a feeling this was all for show—he'd probably insist that Danny stay here in one of his spare rooms. And that was okay. At least I wouldn't be in the awkward position of trying to explain our—mine and Danny's—relationship to anyone else.

Danny accepted Kevin's offer of room and board until he could get back on his feet. He shook Kevin's hand, then impulsively hugged me. We were standing on the verandah, still away from the suspect-finding process going on inside. I hoped it was a safe place to be seen with him, since there was no doubt in my mind that Chief Michaels would know Danny too—and might even know he was my father.

When I was growing up, I thought Duck was the simplest, easiest-to-understand place in the world. I heard visitors say the same thing all the time.

But Duck, like me, had a lot of layers (to borrow a phrase from Kevin). Some of them were long-buried secrets that were known only to a few people. My life seemed to be part of those secrets, just like Rafe Masterson's. I guessed we had that in common.

Before I could move away from Danny's embrace, Gramps came out the front door with Chief Michaels. They both frowned when they saw us. I waited—holding my breath. Gramps didn't say anything—neither did the chief. I wasn't sure whether they were so deep in conversation they hadn't seen us, or they were purposefully choosing not to comment about Danny in front of other people.

They nodded to the three of us and kept walking. I watched them get into a squad car and drive away. It was possible that I was safe for now. Or there might be hell to pay later.

Chapter 28

We stood on the verandah for a few more minutes. I kept expecting that squad car to turn around and come back. I remembered several times when I was about sixteen that Gramps had made that untidy U-turn. There are some things you never seem to grow out of.

Danny didn't seem to recognize Gramps either. But it had been many years since they'd seen each other. He also didn't cringe—at least not too much—when he saw Chief Michaels. I took that as a good sign that he probably wasn't actively in any trouble right now.

I still remembered how all the kids who were in and out of trouble would turn their heads, hunker down in their jackets and otherwise try to hide when Gramps used to take me to school in his uniform. It was embarrassing.

"Come on," Kevin finally said. "Let's get you settled in somewhere."

"If I can do anything to help out while I'm here . . ." Danny offered.

"I'm sure I can find you something to do," Kevin answered. "There's always something to do around here."

I went inside with them. The level of chaos seemed the same as when we'd left. Deputies questioned the conference attendees, who in turn struggled to remember who was and wasn't around them in the lobby during the storm.

This seemed like a perfect opportunity for me to have a look at Sandi's and Matthew's rooms again. Last time, people had been with me—I do my best finding alone.

Despite other people searching the rooms, I still thought they might have missed something only I could find. I knew the rooms would be officially off-limits—part of the crime scene by now.

But if there weren't any officers stationed at the rooms, and I was careful, I couldn't see where it would hurt anything for me to look around. Hopefully I'd find something with more intrinsic value than the ruby ring. It wasn't much help when people had to take my word for what I felt. Even the keys were doubtful as evidence, since I was the only one who could tell Sandi was angry when she threw them.

I crept upstairs past familiar faces who were busy writing down explanations they thought the police would like to see. I made my way back to Sandi's room, opened the door, and carefully slipped under the crime scene tape.

I turned around to start searching—Rafe was sitting on the bed. I jumped a little and he laughed. "You're too nervy by half, girl. You should be expecting my company by now. I'm never far away."

"The way you blew out of the house this morning, I thought maybe you were gone for good," I whispered, not wanting anyone alive to hear me.

"Unlikely," he said. "Just because I was riled by what ye said doesn't mean you're off the hook."

"Then be prepared—you might not like the answers I find."

"Any answers that prove I was unjustly accused and

hanged are fine." He watched me look around the room. "What are ye searching for now?"

"Something to help the police chief figure out who killed Sandi. Either Matthew Wright is guilty or someone else is. The obvious person isn't always the right one."

"That's what I'm talking about. I was the obvious person when they hanged me—but not the guilty one."

"We'll go next door to the museum when I get done here," I promised. "But I'd appreciate it if you could be quiet right now so I can think."

"You're a cheeky wench, by God that's the truth! You don't deserve the information about the murder you find so much more interesting than my own."

"What kind of information?" I asked, not really paying much attention. Ghosts seemed to be oblivious to their annoying habits.

"Only that your chief suspect has crossed over."

"Crossed over what?"

"Crossed over—don't be so thick! I know you understand the King's English!"

I stopped looking in one of the dresser drawers. "You mean he's dead?"

"Most people would assume that."

"How do you know?"

He began rising from the bed toward the ceiling—a movement he made whenever he was upset, I'd noticed. "How do ye think I know? Sometimes it's hard for me to believe you're related to me. It must be the foul air or the strange food you eat that keeps your brain from working as it should."

"Are you sure?" I started thinking about Gramps and Chief Michaels leaving the Blue Whale while the investigation was still going on. They might have heard about Matthew's death. "Where is he?"

"I can't say. Things are different now. I can take you there, but I can't explain exactly where he is."

I thought about my investigation here. If I left now, I might never get back in. But if Matthew was dead—there could be more evidence where he was.

"You can't talk to him, can you? I mean, he's dead and you're dead—"

"I told you, it's not a social club. I don't know where he's gone. If you know one of his relations, you might be able to talk to him through them."

I shrugged. "Okay. Just thought I'd ask."

"Again," he reminded me. "You have no memory either, girl. Mayhap this is why women should be at home—seen but not heard. You waste your time dithering about things that aren't important."

"Okay. That's fine. Insult me when you need my help."

He laughed in a scornful way. "As you need mine to find your dead suspect."

"All right." I decided to leave and investigate Matthew's possible death. "But you better be right."

"Bloodthirsty vixen!"

I realized how my last statement must have sounded and rushed to my defense. "I don't want him to be dead, but if I leave to look for him and lose this crime scene—never mind."

The door to the room opened and Marissa looked around. "Dae?"

"Hi, Marissa." At least it wasn't a deputy.

"You went through the crime scene tape? I hope you don't get in trouble for that. That police officer was kind of specific about not letting anyone in here."

"I was hoping to find something that might help. No one else needs to know. I promise you won't get in any trouble for this either."

"I understand. Did you find anything?"

"No." I walked to the door. The ghost was gone. "I have to leave now and look for something else."

"Can I help?"

"No, I—"

"Dae, who were you talking to in here?" she asked as she glanced around the room again. "Are you alone?"

"Yes. Mostly."

"I thought I heard voices. That's why I came in."

"Oh that!" I laughed. "It's a bad habit—talking to myself." I really looked at her. Her pretty blond hair was messed up and her clothes looked rumpled, as though she'd slept in them. I was going to have a word with Kevin about overworking the poor girl.

Marissa closed the door as we left the room, and this time, she locked it and pocketed the key. "I hope you don't think I was spying on you."

"No. Not at all. I know it's part of your job to keep up with what's going on at the inn. And you're very good at it. I hope Kevin appreciates you. You know how men can be sometimes—they can't see what's under their noses."

She sniffed a little and looked like she might cry. "I know exactly what you mean, Dae."

I hugged her impulsively. "I'll talk to Kevin. You need some time off. I hope everything is okay with your grandfather."

"He's fine, thanks." She smiled wearily. "You're right, though. Between taking care of him and the extra work here, I'm exhausted. Most of the time, I don't know if I'm coming or going. A person can make mistakes that way. I'm trying hard not to let that happen."

I spent a few more minutes trying to cheer her up, but she had other things she had to do. I did too, but I decided to take a minute and tell Kevin that she needed some time off. He probably hadn't even noticed—he was such a workaholic.

I found him cleaning up the glass in the now-dry ballroom. He looked haggard too. We were all stretched too thin, but there wasn't any way but through it. I told him about running into Marissa upstairs and suggested that he either hire someone else to help her or at least give her a few days off.

He handed me the oversized dust pan. "What were you doing upstairs? Please tell me you didn't go in Matthew's or Sandi's room. Because the police have them taped off and they wouldn't be happy knowing you went in and contaminated the crime scene."

"I was just looking around a little. I didn't touch anything."

"Dae, I know you have some extraordinary gifts, but you have to be careful how you use them. You're worried about Marissa—but you're pushing yourself hard too."

I thought about something Kevin had told me—how he'd lost his FBI partner, a woman he'd loved, who also had some psychic talent. She'd had a breakdown of some kind. I was pretty sure he'd quit the FBI because he'd lost her, although he never said as much.

"I'm fine, Kevin, really." I held the dustpan for him to brush glass shards into it.

He stopped sweeping. "You look guilty. What's going on?"

"Nothing." I looked at my watch—I needed to leave if I was going to find out if what Rafe had said was true. "You might not believe it."

He sighed. "Try me. I think I've proven that it takes a lot to surprise me."

"There's a ghost," I whispered, glancing around—more for the living who might overhear us than for Rafe, who I suspected was always listening. "The ghost of my dead pirate ancestor, Rafe Masterson."

Chapter 29

"Are you talking about the scourge-of-the-Outer-Banks-pirate Rafe Masterson? The one who cursed Duck with his dying breath?" Kevin asked. "I didn't know you were related to him."

"I didn't either." I explained from the beginning, wondering why I even tried to keep secrets from him, since he always ended up knowing anyway.

"He's too addlepated to understand," Rafe inserted, showing himself to me.

"You're violating our agreement," I told him.

"He's here now?" Kevin looked around the empty ballroom.

"He wants to know about me. What better way than to hear it from me personally," Rafe insisted. "Besides, you told him about me. That breaks our agreement."

"He can't hear you or see you," I reminded the pirate. "Remember—he's not related."

"What's he saying?" Kevin wondered, giving up trying to find him hovering close by.

"He's not saying anything else—unless he doesn't want my help anymore."

Rafe vanished, but his leaving was like a sudden surge of air blasting through the ballroom. It rattled the chandelier and made the pieces of glass on the floor dance.

"Was that him?" Kevin asked.

"He's kind of a show-off."

"So this ghost is helping you solve Mayor Foxx's murder?"

"Not exactly—he thinks he is. He told me Matthew Wright has crossed over. I was on my way to see if it's true."

"Can I tag along?"

"Sure. I don't see why not." I smiled at him and took his hand in mine. "Trying to make sure I haven't lost it?"

He wrapped his arms around me and held me close. I could hear his heart beating against my ear. "The world you're part of can be dangerous. I worry about you. But I'd also like to know if he's right."

"I can live with that. Thanks." We kissed briefly, then started out of the Blue Whale. I could hear Rafe chuckling, but he didn't make another appearance.

I told Kevin that Chief Michaels and Gramps may have been called to the scene already. "Rafe can't tell me exactly where we're going. He said the area has changed too much."

"Is he here now?" Kevin asked as we got in the pickup parked outside the back entrance.

"I don't see him, if that's what you mean. But I think he's lurking. What are you worried about?"

"Not that you're crazy," he assured me as he started the engine. "How much do you know about spirits pretending to be someone we might want to see?"

"Absolutely nothing—except the little bit of gibberish Shayla shared with me when she found out about Rafe. But there are two things that don't make sense about that. First of all, why would any ghost pretend to be Rafe Masterson? It's not like I would've summoned him to help me. You've heard all the terrible stories about him. And second, what could he hope to gain?"

"Your trust—your help in whatever he wants to do. Spirits can't do things for themselves on this plane. They need human help."

"I told you he wants his name cleared. But even Shayla agreed he could only appear to me since we're related. It's not like I go around seeing ghosts everywhere like she does. Helping him with that doesn't seem so terrible, since he's my great-great-something or other. I've been trying to do some research at the museum, but things keep getting in the way."

"Just be careful. Don't let him talk you into anything that doesn't feel right."

"Okay." I wasn't sure what else I could say. He sounded very ominous about the whole thing.

"He's daft!" Rafe suddenly appeared between us. "The poor sot has no idea what he's blabbering about. What matter of conveyance is this?"

I told Kevin that Rafe was with us. "He thinks you're crazy."

"I'm sure he does." Kevin kept his eyes on the road. "Just have him tell us where we're supposed to go—unless Matthew Wright is out in the middle of Duck Road."

I realized he'd been at the stop sign for a few minutes. Rafe blustered and complained but finally gave me directions. "Follow the road to the right," he instructed. I relayed the information to Kevin. "There's a place on the sound— gad, how amazing that some things stay the same for so long, eh? I had a friend—One Finger Joe—who lived right on that spot. Good fishing there."

"Which way now?" Kevin questioned as we were driving down the road. "There are a lot of places on the sound."

"There is something sticking up out of the water—a quay of some sort. It's beyond a grassy area with walkways of stone." Rafe shook his head. "Beyond that, I cannot tell you."

"The park!" I interpreted. "I think he's talking about Duck Park." There was a small cove at the edge of the park where we'd built a pier for walkers that jutted out into the Currituck Sound.

Kevin pulled the pickup into the parking lot, and we ran down the trails toward the water side of the park. Rafe stayed visibly ahead of us, floating above the path. I felt like I was in an episode of *Scooby-Doo*—pirate ghost and all.

A few Duck residents waved as we went by. A senior group was meeting there for their weekly walk. I smiled and waved back, thinking all the time that the park would become a crime scene if Matthew was found here. Cleanup from the storm would have to be postponed.

The cove was beside the stairs heading up to the long pier, which had such great views of the sound. A few mangled bicycles, a tire and a baby stroller languished in the water.

"I don't see anything—at least not a dead body," Kevin said after a moment. "I'll check from the pier."

"He's down there, girl," Rafe assured me. "Might be weighted down. That's the way we did it. Look hard. You'll see him."

I did as he suggested, as best I could from the shore anyway. I was leery of jumping into the water unless I had to. There was no telling what all was beneath the surface, aside from a dead body.

"I don't see anything," Kevin said again, coming back down the stairs. "I think your ghost might have some bad intel."

"He's here, blast your hides! You're looking all wrong." Rafe paced up and down the shoreline.

"Or you're all wrong," I answered.

"Maybe he's being held down underwater with something," Kevin said. "There's a lot of debris. I wouldn't go in there without some kind of safety equipment. We should call the fire department."

"What will we tell them?" I worried the problem—and my lip. "I can't tell them a ghost told me to come here."

"I don't know why." Kevin shrugged. "People here believe in ghosts. I don't think they'd be that surprised."

"Because I'm the mayor, and people know I have a gift—I find things. Shayla sees ghosts. Mrs. Anson in Southern Shores sees ghosts. Not me. I was really hoping Chief Michaels would be here and I could quietly creep away knowing Rafe was right."

"One of you lily-livered cods jump in!" Rafe yelled, causing the bushes beside us to stir as though a strong wind had come up from the sound. "I'd do it myself, but it wouldn't do no good."

"I left my cell phone in the truck," Kevin said. "I'll call the fire department and tell them we saw something hazardous down here. We won't use your story. Then we'll know if your ghost is telling the truth."

I looked back toward the water and saw something lying on top of the tire. It gleamed in the sunlight. I knew I'd seen it before. "Matthew's car key." I called Kevin back, but he was already too far gone. "I guess you must be right," I said to the pirate. "That's the key I found at the Blue Whale."

"I told you so," Rafe raved. "Now do you believe?"

But there was something else. I walked to the edge of the water, the toes of my shoes getting wet in the process. There was something stuck on the handle of the baby stroller.

I looked around for something to drag the stroller closer to me—even as I heard sirens coming from the direction of the fire station at the other end of Duck.

"What's that you have there?" Rafe came closer, angling to see what I was doing.

I found a stick of some sort—maybe a broken broom

handle—and used it to snag the stroller. It took a few tries to get it close enough so I could grab it from the water.

I knew I shouldn't touch whatever was attached to the stroller handle, so I pushed with the stick, trying to see what it was. I reasoned that it could get lost when the fire department arrived. They would be looking for Matthew, not for debris that might have nothing to do with his death.

My chest felt cold as I brought it closer—it was a small gun. It didn't look real, more like a toy. But I knew it was lethal, probably the .22-caliber the police were looking for. I wasn't the sheriff's granddaughter for nothing.

"What did you find?" Kevin came back, cell phone in hand.

"A gun. Don't worry. I didn't touch it. It looks like whoever killed Matthew threw his keys and a gun in after him."

"I'm sure the chief will give you a hard time for messing with the crime scene anyway," he said. "I guess your pirate was right."

Chapter 30

The cove had to be cordoned off with nets to make sure all the possible evidence was contained. Two police boats kept interested watercraft away from the scene. The fire and police departments worked with sheriff's deputies to pull the terrible, bloated body of Matthew Wright from the waters of the sound.

"Now tell me again how you knew the body was here," Chief Michaels said, licking his small pencil in preparation of note taking. "What I've heard so far doesn't make much sense."

"You know Dae finds things," Gramps added, putting his arm around me. "There's no rhyme or reason for it. But we all know it happens. She saw the keys on the tire and recognized them as belonging to Mr. Wright."

Chief Michaels nodded. "So you and Brickman were out for a stroll and saw the keys in the debris. Based on that, you used this broom handle to fish the gun out of the water. Does that about cover it?"

"The gun was stuck on the handle of the stroller," I explained again. "I was standing here, thinking about Matthew, when I saw it."

"Bag that stroller too, Scott," Chief Michaels called out to Officer Randall, who was in the water. He was wearing protective gear, but the look on his face showed his distaste for the job.

The chief wouldn't let the fire department volunteers do anything but stand around after they got there with the gear. He said they weren't trained to do forensic evidence retrieval.

Sheriff Riley joined us, crouching down near the edge of the water for a minute before he turned back. "Don't look like any suicide I've ever seen. I'm sure he was remorseful for killing Mayor Foxx, though."

"I don't think it was a suicide," Chief Michaels said. "We got a call when we were back at the Blue Whale from a friend of Wright's that his car was up at Nag's Head. It was his car, all right. But he was right here in Duck. Maybe he was trying to get to the inn for the investigation."

"Why didn't you call me?" the sheriff asked, sounding none too pleased. "I should be kept in the loop on this, Ronnie."

"We can process a car, Tuck," the chief said. "I'll let you know if we find anything we can use."

It struck me as odd that Matthew's car keys were here in the water with him while his car was in Nag's Head. I decided not to mention it—at least not right then. I was sure they weren't done with us yet.

"What are *they* doing here?" The sheriff confirmed my suspicions. He glared at me and nodded to Kevin and Gramps.

"They found the body." Chief Michaels filled him in on our story. "Want to question them?"

"Not right now," the sheriff said. "Maybe later. But get 'em off my crime scene, huh? No civilians."

"*Your* crime scene?" Chief Michaels snorted. "I called you in to help with the questioning at the Blue Whale. Maybe you've forgotten that you're not out in the county, Tuck. This is Duck jurisdiction."

"That makes this my case now too, Ronnie." Sheriff Riley glared at us again. "All right. Get them out of *our* crime scene."

I was happy to get out of there. They didn't have to tell me twice. I took Kevin's hand and we walked away from the water. Gramps didn't follow—maybe it was okay for him to stay, since he used to be Riley's boss.

Gramps hadn't even tried to talk to me about Danny. Apparently, he hadn't recognized him. I thought that was a good thing. It eased the knot in the pit of my stomach that came up when I thought about explaining everything to him. I didn't like keeping secrets from Gramps—but lately, there seemed to be a lot of them.

"Mayor?" Chief Michaels hailed me before Kevin and I got to the pickup in the parking lot. "If I could have a word or two in private."

Kevin nodded and got in the pickup while the chief kind of nudged me into one of the park shelters. "You know, you've always been like a daughter to me. I always wanted a little girl, but Marjory and I were blessed with boys. I'm telling you this because I think you're in way over your head with Danny Evans."

"I don't know what you mean," I replied. "He was at that wreck Kevin and I helped out on. I felt sorry for him."

"Tim told me he was staying at your shop. He's bad news, Dae. You need to put some distance between you and him. I don't like the thought of you getting mixed up with Danny."

I put on my big mayor's smile. "I appreciate the thought, Chief, but—"

"I know who he is. Even more important, I know who he

is to *you*. I don't think Horace recognized him back there. But *you* know, don't you?"

I shrugged, but my heart was pounding. I wanted to tell him to mind his own business, but it was better for me to deal with this than to have him go to Gramps. "I know he works at the Sailor's Dream and that his place was flooded. He had nowhere to go."

"So you took him in." The chief's brown eyes narrowed. "Why not take him home? Why take him to Missing Pieces and the Blue Whale?"

"It seemed easier at Missing Pieces because I met him there." What kind of game was this? He obviously knew the truth—but he was still trying to decide if I knew that Danny was my father. "Kevin offered to let him stay at the Blue Whale. I thought he'd be more comfortable there." I wasn't giving away anything either.

"You mean after you and Brickman went and got him out of the county lockup? Come on, Dae! How naïve do you think I am?"

I raised my chin and looked him in the eye. "That's right. I went to get him because Tim arrested him after I'd said he could stay at my shop. What's wrong with that?"

He nodded. "Okay. Have it your way. You know you can talk to me if you need to—if there's something you can't say to Horace. Whatever that may be."

"And I appreciate that."

He cleared his throat, brushed a blade of grass from his shiny black shoes and set off back to the crime scene.

"What was that all about?" Kevin asked when I climbed in the pickup.

"He knows that Danny is my father. Gramps didn't recognize him at the Blue Whale—but the chief did."

"It's a very small town, Dae," he said, starting the engine. "You've told me that before. Everyone knows everything."

"Maybe. But why didn't I know, Kevin? They managed to keep my father a secret from me all these years."

"I don't know." He covered my hand with his. "I'm sure they thought they were protecting you from him. You have to admit, your father doesn't have the best reputation. And you're talking about lawmen. They tend to get more protective when someone they love gets involved with a criminal."

"It just makes me wonder what else they know that I don't."

"You should tell your grandfather, Dae. If you don't, you risk all of it blowing up in your face—like it would have at the inn if Horace had recognized Danny."

"Well, he didn't recognize him. I think it's better this way. He'll only get upset, and we'll have another big fight. I'm not giving up being with my father because of things he did wrong in the past. And right now, I'm not really sure if Gramps is all that innocent either. He drove Danny away when my mom needed him. That might not make him a convicted felon—but it makes him wrong."

There was a white SUV parked to the far right of us—almost in the bushes. I recognized the driver. Shawn Foxx. "What is he doing here?"

"Who?" Kevin followed my gaze. "Mayor Foxx's husband? Maybe he has a police radio."

"Maybe." I told him about Shawn's visit to the Blue Whale.

"I don't think it's unnatural for him to want to know what's going on," Kevin said. "I'd be following the chief around if I knew he was looking for the person who killed my wife."

"Maybe," I agreed. "Should we go and talk to him?"

"I don't think so," Kevin answered. "Let's leave the poor guy alone. He has enough problems."

We talked about Shawn a little more on the way back to the Blue Whale. Since Kevin didn't find Shawn's actions suspicious, I reserved judgment.

Kevin didn't press me any further about telling Gramps about Danny. I might have sounded hardheaded about my position. I just wanted a chance to get to know my father better before I decided if I should let him into my life and my heart. I wanted to know the truth about him without the outside interference.

Shayla was waiting for us at the Blue Whale. She and Kevin nodded to each other without speaking before he went inside.

"Is the ghost still bothering you?" she asked.

"Bothering her?" Rafe put in an appearance. "I'm helping her solve her lady friend's murder. I would hardly call that being a bother."

Shayla rolled her expressive eyes. "I wasn't talking to you, blowhard. Dae, I think I can get rid of him for you, if you want me to. I found some old text and talked to my Aunt Marie in New Orleans. She thinks we can send him back."

"Don't I get a bloody say in all this? You summoned me. I'm not some random spirit ye can call up and put back without so much as a by-your-leave."

I listened to them bickering. I knew Kevin understood what was going on. I hoped no one else was listening, since it would be a weird conversation to hear on the outside. "I'd like to say something."

"Well, spit it out, girl," Rafe said. "We haven't got all day."

"I've decided to help him," I told Shayla. "He's helped me, and I owe him that much. So I guess he stays for right now. Let's talk about it later if he doesn't go away once we figure out the truth about his death."

Rafe pounded the side of the inn with his fists. Birds flew up around us, and several people inside looked out to see what was happening. "It's about time! Let's get to work!"

Chapter 31

Since I knew Mark Samson would be my best source for Rafe Masterson lore, I set out for the Rib Shack with Rafe and Shayla on my heels. I explained why I needed to talk to Mark, but when we got to the Rib Shack, it was closed. There were no visible signs of damage to the old, squat building. It had been built out of cinder block in the 1950s. Those old structures like the Rib Shack always seemed to emerge from even the worst storms unscathed. It would probably take a car smashing into it to make a dent.

"He lives a few doors down from here. Let's try there," I told my companions. "He's the one we need."

"You think he's the magistrate's descendant?" Rafe asked.

"I don't know," I admitted. "The magistrate's descendant might not even live here anymore. People move around a lot more now than they did in your time. He could live anywhere in the world."

"Can't you do a spell or something, witch?" he asked Shayla. "We could get these answers faster."

"I'm not a witch," she protested. "I'm a medium. So unless you want me to contact the magistrate's spirit, you're out of luck."

Rafe didn't reply—we were at Mark's little house by then. It looked much like the Rib Shack—pale green-painted cinder block with a dark green roof. I felt pretty sure the two buildings must have gone up at the same time.

Mark was working on his roof, pushing off tree branches and hammering down loose shingles. He waved when he saw us and came down with a smile.

"You know Duck history is my favorite subject," he said after I'd told him the reason for our visit. "I need to wash my hands. Then we can talk. I'm afraid all I can offer you for refreshments is some warm Coke and a few Twinkies."

He smiled at us in his warm, friendly way and ushered us into his home. He was a short, older man with gray hair and glasses who looked more like a librarian than someone who roasted pork for a living.

Shayla and I had some warm, flat Coke—it would have been impolite not to. Rafe paced and fumed at the interruption as we all sat in Mark's tiny living room. There was a big masking tape X on the front window, but the glass was all in one piece.

We talked about all the gossip involving the storm—how the Harris Teeter grocery store was almost empty, and several residents weren't able to get the prescriptions they needed with the road blocked. Mark knew some things I hadn't heard, and I gave him some tidbits that surprised him.

When we were all caught up, Mark brought out his research into Rafe Masterson's life. "Well, like I was telling Dae earlier, Masterson was a pirate—no doubt about it. He was a particularly nasty pirate too. Some historians feel certain he robbed and sank at least twenty ships."

"That's a lie!" Rafe roared at the man who couldn't hear him. "I sank a hundred if I sank one!"

"He probably killed several dozen people too." Mark leafed through his documentation and cleared his throat. "People around here were scared of him. They had good reason to be."

"But you said he might have been hanged for something he didn't do," I reminded him.

"Oh yes. I have reason to believe from the old records, that he retired—if that's what pirates called it. He kind of went underground for a few years, and no one knew what happened to him. Many people thought he was dead."

I thought of the dream I'd had about Rafe's ship being destroyed. Maybe that was when he disappeared.

"He reappears in a county document." Mark handed me the copy of the old paper. "He got married. Looks like he tried to start a new life. But I have a feeling he couldn't get away from his past. He and his wife had two boys in quick succession. I have their birth certificates, of sorts. They're handwritten notes made by the local midwife who kept glorious records of the children she delivered, bless her soul. Her notes have been invaluable to anyone interested in Duck history."

Shayla and I looked at the records and passed them back to Mark. "So what happened?" she asked. "Did people forget who he was?"

"There's no way of knowing that," Mark answered. "It doesn't appear he was a landowner, probably kept a low profile, since the local law enforcement—probably a magistrate—would've remembered him too well."

"What about the hanging?" Rafe yelled, swinging his arms. "Tell them I was innocent."

"The next time we see his name, it's on a docket at the prison. He was sentenced to die by hanging." Mark looked up and smiled. "I'm not sure how he managed not to be drawn and quartered. It was popular at that time for pirates."

"You know, I thought everyone always said he was drawn, quartered and hanged after being tricked into coming to shore," I said.

"That's just folklore," Mark said. "This is what really happened."

"And what makes you think Rafe wasn't guilty?" I asked.

"Well, I found a few documents on other prisoners who were being held at the same time. One of them—I can't make out his name—was released, and Rafe's name was put over his for smuggling. I think someone just wanted him dead."

Shayla looked at her bright red fingernails. "Who can blame them? I mean, the man was a thief and a murderer. He might've been killed for something he didn't do, but it sounds to me like he deserved it."

"Mind your tongue, witch!" Rafe yelled at her. His anger blew all of the documents we'd been looking at on the floor. Two of the windows (probably damaged in the storm) blew out, and the door that had been open, slammed shut.

"What was that?" Mark asked, looking around. "I didn't even realize those windows were bad."

I got on the floor and picked up all the papers. "Do you know the name of the magistrate who condemned Rafe to death?"

"I think it's here." Mark took some of the papers from me and started looking through them. "He was involved in a lot of cases around the Outer Banks—probably the only magistrate for miles. There wasn't a lot of society out here at that time. That's why they had to send men down from Virginia to kill Blackbeard. Not much by way of government."

Mark shuffled through the documents, squinting at them despite his glasses. Rafe frowned and looked over his shoulder.

"Here it is!" he said after a few minutes. "His name was William Astor. He tried and convicted more than one hundred pirates in his time. Some of them were probably just smugglers, but he wanted his convictions to sound more impressive. From what I can tell, Rafe was his biggest catch. He wasn't exactly merciful with his executions either—another reason I'm surprised Rafe was only hanged."

I took all of it in, borrowing a pen and paper to write down some information. "Do you know if William Astor has any living descendants here?"

"I haven't gotten that far in my research," Mark said. "Although, I might not even go in that direction. I'm kind of only interested in Rafe. I think we might be related. How cool would that be—to be Rafe Masterson's descendant?"

"Probably not as cool as it sounds." Shayla got to her feet. "I have to go. I have an appointment."

"Thanks for your help, Mark." I shook his hand. "I hope you find out you're related to Rafe."

"No problem, Dae. There's supposed to be a journal or diary left by William Astor. You could ask Mrs. Stanley about it. She might know where it is. That might give you some idea whether any of Duck's current residents are related to the old magistrate."

Shayla and I walked back out into the sunshine with Rafe floating along in front of us.

"Why isn't he gone?" Shayla asked when we were a few yards from Mark Samson's house. "Mark said he probably wasn't guilty of smuggling. He should be gone."

"You understand very little," Rafe said. "I need the real proof—I need that diary wherein the man himself admits he killed me dead for naught. Nothing less will give me peace after all these years."

"Whatever." Shayla shrugged. "Say the word, Dae, and I'll give Aunt Marie a call."

"I want to get rid of him as much as anyone—"

"Lucky Mark Samson isn't related to the pirate blowhard or he'd be taking up residence at the Rib Shack," Shayla added.

"Anyway, it sounds like Rafe might not be guilty. All we have to do is figure out if someone here is still related to William Astor and has his diary." I smiled at her.

"Sounds like fun," she said. "Give me a call when you're done. See you, Dae."

Chapter 32

I decided to go to Missing Pieces and spend some time alone to think about everything. Being alone meant Rafe could be in the shop with me—according to our agreement—but I was hoping to persuade him otherwise. I thought of several convincing reasons why I needed some time without him.

But it turned out he had other plans anyway. Without any explanation, he vanished down a set of concrete stairs that led into the sound. Watching him disappear into the water gave me shivers.

Gramps had told me once that those stairs had been part of a pier that was destroyed during a hurricane years before I was born. No one had ever bothered to pull them up—they made for interesting stories to tell children and tourists.

Maybe hearing about his past from Mark Samson had left the old pirate in need of some time alone too, I speculated as I opened the door to Missing Pieces. I certainly wasn't complaining. I sat down on my burgundy brocade sofa with a relieved sigh.

There was always something about the days following a bad storm—as though time stood still for a while as we recovered from the assault. Life, *normal* life, came back slowly until one day everything was working and where it belonged again. That transition was as much a part of the rhythm of the Outer Banks as the horses and the lighthouses.

I took a hand cloth and began dusting and rearranging all my treasures. This was one of my favorite chores. I was surprised and pleased to be interrupted by a customer.

"I'm looking for a birthday present for my sister back home," the woman told me. She was tall, thin, very blond, and dressed expensively. "I was supposed to be home already, but the storm stranded me here for a few more days. She's picking me up at the airport when I leave next week. I thought it might be a nice surprise if I came back with something for her."

"Where's home?" I asked with a smile, quickly hiding my dust cloth.

"St. Louis. All my family is there. But I've had a wonderful time down here. My friend who comes every summer with her family recommended Duck—and your shop."

"I'm glad you've had a good time, despite the storm. And I'm glad you stopped by. What did you have in mind?"

"I don't know. She likes antiques." She shrugged and looked around like she was lost. "I don't know anything about them. I'd love it if there was something that has a story. She's a writer and she loves history."

"Really? What does she write?"

The woman laughed, showing perfect white teeth in her tanned face. "She writes murder mysteries set in the past. Crazy, huh? But she's successful at it. My brother and I tease her all the time about it. She doesn't care. She's happy."

I thought about the gold makeup case and dug it out. Apparently my previous buyer had changed her mind, since I hadn't heard from her. "This belonged to Lady Suzanne Forester, and there is a story that goes with it. She spent some time here off and on with her uncle during the late 1700s and early 1800s. She was a writer too."

"Murder mysteries?" The woman carefully examined the case.

"No, I'm afraid not. She wrote wonderful journals about her life and the people around her—what it was like to spend time in this area when it was still basically a wilderness then return to England and her life there. She was an early suffragette. She was very accomplished as an artist too. A Renaissance woman. Your sister can probably find some background material about her in books."

"Really? How fascinating!" She turned the makeup case over, opened it and peered inside at the old mirror. "I think you're right. I think she'll love it."

The woman had already successfully passed several of my tests for buying my real treasures—like this makeup case. I wanted my important items to go to people who'd really appreciate them. And I charged a steep price when anyone asked how much they cost.

She not only didn't ask before she pulled out her Visa card, she also didn't blink when I told her how much. She was the perfect buyer.

"Can you gift wrap?" she asked.

"Of course." I pulled out a sheet of pirate-themed wrapping paper. "What do you think?"

"Perfect! Thank you so much."

I waved to her as she left, amazed and thrilled to make any money at all this week. I was even more pleased to have sold the makeup case to someone like her. As sad as I always was to see my treasures leave, I knew this one was going to a good home. I picked up the dust rag again and hummed as I finished straightening and dusting everything in the shop.

After I was finished, I sat down with a cup of tea and tried to work out what could have happened to Sandi and Matthew. It seemed obvious to me that Sandi's husband made the perfect suspect—like my perfect customer. Unless Shawn Foxx had a remarkable alibi, I knew Chief Michaels would be thinking the same thing. What man would continue looking the other way as his wife had affair after affair?

Of course, that didn't make Shawn a killer. Jealousy and anger were powerful emotions, but it was only two days ago that we thought Matthew Wright had killed Sandi. Not every hypothesis proved true.

But who else could do something like this? I knew from listening to the chief talk that he thought it was possible the two murders were committed with the same gun—the one I'd found at the park. Part of me wished I'd had the opportunity to touch the gun, but most of me was glad I didn't.

My gift of seeing events by touching articles connected to those events came with a terrible price sometimes. Even the gift I was born with—finding missing items by touching people—could be painful. I'd learned to live with these abilities, but it was difficult.

I admired and envied Shayla's calm acceptance of her abilities. She never questioned if what she saw was right or wrong. She never doubted herself. We were raised similarly, with family and friends accepting our abilities. But there the resemblance ended. I don't know why I didn't have her confidence. She was so cool and laid-back about what she could do that I often wondered if it affected her at all.

Finally tired of being alone and realizing that sitting here wasn't getting me any answers at all, I closed up shop around five P.M. and headed back to the Blue Whale. I wasn't ready to spend much quality time with Gramps—another sore point in my life. We were so close. It broke my heart to hide things from him and distrust his word. But that's the way it was, at least for right now. I knew we'd find some way to work it out.

I was surprised to see that town hall was closed as I walked by. Glad, too, because it meant Nancy had gone home. She worked too hard for the small salary we could pay her. She was really too good for us—but I didn't know what we would do without her.

The boardwalk and parking lot seemed strangely empty to me. Even though this time of year was normally quiet, I never really got used to it. After a storm was even worse than normal. Next week, things would be better. Shops would be open again and people would be out walking around, visiting friends and buying. It would stay busy until the Jazz Festival in November. After that, it would be empty again until spring.

Phil De Angelo, who owned the Coffeehouse and Bookstore, was inspecting the damage to his place. The little shop was very popular and sat off to one side in the Duck Shoppes parking lot.

"Mayor." He nodded when he saw me. "I'm getting too old for this. I don't know how you people go through it all your lives."

By "you people" he meant people from Duck. Phil was a recent transplant from New York. He'd chosen to retire here after many years serving the city of Buffalo.

"It doesn't look so bad," I commented. "This wasn't even a real hurricane. There's a lot of damage, but we'll be fine."

He shook his head. "Not me. I can't keep doing this. I decided yesterday to put the place up for sale. I got a sister who lives in Atlanta. Her husband recently passed, and she needs help keeping her place. I'm moving there. Not much going on there with the weather. And no earthquakes, like my brother in Seattle. I'll miss you people, though."

I hugged him, and he looked a little embarrassed. "I wish you wouldn't leave. We'll miss you."

"Thanks." He sniffled and wiped his eyes. "I really enjoyed being here. But sometimes things don't work out the way we want them to. You take care now."

I was going to miss Phil—his mochas and his stories about his life. I hoped someone else would reopen the coffee shop. It was a favorite around here.

The day was over for most people by the time I got to the Blue Whale. Most of the cars—police, sheriffs, and guests being questioned—were gone. I hoped that was a good sign. Chief Michaels was too thorough to let everyone leave just because Matthew was found dead. I wondered about his new strategy.

Good smells were emanating from the kitchen as I opened the front door. "Anyone here?"

"He's in the kitchen," Marissa told me, bustling by. "Thank God the investigation seems to be over. Maybe we can get back to normal now."

I agreed and felt a little embarrassed when my stomach growled loudly. "I haven't eaten since breakfast," I explained. "I guess I'm hungry. I hope Kevin made enough for me too."

Marissa swung her long blond hair away from her face. "You know him—he makes enough to feed an army. I'm on my way out. See you tomorrow, Dae."

I said good-bye and went into the kitchen where Kevin was stirring something in a big pot. "I'm glad you're back," he said with a smile. "I was about to open some wine. Want some?"

"Only after I eat everything in that pot. What is it?"

"Just some leftovers I threw together. After feeding everyone today, I had enough to make some stew."

"I'll take some of that and some wine, thanks. It's been a long day."

The wine was a sweet, muscadine blush made from grapes harvested from the Mother Vine in Manteo. The vine, cultivated for more than three hundred years, had almost been killed by power-line workers spraying pesticide on weeds. But it was healthy again now and producing grapes.

"So how did it go?" Kevin asked as he poured the wine.

I told him about my meeting with Mark Samson and my wonderful sale at Missing Pieces. "That's it for me today. I'm going to eat some stew, drink some wine and spend quality time with my favorite person. Then I'm heading home for the night. Gramps texted me on the way over to let me know he wouldn't be home until late."

"You're going to have to talk to him sometime, Dae." Kevin ladled the fragrant stew into bowls. "Now that Chief Michaels knows, how long will it be before Horace knows too?"

"I don't have to live with Chief Michaels. And I don't think he means to tell Gramps. I think that's what our secret meeting at the park today was all about."

"And this from the woman who warned me about the Duck grapevine?"

"Like I said, apparently we can keep secrets from people who are involved in them. Just ask me. I know all about it." I tasted the stew and smiled. "You are the best cook in Duck! Even when you're only throwing things together."

"Thanks." He tasted the stew and added salt to his. "What about the pirate?"

"Still lurking. It wasn't enough that Mark thinks he's innocent. We have to prove it. Probably the only way to do that is to find the magistrate's diary. At least we know his name now. All we have to do is trace down his family tree and hope one of his descendants lives around here. If not, I might have a pirate living with me forever."

Chapter 33

"Anything new in the murder investigation?" I asked.

"The chief is questioning Shawn Foxx."

"Seriously? He thinks Sandi's husband killed her? It's a long drive between here and Manteo."

"It makes sense, unfortunately," Kevin explained. "Sandi was killed—then her lover. Husbands and wives make good suspects in a case like this. Since Matthew wasn't married, that leaves Shawn Foxx."

"I understand." I sipped wine and ate freshly baked crusty bread with my stew. "What about Matthew? I wonder if he had someone special in his life."

"What do you mean?"

"He was really intent on leaving Sandi. Maybe he wasn't just tired of her and ready to move on. Maybe he'd met someone else."

"Maybe," he agreed. "But the chief has Shawn Foxx on his radar right now."

"Well, we know he was in Manteo with his kids during the storm, right?"

"Apparently not. He'd driven down to some kind of sales meeting in Kitty Hawk. The kids were with their grandmother. When his wife was killed, he was sleeping alone in his car, waiting for the storm to pass. Not much of an alibi."

"No."

"It was enough to make the chief drive over to Manteo with the sheriff to question him."

"Glad I'm not with them. The two of them together are too much."

He laughed. "That's the way competing law enforcement agencies always are."

"I hate to think that those two little girls could lose their mother and their father."

He got up and put his arms around me. "No one wants to think that, Dae. But if he killed her—"

"I know—granddaughter of a sheriff, remember." I shook my head, glad that he was near. "And daughter of a petty criminal, I guess. Maybe that's what makes me so divided." I looked into his eyes and asked, "What made you ask me if my father had stolen something?"

He shrugged. "Habit, I guess. For him and me. Did he steal something from you?"

I started to answer, but Danny came into the kitchen. He sniffed appreciatively. "Smells good! Hi, Dae. I mucked out that cellar, Kevin. Most of what's in there—except the whiskey—was probably ruined by the mud and water."

"I thought so. Thanks, Danny." Kevin let me go. "Help yourself to some stew. There's bread in the oven too. Don't be shy."

"Thanks. I feel like I could eat a few wild horses."

Watching Danny dip stew and cut bread in Kevin's kitchen made me feel guilty. I was being unfair lying to Kevin about Danny stealing from me. What if Danny took something from Kevin too? In all honesty, I didn't know if Danny would have returned the makeup case if I hadn't found him trying to spend the night behind the trash bin. Kevin might not be that lucky.

Since I'd started this quest to get to know my father, I'd told so many lies that I wasn't sure anymore where one began and another ended. I wasn't happy about that, but I had no other choice. Somebody had to give him a break and show him that they cared about him. I wanted to be that person.

Maybe Kevin was right and I should tell Gramps everything too, instead of treating him like the enemy. He'd taken care of me my whole life. I owed him something too. I loved and respected him. I didn't want to lose him while I found my father.

"I'd better get home," I said, hoping Kevin would take the hint. "Walk me outside?"

"Let me take you home," he offered.

"Okay. Good night, Danny. I'll probably see you tomorrow."

"See you, Dae. Thanks again. You know, you're my guardian angel."

My heart swelled when he said that, and I smiled. And seeing his return smile reminded me that we shared that trait—I had his smile. When I'd first started watching him, I noticed it right away. He might not have been there when I was growing up, but he was still my father. How could I feel any different?

"You were saying?" Kevin prompted when we were on the verandah.

We both knew what he was talking about. "I'm sorry. I know I keep saying that, but I'm really sorry I lied to you. Yes. He took something from me. But he was alone and desperate. I don't know what I'd do in that situation."

Kevin's face took on a hard look that I'd never seen before. "I can tell you what you wouldn't do—you wouldn't steal from the woman who'd helped you in an accident the night before. I hate that he's your father, Dae, but he is what he is."

"I don't believe that," I disagreed. "He's been working and honest for years—you said so yourself. He hasn't been in jail for a long time. That whole 'once a thief, always a thief' thing isn't necessarily true. What about rehabilitation?"

"You're right. He hasn't been in jail. But that probably means he hasn't been caught at anything. You can argue that he's not that kind of person anymore, except that he stole from you, and he'll probably steal from me if he gets a chance."

I stopped short from getting into his pickup for the ride home. "This isn't you talking, Kevin. This is the FBI. I know you worked for them for a long time, but you aren't an agent anymore. I guess that would mean the same thing—you automatically revert to the person you were before and judge people by what statistics tell you."

He leaned against the side of the pickup. "Dae, I know he's your father. I know you feel a bond with him. But that doesn't make him a good person. Horace knows that too. I guess Chief Michaels feels the same way. Doesn't that tell you something?"

I nodded, almost too angry to speak. "Yes, it does. I know way too many people in law enforcement, where they teach you to be cynical and suspicious. I think I need to walk, Kevin. I'll talk to you tomorrow."

"That's not fair, Dae. And I think we should talk about it."

"Good night, Kevin. I'll call you when I think I *can* talk about it."

I started walking, hoping he wouldn't try to join me. I kept my head down until I reached Duck Road. I was still alone. I was glad he gave up. I needed some time by myself.

"You spoke rightly, girl," Rafe assured me—not as alone as I'd thought. "People change. Look at me! I was a husband and a father. What did people see—a pirate. I guess I'm like yer old man, eh? Now that you don't have to spend so much time with your lover, mayhap you can work harder on my situation."

"Maybe so." I realized he wasn't empathizing with me so much as wanting my full attention.

"What plans have we for finding the magistrate's diary?"

"I don't have any plans right now except to take a hot shower, put on my pajamas and have a cup of hot chocolate. I might even watch some TV."

We crossed Duck Road together, the pirate floating beside me. Traffic was back to normal—a car honked its horn at me—and not because the driver knew me.

"Throw some rum into that mix and I might join you," Rafe said with a laugh.

"I don't think so, but thanks for the offer. This is private time, the kind where you go off and do whatever ghosts do."

"Have I mentioned that I'm willing to show you where I buried my treasure?"

"No. You still have a treasure?"

"Aye! And a right good bit of booty it is. Enough to keep a girl in geegaws for a long time. Interested?"

Chapter 34

"This is for finding the diary, I guess?" I wondered if he thought a bribe would make a big difference. Of course—he was a pirate—he'd think to grease my palm.

"It is," he admitted. "Ye don't seem to be motivated much to the task. I thought my presence was onerous enough, but that hasn't done it. What about treasure? Aye, that's the stuff dreams are made of. It means little to me now."

"I suppose not." We had reached a bend in the road that was protected from prying eyes by thick bushes. I felt comfortable looking at him as I spoke. "I'm sure anyone would like to have your treasure—and I'm your descendant, so I guess I'm entitled to it. But I can only do what I can do. The world won't stop turning for me to find the diary in the next five minutes. I'm doing the best I can."

I realized that I was crying during that last part and started walking faster toward home. I didn't want anyone to see me this way.

Rafe followed me—there was no getting rid of him.

"Women! A man can't say what's on his mind without a woman blubbering all over. My own blood relation is a watering pot. And you're not even angry with *me*—it's your lover that's bothering you. He told you your pa is no good and that hurt your bloody feelings."

"Go away!"

"I will when you take care of my need."

"I told you—I'll handle it tomorrow. Believe me, a treasure is nothing compared to getting rid of you."

"Stop your bawlin'! How can you be related to me?"

I took out my cell phone as though I were taking out a pistol. "If you don't leave right now, I'm calling the witch. She'll send you away without the diary."

"Ye made your point. Good night to you then." And he was gone.

I sat down on the front stairs leading up to the house and stared at the night that was closing in around me.

I hadn't wanted to fight with Kevin about Danny. Would he even let him stay at the Blue Whale now? If the universe was trying to show me that it was better to tell the truth than to lie—it was doing a poor job of it.

"Dae?" Gramps called as he opened the door behind me, golden light spilling out into the darkness. "I thought someone was out here. Old Roger was barking up a storm. Are you okay?"

Old Roger was the next-door neighbor's German shepherd. He'd been faithful in announcing visitors to our home for the last ten years.

"Fine." I wiped my eyes and tried to stop sniffling. "I thought you were going to be late."

"I thought so too. But Tim swung by—looking for you—and he offered to help me get the tree out from in front of the garage. I took him up on it. Are you coming inside?"

"Yes. We have to talk, Gramps."

"Okay. Let me put some coffee on. It sounds bad."

Over fresh coffee and stale cinnamon rolls, I told him

everything, from watching my father at the bar a few times each week to letting him stay at Missing Pieces. I didn't know what the universe would do to me in this case, but I knew telling Gramps was the right thing to do.

When I was finished and had stopped crying—maybe Rafe was right about me being a watering pot—I waited to hear what Gramps had to say. He was silent for a long time, thinking it over while he chewed and swallowed. His blue eyes didn't give anything away.

This was how I remembered him from when I was a teenager. My mom would ask him to speak to me about some escapade or another—like the time I went to a beach party I was forbidden to go to.

He'd come home, change his uniform for a T-shirt and old jeans. Then we'd sit at the table until we talked about whatever it was. And we'd all feel better. I hoped we'd all feel better this time too.

"Do you like what you've seen so far?" he finally asked after a swallow of coffee (there was no other way to get the dry cinnamon roll down).

"Do I—what?"

"Your father. Now that you've met him and talked to him, do you like what you've seen of him?"

It was a difficult question to answer, and one I wasn't expecting. "I don't really know him that well yet."

"Come on, Dae. I've heard you make decisions about people much faster than this. Don't bail on me. You've told the truth. I thank you for that. Tell me the truth now—do you like him? Do you think he's a good person?"

"I think he's had a hard life," I ventured in my father's defense.

"He comes from a well-to-do family. Never had to work a day in his life—until they finally disowned him after he'd been in and out of jail a lot. He had a life you could only dream of."

"Okay. Not a hard life financially, but maybe a hard life in other ways. Money isn't everything. You taught me that."

"Dae, I know you love him—or at least you think you do right now. He's your father and you've always felt cheated because you didn't know him. But he's not a good person. He'll only leave you to ruin like he did your mother."

"You didn't give him a chance to do anything else," I accused.

He nodded. "Guilty as charged. I protect the people I love, and I won't apologize for it."

"I don't think I need that kind of protection anymore, Gramps. I can make my own decisions about people."

"How does Kevin feel about him? I'm assuming he knows the truth. Did you tell Danny yet that he's your father?"

I got up from the chair and calmly put my cup in the sink. "Kevin feels the same way you do—all based on Danny's past record. And no, I haven't told Danny yet that he's my father. I thought I should get to know him first before I spring it on him."

"At least you're trying to use the brains God gave you. I'm glad about that."

"But you know I'll have to tell him sometime. I don't think you and Kevin give him credit for not being the same person he was thirty years ago. You're both wrong about him, and I'll prove it to you."

"Please don't do anything foolish, honey. You don't have to prove anything. Don't get involved in his life. You've made a wonderful home for yourself. People like and respect you. Don't throw all that away on someone who doesn't deserve it."

There was nothing more to say here either. For Gramps, as with Kevin, actions would speak louder than words. And yes, I hadn't come completely clean about my father. I'd left out the part about the makeup case. I had no doubt

Kevin would enlighten Gramps, but he wasn't going to hear it from me.

Maybe by that time, Gramps would begin to see that Danny was just someone struggling through life. He wasn't a bad person—he had issues that I felt sure time and love would solve.

"I love you, Dae," Gramps said as he stood up and hugged me. "I hope you know that. We haven't been so close lately. I miss that. Please don't shut me out of your life."

I hugged him back. He was wrong about Danny, but I still loved him too. "I'm sorry it's been so weird lately. Strange things have been happening."

"Such as?"

"Did you know the Bellamys are related to Rafe Masterson?"

"The pirate?"

"You got it."

"How did you find out?"

I laughed, glad that I'd told him most of the truth and cleared the air between us even though doing so had been hard. "I think that's going to take another cup of coffee."

Chapter 35

Gramps and I talked until midnight about the pirate ghost and the things he'd told me about the past. It was as easy as ever talking to Gramps—about that subject. I tried to get Rafe to appear and do some little trick to show he was there, but no such luck.

We didn't touch on my father again. That was good. I realized that I didn't want to exclude Gramps from my life—I just wanted to include Danny too. My optimistic heart believed that could happen.

It was raining the next morning—a definite hindrance to getting Duck back in order. The maintenance people would have to sit around and wait for the weather to clear. But every Banker knows to expect bad weather this time of year.

I put on my rain poncho and boots and headed for the Duck Historical Museum early, when I'd be most likely to catch our town historians there. They met for tea and cookies several times a week to debate Duck history. I needed to pick their brains if I was going to have a chance of finding the magistrate's diary.

I wondered how I'd managed to escape Rafe's company this morning. I kept expecting him to pop up. I knew he was still here somewhere. Who knew that pirates pouted?

I couldn't help glancing next door at the Blue Whale as I reached the museum. Kevin's pickup was gone, but I saw Danny outside working on replacing glass in the lower-floor windows. He didn't see me, so I got to watch him for a while. I thought about his age—he had to be in his fifties. It had to be hard for him to be thrown out on the streets. At least Kevin had let him stay. I was happy about that. I wasn't looking forward to talking to Kevin again just yet. In some ways, I was glad he wasn't home.

I could hear our local historians arguing inside the museum before I even opened the door. Mrs. Euly Stanley was making a point as she poured herself another cup of tea. Mark Samson was eating a blueberry muffin, and Andy Martin was sitting back in his chair shaking his head.

"I'm telling you the *Andalusia* sank in 1721, not 1720. All my research points in that direction," Andy said. He looked up when he saw me and smiled broadly. "Mayor! What brings you out this early?"

"Good morning, Dae," Mrs. Stanley said. "We have plenty of goodies here. Please help yourself."

"I guess I'm the only one who knows what you're after." Mark grinned and got up for another muffin.

"Sit down, Mayor," Andy said. "Tell us about your mystery."

I took a cup of tea and a muffin, then sat down with the group. "I thought Mark might have told you already. I'm looking for information about the magistrate who condemned Rafe Masterson to death."

Mrs. Stanley sat down beside me and sipped her tea. "You know, I remember hearing about that."

"From me," Mark said. "I told you all about the documents I'd found. The magistrate's name was William Astor. Some people have called him the hanging judge—but he was a lot worse than that. Dae is helping me prove my theory that Masterson was hanged for something besides piracy."

I didn't remember saying that I was helping him—but whatever worked.

"That's crazy," Andy said. "Everybody wants to rewrite history. We all know Rafe Masterson was one of the worst pirates in the area. He cursed Duck. How much worse can you get than that?"

"Technically, he might've cursed the area, but Duck wasn't officially here yet," Mark reminded him. "The only thing worse than rewriting history is believing mythology is history."

Before this got into a daylong argument, I stepped in to smooth the waters. "What I'm really looking for is one of William Astor's descendants."

"What for, dear?" Mrs. Stanley asked.

"I'd like to find his diary." I nodded at Mark, who gave me a secret smile. "I've heard that all of his deeds are faithfully recorded in that diary. I'm sure there would be some interesting historical notes, if we could find it."

Mrs. Stanley sipped her tea and carefully dabbed a napkin on her lips. "I don't know exactly who that would be, but we could certainly trace down the Astor lineage. Maybe that would give you some idea. Though it's likely whoever it is doesn't live here anymore. You know young people tend to leave."

"I know." It was something everyone talked about. Mad Dog Wilson was using it as part of his campaign for mayor. He said we needed manufacturing jobs to keep young people in Duck after they graduated from high school. It wasn't that I didn't want to see young people stay in Duck—I just didn't know where we'd put manufacturing companies.

"But we could check anyway," Andy said. "It would be fun. And you never know, one of the old magistrate's descendants could be here. It happens. Look at us. All of us were born here."

"I agree," Mrs. Stanley said. "I'll start calling members of the historical society today. Someone in the group is bound to know something—even if it's that the magistrate's descendants aren't here anymore."

"This is exciting!" Mark got to his feet. "This information could really help with my Rafe Masterson project too. At least I'd know if he was hanged for legitimate crimes. Once I get all the information together, I plan to publish."

Andy made a scoffing sound. "Who would want to publish *that*? I don't think a publisher would be interested in something that happened here a couple hundred years ago. They aren't even interested in what's happening here now."

"Nonetheless," said Mrs. Stanley, interrupting. "I think it's a wonderful idea, Mark. Even if we only sell copies locally. We could have copies here at the museum."

While they were discussing the merits of publishing Mark's work, I noticed a box of various bottles on a side table. They were dirty and unsorted. They had to be a new find for the museum. Something in that box seemed to be calling to me. It was almost as though I could feel it urging me to pick it up.

"Are these for a new exhibit?" I got up and went over to the box.

"Yes, well, maybe." Mrs. Stanley joined me. "It's part of some things Martha Segall had on her porch from her father's old house. You know he's in sorry shape, bless his heart. She had to put him in a nursing home in Manteo. She and her brother cleared out his house and put it up for sale. They had an auction, but no one wanted this stuff. She thought the museum might want it."

"I hope you told her we have plenty of old Mason jars and whatnot," Andy said. "People can't just drop off their old junk here because they don't have anything else to do with it."

"May I take a look?" It was all I could do not to push past her and grab the box to examine it.

"Of course," Mrs. Stanley said. "If something looks interesting to you, Dae, please take it as a donation to your shop. We already have a lot of old bottles."

I heard her as though she were talking from the other end of a long tunnel. I reached for the dusty bottle that was calling me. It had a faint rose tint to it beneath the grime. I realized it was a perfume bottle with a top that was shaped like a rose.

As soon as it touched my hand, I was transported back to where it was made—somewhere in England. It came here as part of a trousseau, but never made it to the wedding. Pirates boarded the ship and took everything before lighting the ship on fire.

The glass perfume bottle lay in a trunk, unused for several years until it was given to a woman with red hair and a rosy complexion. Her husband leaned over to kiss her bare shoulder as she used the stopper to apply her perfume. I could see both their faces joined in the mirror on her vanity.

I came back to myself with a rush of awareness and a weakness in my knees that threatened to send me to the floor. The woman in the mirror was Mary Astor—the wife of the magistrate. The same magistrate who had hanged her first husband—Rafe Masterson.

Chapter 36

I gasped as I realized what had happened. Looking into Mary's beautiful face in the mirror—it was as if I were Mary, with the rose-colored perfume bottle still in my hand.

I knew everything. It all came to me in a wild surge of emotion that lay locked behind her brilliant green eyes.

The magistrate had given her a choice—she could become his wife, lovingly and faithfully, or she could watch as Rafe was horribly tortured in front of his children and the people of the community. Mark was right when he'd said hanging was the least of the things they could do to a pirate.

"She loved him," I said out loud on a sob without really knowing what I was saying. "She begged for mercy and gave herself to him."

"What did you say, dear?" Mrs. Stanley asked.

I realized where I was, looking at all the surprised faces around me.

Mary had been the reason the magistrate had decided to

get rid of Rafe. William Astor had fallen in love with her. He wanted her and was willing to kill Rafe to have her.

This was a whole new spin on Rafe's life. He was telling the truth about being a changed man. I felt that from Mary. He had been a good husband and father. She had loved him.

"Are you all right, Dae?" Mark asked. "You're as white as the proverbial sheet."

"Yes! Sit down, Mayor." Andy pulled out my chair. "You do look a mite peaked."

I did as they suggested, drank tea and nibbled on a muffin while they argued again about the date the *Andalusia* sank—all the while I still felt Mary's pain at losing Rafe. They'd been happy together and had looked forward to raising their children together.

But she knew she had no choice. She'd stood, unemotional, with her sons beside her as she watched them hang Rafe for a crime he didn't commit. The night before, she'd begged for mercy for her husband—allowing the magistrate to do terrible things to her in exchange for his leniency.

She never let on—never even blinked. Her life was over in that moment, but she wouldn't give William Astor the satisfaction of knowing.

"We're leaving now, Dae." Mrs. Stanley had put on her jacket. "You're welcome to stay, of course. But maybe you should go home and lie down for a while. Poor dear. It must be all the strain from the storm. It can't be easy being the mayor of Duck at a time like this."

"No offense, Dae," Mark said, "but maybe Mad Dog is right about a man being better able to handle the job of mayor."

That shook me up and made me get to my feet. "I'd like to keep this bottle," I told Mrs. Stanley. "And as far as being a woman mayor, I think I can handle a storm as well as Councilman Wilson. Thanks for your help. I hope to hear about that magistrate soon."

I walked out. My rudeness left them all a little stunned, I'm sure. It wasn't easy to propel myself out the door. I still felt lost in the past—it was a difficult feeling to pull away from. I wanted to cry for Mary Masterson and her children. Knowing these people were related to me made me even sadder but also more determined to prove that for once in his life, Rafe was innocent.

"I can see you learned something valuable in there." Rafe joined me as I walked away from the museum.

I didn't answer until I'd walked behind the Blue Whale. I was worried the three historical society members would see me talking to myself and think I was crazy. "There was something," I told him finally, not sure what I should share with him. Did he realize what Mary had gone through? How would it affect him?

I studied my ancestor's face. It wasn't exactly like looking at a living man's features. He wasn't solid looking—more opaque. No one could mistake him for anything but a ghost.

I wanted to see in him what Mary saw—I wished I was still seeing through her eyes. There was something more to him than his terrible past and the dastardly deeds that he ended up paying for at the end of a rope.

"You're scaring me, girl, and that's not easy. What are ye looking for? You act like you've never seen me before. Are you in your cups? I didn't know they were serving spirits in there—I might've joined you."

A concrete bench sat nearby, between two large bushes. I could see the gray of the Atlantic, stretching on beneath the dark sky that still threatened more rain. It was there that I told Rafe what I'd seen—what I knew about Mary. I didn't know what to expect from him.

To my surprise, he knelt on the ground and began to weep, huge choking sobs that shook his already unstable frame from head to toe.

I put my hand on his shoulder as I would have any other

person in such distress—but there was nothing there. And an instant later, what was left of the man Mary had loved disappeared.

"Dae?"

I heard my father call my name. I wiped my eyes, put the perfume bottle in the pocket of my poncho and tried to clear my mind. "Danny! How's it going?"

"Good. Good. Your friend is a decent man. There's not a lot of people who would take in a stranger this way."

"I saw you working on the windows," I said, grasping for a topic.

"Yeah. Kevin keeps me busy. But I talked to the owner of the Sailor's Dream this morning. He hopes to be open again by the weekend. He says if my place isn't ready yet, I can stay in the back room of the bar after that. Things are picking up."

"I'm glad to hear it."

"You know"—he sat beside me on the concrete bench— "I don't want you to take this the wrong way—I'm not coming on to you, I swear—not that you aren't a beautiful woman."

"Thanks."

"Anyway. There's something about you—I felt it from the beginning. Something almost familiar. I guess it's because I knew your mother. I don't know. I guess I'm kind of crazy. But it's more than the short time I've known you. It just feels like I've known you all my life. Weird, huh?"

I put my hand on his arm—too emotional from what I'd seen about Rafe not to tell him the truth. He should know. He deserved to know I was his daughter. It could change his life the way it had changed mine.

"Dae!" Tim Mabry said as he ran up to us. "There you are! I've been looking for you everywhere!"

The moment had passed—sanity returned. I knew I couldn't tell Danny the truth yet.

"What's up?" I asked in what I hoped was a normal voice.

"They need you up at town hall. We're gonna be on TV! The Weather Channel is here, following the path of the storm. Can you believe it?"

Chapter 37

I had to run home and change clothes. No one wants to see a sandy, rumpled mayor on TV! Tim's announcement was like a cold slap of seawater in the face, jerking me away from the past and into the reality of the present.

I put on a little lipstick and made sure there was nothing stuck in my teeth, then I sailed out the door.

I saw the TV vans in the Duck Shoppes parking lot. I was sorry the bad weather had brought them to us, but I wasn't going to waste the opportunity. One of the vans was from the Weather Channel amd the other was from our local station in Virginia Beach.

Town hall was packed with residents, TV crews and members of the town council. Like me, they had changed their everyday clothes for suits and ties. Nothing but our Sunday best to show off Duck!

I was excited and happy to be there—until I saw Mad Dog talking to a reporter on air.

"And this is why we need new leadership in our town," he said, waving his arms like a crazy octopus. His dark blue suit was too small for his large frame, its brass buttons threatening to pop off his jacket. "Two murders in Duck within days of each other, following a terrible act of nature. And what has Mayor O'Donnell done for us?"

I disliked the way he made it sound as though I were responsible for the murders as well as the storm. After going through an emotional wringer all morning, I was tempted to just walk back out the door.

But I wouldn't let him get to me. I straightened my black suit, plastered on my mayor's smile and pushed my way through the crowd that surrounded Mad Dog.

"What I'd like to know, as mayor and as a citizen, is what Councilman Wilson has done about the things that have happened in the last few days. Not once while I've been out helping with cleanup after the storm or aiding the Duck Police with these terrible crimes, have I seen Councilman Wilson. Where have you been, Mad Dog?"

"Mad Dog?" The smiling TV personality looked back at him. "That's an unusual nickname."

"He got it racing cars around the Outer Banks when he was younger," I told her.

"So you were one of the infamous moonshine runners, huh, Mad Dog?" she asked with a practiced smile of her own.

"I was a stock car driver," he corrected her. "I never ran moonshine. Not once. Not in my whole life."

His words added fuel to the allegation, and the reporter put a match to the whole thing. "Was that during the time of prohibition?"

Mad Dog frowned at me. "I'm not that old. What do you take me for? It's Dae's fault—she twists words around."

The reporter turned away from both of us and laughed as she faced the camera. "Sometimes history gets a little *too* real down here in the Outer Banks. Reporting from Duck,

North Carolina, I'm Christine Thomas and I'm out and about!"

The cameraman lowered the lens, and Christine Thomas put away her microphone.

"Wait a minute!" Mad Dog tried to stop her. "I haven't finished. There's more to say about the mayor and all of the mysterious goings-on right here. Maybe we should do an in-depth piece."

Christine smiled at him and kind of patted him on the shoulder. "Maybe—once Duck gets to be more important. Right now, it was all I could do to get my boss to let me come down here with the Weather Channel. Sorry."

The expression on Mad Dog's face reminded me of a hound dog on an old calendar. He shook his head like he couldn't believe his time on-air had been for nothing. "You know, one day, Dae O'Donnell, the world is going to hear how you and your grandfather manipulated the last election. Then I think you won't find it so funny."

I started to tell him that I didn't think it was funny now, but he made a *humphing* sound and stormed out of town hall. Really, I couldn't believe our little election could turn so dirty. Again I thought it might be best to leave the race and let him have it. I didn't want this to turn into a campaign of dragging each other's dirty laundry through the streets of Duck.

But I didn't have time to dwell on it then. The Weather Channel crew wanted me to walk them through some streets that would show off the damage done to Duck. They also wanted to know what it was like the night of the storm, how the cleanup was going and what our normal precautions were during emergency weather.

I was amazed at how thorough their questions were. We had nothing to hide, as far as I was concerned. Our emergency personnel and policies were as good as any other town around here. And I was glad to talk about them.

The pace was rigorous as we drove to some spots for

photos and video, then walked to other areas where I answered questions and we talked to Duck residents about their experiences.

I saw Shawn Foxx standing outside Carter Hatley's Game World and wondered what he was doing there. Given that Kevin had said the police were questioning him about Sandi's death, I was surprised to see him in town. Was he doing his own investigation? The arcade seemed a strange place to start. But I'd be investigating if I were a suspect in a murder investigation.

There wasn't time to stop and ask as the Weather Channel van sped by. I was glad to hear that not a single resident thought the town had done less than its best. That made me feel proud even though I certainly couldn't take all the credit. I told the TV crew the same thing—the aftermath of a few minutes from the hurricane feeder bands would take months for our public works people to take care of. "There aren't many of us here, but we all pitch in."

At one stop, I found Kevin working on the roof at Betty's Boutique and Floral along with a group of volunteers. I pointed out to the TV crew that Kevin—and probably the others as well—was helping out Betty even though his own business needed repair too. Betty's situation was more urgent, since there had been a dinghy on her roof.

The volunteers all shook hands with the camera crew. Kevin looked across the crowd at me. I smiled and he kind of smiled back. I thought it was a good sign. But I felt pretty sure we wouldn't get to talk today. Maybe a little space would be good for us.

It was going on evening when the Weather Channel crew finally wrapped up their taping. I suggested going to Wild Stallions on the boardwalk, since they were all hungry and thirsty. We had a good time comparing notes on storms in the Atlantic. One of the crew was from Wilmington, North Carolina, so we had a lot in common.

By the time everyone had eaten all the French fries and seafood they could hold and had plenty of beer (except the cameraman, who lost the toss and became designated driver), it was almost ten P.M. I stood in the Duck Shoppes parking lot and waved to them as they left. The program about the aftermath of storms would air in January.

I had just started walking home, sorry I hadn't worn more comfortable shoes, when Rafe rejoined me. "It's not as if I had much choice in the matter," he said as though we'd never stopped talking from earlier in the day. "You've done good work, girl. But we need that diary if I am ever to lay down this blasted existence."

"I have everyone I know working on it," I told him with a new feeling of camaraderie. "We'll find the diary."

"Aye, I know ye will."

I kept walking and he stayed beside me. There were so many questions I wanted to ask, but I didn't want every one of them to be like a dagger to his heart—even though he was dead. "Will you ever see Mary again?"

He looked up at the stars. "I'm hoping so. We've been kept apart all these years. But I'm hoping, once I'm free, to be able to join her. My children too, for that matter. It's been a long, lonely punishment for my crimes."

"What about William Astor? Will you see him too?"

"I hope so, girl. I'd like to rip off some of his dead flesh and take the pieces—"

"I think that's how you got here in the first place, Rafe. Maybe you should be forgiving too."

"And who are ye to give me advice?" he demanded. "You haven't even lived two score yet and you're a *woman* to boot. I think I know what's best for me."

Traffic was light this late, and I considered my next question carefully before I asked. "Will I ever see my mother again? I've tried to contact her for the last few years. Maybe she doesn't want to see me."

"There, there." His ghostly hand sort of patted my shoulder. "It's probably nothing to do with you. Maybe yer ma's not ready yet."

"Could you ask her for me?"

"I could," he agreed. "If I had any blasted idea of who she is."

"She was a Bellamy on my grandmother's side. Maybe you could look her up."

He kind of snarled. "It's not that easy. But I'll try."

I could've hugged him, but I knew there was nothing really there but hot air and attitude. We reached the turn in Duck Road right before my house. Two police cars and a county sheriff's vehicle were parked in the street and in the drive.

"It looks to me like you've got company," he said before he disappeared.

I blinked my eyes, amazed again at how fast he could be gone. I wished I could disappear too.

Chapter 38

I've always known that once a lawman, always a lawman. Even though Gramps was retired, he had almost as many late-night meetings with Tuck Riley and Chief Michaels as he'd had when he was working.

I grew up knowing my grandfather (who stood in as my father on many occasions) was different than other class-mates' fathers. Trudy's father was an accountant. Tim's father was a dentist. None of them seemed to worry about what was happening to the FBI or if there were more guns available on the island than there were twenty-five years ago.

He also used a secret code for things my mother didn't want me to know about. Gramps would come home and talk about problems and situations that to my ears didn't make any sense. I learned later that, on those occasions, he used code words to describe nabbing a bank robber or a drug smuggler. My mother worried that these were issues that were too adult for my eight- through twelve-year-old mind.

I remembered listening from the stairs to the lawmen gathered in the kitchen as they talked openly about getting shot, losing partners and dealing with other everyday life crises. Everything from murder to shoplifting was discussed during these sessions, which could last most of the night. Smuggling, from artwork to drugs and Cuban cigars, was always a popular topic. Being so remote, Duck had always been a target for smugglers.

At the time, I romanticized smuggling, thinking it was like being a pirate. My mother would catch me on the stairs and tell me I shouldn't listen to that kind of talk. I should be thinking about new dresses and dolls, boys and parties. I always reminded her that *Batman* was my favorite comic book. Her argument was that Batman wasn't real—while what Gramps and the others talked about was.

By the time I was a teenager, I knew more about law enforcement than most kids. But by then I'd lost interest, and boys and parties took priority. It was enough to know what was going on out there without hearing the boring details.

So tonight, I walked into the house knowing exactly what to expect—anticipating the hot air and tense moments as the lawmen discussed whatever this evening's subject was. But I was surprised to find that they weren't talking only about old times.

"Dae, will you put on another pot of coffee?" Gramps asked when he saw me, a frown furrowing his forehead beneath his old fishing hat. He looked like he'd just come in from fishing on the *Eleanore*.

I knew that meant it was going to be a long night. Sometimes they went through three or four pots.

Tim Mabry nodded to me but kept a low profile. Even more than Gramps's expression, the fact that Tim didn't flirt with me indicated a serious subject was being bounced around the kitchen table. Fresh donuts were present, but no one was eating—another bad sign.

Sheriff Riley was walking around the room, his hand resting on his gun as he spoke. "This affects all of us, Horace," he said. "That's why we're here. Two and two don't always make four."

"In this case, I'd say they have no choice," Chief Michaels said. "We had the gun and bullets tested twice. This is ballistics' final report. There's no doubt about it."

I measured the coffee carefully, taking my time, wishing they'd get on with it. Usually I didn't want to hear their discussions, but tonight was different. I could feel it in the clipped sound of their voices and tense body language. Something else bad had happened.

I was afraid they might decide not to continue until I left the room. I felt like a kid again, urging them silently to get to the point before my mother found me eavesdropping and ordered me to my room.

"The .22 pistol that killed Matthew Wright and Mayor Foxx is the same weapon that killed Wild Johnny Simpson over at the Blue Whale more than thirty years ago." Sheriff Riley stopped pacing and glared at the chief and Gramps as if they were at fault.

The gun that killed Wild Johnny Simpson? I couldn't believe it.

"I thought we knew old Bunk Whitley killed Johnny?" Chief Michaels asked. "Maybe Bunk planted that gun to be found someday. Like now."

"Any prints on the gun?" Gramps wondered in a hopeful tone.

"Wiped clean," Scott Randall said as he smiled at me. I smiled back, and he looked away, his face stained red. Tim nudged him with his elbow as a warning not to flirt with me.

"I don't believe old Bunk came back to kill this Wright fella and his girlfriend," Sheriff Riley stated like he was saying it for the record. "I'd say old Bunk has bigger fish to fry."

"But if not him, who?" Gramps demanded. "And how many times are we gonna ask this question about who killed Johnny Simpson?"

Wild Johnny Simpson was a mythical kind of figure in Duck—like Blackbeard or Rafe Masterson. He didn't start out that way. He seemed to lead a normal kind of life, building a house and marrying Miss Elizabeth Butler.

Then something happened and he vanished, almost never to be seen again. If Kevin hadn't reopened the Blue Whale, what happened to Johnny might still be a mystery.

Kevin had been showing some of us around when we found Johnny's long-dead body in one of the top-floor rooms. He'd been shot and left to die—the Blue Whale closed up around him as old Bunk Whitley mysteriously vanished the same night. No one had ever known for sure what happened to either man.

Then I ran into Bunk Whitley on one of the supposed-to-be uninhabited coastal islands. Before he made another mysterious exit, he'd told me he'd left Johnny Simpson in charge of the Blue Whale and would never have hurt him. That left Johnny's death still a mystery to some—while others, mostly the police, still accepted Bunk as Johnny's killer.

What Bunk had said made sense to me. He was also the one who told me my father was still alive after years of Gramps, and even my mother, lying to me. I guess I felt like I could trust Bunk to tell the truth about Johnny, since he'd been honest with me about my dad.

Now the gun that had killed Johnny was involved in two more deaths—deaths that had no connection to Johnny or Bunk Whitley.

"We'll keep bringing it up until we have an answer!" Sheriff Riley banged his fist on the table. "You couldn't solve this case when you were sheriff, Horace. Now, when this comes out, it's gonna make us all look like monkeys. We have to figure it out before that happens. Any suggestions?"

I finished the coffee and saw a look pass between Chief Michaels and Gramps. *I knew that look.* They were thinking about having me hold the gun and see what I could find from it.

It would be an easy answer—if what I saw made sense—and if they could convince Sheriff Riley to go along with the experiment. It wouldn't be an answer they could take to court, but it might be something that could put them on the right track.

Am I willing to hold something knowing it was used to kill three people? I considered the difficult question even before they asked me. I wanted to help. But the emotional strain would be terrible. Just handling Mary's perfume bottle had been enough to make me feel the agony she went through for Rafe.

What would it be like handling a weapon that had committed murder? How would I deal with *that* emotional pain when it was over? It was a terrifying thought.

And I never knew exactly whose emotion I'd be feeling. In this case, it could be the killer's—or the victim's.

"Excuse me, gentlemen." I smiled at all of them and acted as though I didn't know what the discussion would be about after I'd left the room. I just didn't want to hear them discuss it—*"Dae won't mind, will you, honey? She'd be glad to help."* Or, *"That's the craziest thing I've ever heard, Horace. We need real facts."*

And I didn't want to feel pushed into making a decision right away, which I might be if I stayed in the kitchen.

"I'm turning in for the night," I told them with a calm demeanor I was far from feeling. "I'll see you tomorrow, Gramps."

Chapter 39

I wished I hadn't argued with Kevin. He was the one person I could turn to—the one person whose advice I trusted about these things.

But I couldn't call him and tell him I wasn't angry anymore—*Oh and by the way I have a problem I need to discuss*.

I went up to the widow's walk and sat there looking out at the perfect night sky. When I was young, I would've gone to Gramps and we could've talked about this. But not anymore.

Not that my innocent gift of helping people find things ever had such serious consequences when I was young. I used to help Miss Elizabeth Simpson find her car keys, which she managed to misplace every week. Or I helped Cailey Fargo find her missing earrings. People in Duck loved my gift and enjoyed using it as much as I did. It was one of the perks of living here, I thought.

But now life was more complicated. The adult me understood that though Gramps loved me, he'd expect me to use my gift for the betterment of the community—even if there were personal costs. People sacrificed for the greater good sometimes—like his suggestion that I should give up my relationship with Kevin to be mayor again.

I understood his point of view, although I didn't necessarily agree with it. Every police officer was willing to sacrifice for the greater good. Many times those sacrifices included their families, marriages, even their lives. Why would Gramps even hesitate to volunteer my services, when it might only make me uncomfortable?

I knew I couldn't talk to Shayla or Trudy about this either. Shayla would balance my chakras and tell me to make my own choices. And though Trudy had been my friend since childhood, she'd never been comfortable with my gift. I couldn't ask her to help me with this.

"Feels like standing on the bow of my ship," Rafe said, appearing on the cast-iron rails that surrounded the widow's walk on the roof. "Aye, you could look out and see forever. That was true freedom—true happiness."

"That you lost when the British destroyed your ship." I was glad to be diverted from worrying about Gramps asking me in the morning to hold the gun.

"Damn fools!" he yelled, causing some bats to change course. "They thought they'd killed me. They thought they could find my treasure. But I was too smart for them."

"So the story I dreamed about you was true. You buried your treasure, killed your sailors and sent that poor cabin boy to swim away from the island. No wonder they called you a scourge."

"That was me," he admitted. "But allow that a man may change. Death and destruction—even plunder—gets old as the bones ache in the night and the body wears. I made my peace with what I'd done. God blessed me with a woman who loved me, despite my sins, and two fine sons. I was happy for a time—at least until the magistrate hanged me."

"Rafe—I'm so sorry about Mary and your sons." I hoped he wasn't going to break down again as he had during the day. I didn't think I could hold it together if he did.

He frowned and took out his cutlass, making some stabs at the night sky. "'Twas what I deserved, no doubt. But she deserved better."

We didn't speak for a few long minutes as he walked along the edge of the metal rail around me. Then he said, "You know, you remind me of her."

"Me?"

"Aye. Pluck to the backbone. She never took nothing off of me. Told me what she thought, she did. But with a loving heart and a beautiful smile."

"Thank you." I thought again about the beautiful, sad woman in the mirror who'd tolerated the magistrate's hand at her breast for the sake of her husband and sons. I didn't mind the comparison.

"Don't let them make you do anything ye don't want to do," he spat out. "They need you, my girl. You don't need them. Make them pay—or tell them to go away."

I was amazed at his understanding of the situation without one word of explanation. "How do you know?"

"Bah! I'm not an imbecile. I know what you can do. I saw the greedy looks on their faces. It doesn't matter if you're a pirate or a king. Those looks are on everyone's faces who want their way. They need yer aid in this investigation. They don't care about what happens as long as they win the plunder. It's all the same—my time and yours."

He had summed it up remarkably well. I wasn't sure I could be as fast to turn down what would surely be presented as my duty, but I was glad he comprehended. The two of us up on this lonely rooftop had found a way of understanding each other despite the centuries (and so many other things) between us.

"I appreciate that. I know you're right. I don't know if I

can just say no. I want Sandi Foxx's killer to be found. That might not happen without me."

"The hell with that," he roared. "That girl is dead. Finding her killer won't bring her back. You think on that, girl. Think about what ye will give up to do this thing. You can only lose so many pieces of yourself before there's nothing left."

And with those pirate words of wisdom, I was alone again.

He was right about losing myself. It was what I feared most from this part of my gift that took me into other people's emotions. I could handle most of the day-to-day things—towels manufactured at a sweat shop in China, cars that had been used for smuggling. But things like the perfume bottle, and probably the gun that had killed Sandi, were more difficult. The effects from objects like those were hard to recover from. The strong emotional undercurrents sometimes dragged me down like the cold Atlantic and didn't want to let go.

I smiled thinking that Rafe was probably a good source of wisdom when it came to losing pieces of yourself. Wasn't that what happened to him? Mary and his children had redeemed him, given him a lineage and legacy that he wouldn't have had if he'd died on his ship at the hands of the British.

But I wasn't a pirate, and I'd been brought up with a strong sense of right and wrong, duty and honor. I didn't know if I could look the other way when the time came.

I went back down the secret stairs that led from the widow's walk to my bedroom. Even though I was used to Rafe popping in and out now, I took a step back and gasped as a figure separated itself from the shadows in my room. "Kevin?"

He put his arms around me and we kissed in the darkness. "I missed you. I don't ever want to argue with you again."

I felt the same, but I wasn't necessarily ready to let it go. "Is that something like an apology?"

"It's whatever you want it to be. Do you feel like walking?"

Gramps was already in bed—probably having ended the discussion with the sheriff and the chief by volunteering my help with the gun. Kevin and I slipped out the front door without disturbing him and started down the dark, wet street.

"I know you were supposed to call me," he began. "But I waited all day and you didn't call."

"I was busy with the Weather Channel thing and everything else." I told him about what happened at the museum with the perfume bottle. "But I'm sorry I didn't call. You were right. I should've admitted that my father stole from me. I just believe that anyone could be desperate enough to do it."

He wrapped his arm around me as we walked down deserted Duck Road toward the center of town. "Maybe I was right—but so were you. That's one of the reasons I gave up being in the FBI. It does make you see the worst in people. I came to Duck to see the best in people. But old habits die hard. I trust your father because you trust him. Let's leave it at that unless something else happens. See? I'm learning to have faith."

I hugged him hard. "I'm glad." I admitted to being tired of lying and sneaking around where my father was concerned. "I'm going to talk to Gramps again too. I'm a grown woman. We have to work this out as adults. I'm going to see my father, and I'm going to tell him who I am. I'm sure we'll all feel better when it's over."

"Good for you!"

The winds from the ocean and the Currituck Sound were screaming across the open spaces where there were no bushes or buildings to slow them down. We ran through those areas and ended up at the Curbside Bar and Grill. I was surprised to find it open so late.

But Cole and Molly Black, owners of the grill, were feeding whoever came in for free. The place was packed, of course, but Kevin and I managed to find a corner to drink some coffee and warm up.

"This whole thing with Rafe has turned into a bigger deal than I'd thought it would be," I explained. "That perfume bottle really knocked me over this morning. I'm still amazed at how real those emotions can be."

He took my hand, his face unusually serious. "I admit to having another reason for finding you besides apologizing," he said. "I heard about the pistol this afternoon—and a crazy idea to have you get whatever information you could from holding the gun."

I shrugged. "They haven't asked yet. But I got that drift too."

"Dae, don't do it. The perfume bottle was nothing compared to the emotions of a killer pumped up with rage and jealousy. Not to mention the terror of a person being killed. Please promise me you won't agree to this."

"It sounds even worse when you put it like that," I joked, but he didn't return my smile.

I knew Kevin was overly cautious about these things. He was probably afraid of losing me like he had his FBI partner.

Not that the idea of losing myself completely wasn't scary. Holding the perfume bottle almost made me forget who I was and where I belonged. I was so much a part of Mary that I wasn't me anymore.

But I had to feel like I could control my gift—not the other way around. Otherwise I'd have to walk through life wearing gloves—literally. That just wasn't me.

"You've already decided to help your grandfather, haven't you?" Kevin asked, sitting back in his chair.

"No! I haven't decided anything," I replied. "I'd like to find out who killed Matthew and Sandi. This is my home town. I don't want to think of it as the murder capitol of the Outer Banks. But I know there are risks. I feel them every day—every time I touch something with an emotional past."

"You can't let them bully you."

"I won't."

"They need you—you can call the shots."

I grinned. "You sound like Rafe. He was basically giving me the same advice while I was up on the widow's walk. You know, I don't think he's as black as he's painted. Well, not anymore anyway. He was definitely a scourge when he was younger."

"Are you getting to be friends with him?"

"He's more like some uncle who was in prison but you think he might have reformed, if that makes sense."

"If talking to a ghost makes sense, anything is possible." He smiled and kissed my hand. "Just be careful, Dae. Ask for help if you need it."

"I will. Don't worry."

Before we could say anything else, Cole Black came to the table and asked us for help. "I never expected so many people, Mayor Dae! Think you could give us a hand? Molly has that bad lumbago. I'm worried she might wear herself out."

Cole and his wife had retired here a few years back, claiming they were looking for some relaxation—but they worked harder than most people half their ages.

"Sure!" I agreed. "We'd be glad to help. What do you need?"

"See those tables over there by the windows? Could you bus all of them and do some dishes?"

Chapter 40

"Well, that was interesting," Kevin said when we were done cleaning up the restaurant. "If I'd known we were going to work in a kitchen, I would've stayed home and cleaned mine."

I laughed at him and gave him a towel to dry his hands. We'd done several loads of dishes, pots and pans and silverware by hand. "But so many people were fed tonight. Isn't it wonderful to see everyone pulling together?"

"Marvelous." He flicked water at me.

I snapped my towel at him. Cole and Molly found us horsing around in the kitchen as they got ready to close up.

"You two remind me of us when we were young," Cole said with an affectionate smile at his wife.

"Or that nice young couple who stop in every so often, right?" Molly shook her head. "Not that they were married, we've come to find out. I'd hate to live with that kind of guilt. His wife is dead now, you know. That young lady mayor at the Blue Whale. What a shame!"

"Shawn Foxx?" I asked sharply. "He ate dinner here with someone besides his wife?"

"Regularly," Cole confided. "He was here the night of the storm. We didn't even know that was his name until we saw his picture and heard his wife had been killed. It was a real surprise that the other woman wasn't his wife. The two seemed very close."

"What did his girlfriend look like?" I asked.

"Kind of tall," Cole said. "A real looker too."

"Never mind him—he thinks everyone looks tall and every woman under thirty is a real looker," Molly added. "But it seems to me they were about the same height."

"Did you ever hear him call her by name?" Kevin questioned.

"Nope. Like I said—we didn't even know his name until we saw that his wife had been killed. But they tipped well. I can tell you that," Molly said. "And always paid with cash."

"My favorite people!" Cole smiled.

"Was she blond? Have you ever seen her around in Duck?" I asked.

"No, she had long, dark hair," Cole assured me. "This woman was late twenties, tops. Thin, like a model."

"Now that you mention it, Mayor Dae," Molly added, "I have seen her before. I think she might work at the skee-ball place. I've seen her smoking outside there. Or it was someone who looked just like her."

"Thanks." I hugged them both, not wanting them to feel we were interrogating them. "See you later. And thanks for sharing with so many people."

"Please! We didn't want all that defrosted food to go to waste," Molly said. "And it's a tax deduction. Don't make us heroes."

Kevin and I said good night and walked back out into the cold early-morning air. "So Shawn had a girlfriend."

"It sounds like it." I wrapped my jacket closer around me. "Someone who probably lives in Duck."

"If you're thinking she could be the killer, that would mean she had to be in or around the Blue Whale during the storm."

"That's true. Although Game World isn't that far to walk from the inn. I guess that's why Shawn had such a lame alibi about spending the night by himself in his car. He might have been here in Duck—with his girlfriend—at the time Sandi was killed. I can see why he wouldn't want anyone to know about that." I yawned after I told him about seeing Shawn at Game World. "But I don't know if I'm thinking at all, to tell you the truth. I think my brain stopped working about an hour ago."

"Maybe that means we should call it a night." He wrapped his arm around me, and we headed down Duck Road—again.

I hated to say good night once we reached the house. He kissed me, and we clung to each other for a long time while we stood on the front porch. I was freezing, but I didn't want the moment to end.

"Call me if you need me," he whispered. "I'm good at reinforcing 'no' if that's what you decide."

"I will." I kissed him one last time. "It'll be okay, Kevin. However it works out."

Gramps met me on the way into the house. I didn't even make it to the stairs. "Dae, we need to talk."

"Not right now, if you don't mind. Maybe tomorrow."

"This is important, honey. Chief Michaels needs your help."

"I know. But I'm tired, and I don't think I can make a decision about the gun tonight."

He raised his eyebrows, his only sign of surprise. "Are you reading minds now?"

"Gramps, I knew when I heard the three of you talking

in the kitchen. Kevin knew too. You aren't very good at keeping secrets."

He sat down in his chair, ignoring his favorite dancing show on TV. "But you'll do it?"

"I think so. But not because it's my duty. I'd like to know who killed Sandi. And this might be the best way to find out."

"I understand."

"And while we're talking"—I squared my shoulders like a prizefighter preparing for a bout—"I've been spending time with Danny—my father. He doesn't know yet that I'm his daughter. But I plan to tell him."

"I think that's a mistake." He shook his head. "But you'll have to make that call—and live with the consequences."

"I know. I really think he's changed, Gramps. And I'd like to have him over for dinner one night."

"I suppose you would." He stroked his white beard. "But I don't think I'm ready for that yet. Maybe someday."

"It's been thirty-six years, Gramps. That's a long time to hold a grudge."

"You didn't see the look on your mother's face when he abandoned her. Or know that he killed your grandmother as sure as if he'd held a gun to her head. I know I had my part in all this too. God knows I'm no saint, and maybe I was wrong about what I did. But he could've stayed. I wouldn't have left you because someone threatened me. Or he could've led a decent life that was fit for your mother and you. I don't know if I can ever forgive him for taking your mother's innocence and leaving her to suffer. Not even for you, Dae."

Well, I'd wanted the truth out between us. I realized Gramps had his own truth about things too. Just because I wanted to know Danny—as my father—didn't mean Gramps wanted to know him at all. I had to respect that.

I hugged him to let him know it was okay. "You took that

news way too well, you know. You'd already heard about me and Danny, right?"

He shrugged. "Duck is a small town, honey. A lot of people around here have long memories."

I knew that was true—and had no doubt that Chief Michaels had told Gramps what was going on, for my own good. "Good night. Have someone bring the gun to Missing Pieces tomorrow. I'll look at it there."

"Thanks, Dae. I love you, honey."

I went up to bed, but my dreams were restless. I was again that cabin boy who had been ordered to swim for his life.

He was lying on a beach—washed up after so long that he wasn't sure he was going to make it. He opened his eyes and looked around, surprised to find that he was alive and that he had managed to escape Rafe.

He had no idea where he was or where he would go. His parents were long dead. There was no one to care if he lived or died. That was what had taken him to the pirates in the first place. He sat on the sand, his clothes crackling with dried saltwater, his skin puckered like a briny pickle.

The sun was hot overhead. He knew he had to find shelter, something to eat and drink if he wanted to stay alive. He already felt sick and weak. If he was going to survive to get his revenge on Rafe Masterson, he had to get up and find somewhere to recover.

He stumbled to his feet, and as he did, a huge black horse raced past him, knocking him down. He coughed into the sand, not knowing if he could get up again.

To his surprise, the horse turned around and a woman dressed in a lavish blue velvet riding habit with flowing white lace at her throat and wrists jumped down to check on him.

She was beautiful—like an angel with her crystal blue eyes and black hair. She ran her hands over his arms and

*legs with a serious frown on her face. "Are you all right?"
she asked. "Poor thing. You look nigh starved to death."*

*Another horse came up behind them and a man climbed
quickly down. "You shouldn't stop for rabble, your lady-
ship," he told her. "These urchins are everywhere. They call
themselves Bankers, and they prey on anything that moves.
You're not safe here."*

*The beautiful lady shot to her feet. "This child can't prey
on anyone, Mr. Fipps. I knocked him down with Vulcan. See
that he gets to my uncle's estate safely. I want him nursed
back to health. Is that clear?"*

*He nodded. "Yes, Lady Forester. Right away." He knelt
close to him and whispered, "This is your lucky day, whelp.
Be glad of it and give thanks."*

Forester! Lady Suzanne Forester!

Chapter 41

I woke up thinking about the makeup case I'd sold and the vision I'd had from it when I first acquired it. I'd seen her son as an adult giving her the makeup case for her birthday. I felt sure this was the same boy. Even as an adult, he had similar features.

If my dreams were right, the cabin boy that should have died trying to escape from Rafe not only survived but may also have been raised as a member of the English aristocracy. This was another piece in the puzzle that pointed to this boy being William Astor.

It would've been difficult, maybe impossible, for that cabin boy to become a magistrate without some family background or a patron to get him there. I had to look further into this, even if my dreams didn't turn out to be true.

It was barely dawn, but I couldn't go back to sleep. I showered, got dressed and went downstairs. Gramps was making French toast with the last of some stale bread. We spoke about repairing the windows in the house and some work he had to do on the *Eleanore* before he could take her back out on another chartered fishing trip.

Neither one of us mentioned the gun or my father. I ate a slice of French toast, then walked down to Missing Pieces alone.

I was surprised and pleased when our UPS delivery man, Stan, brought in some packages. "Morning, Dae. Things are starting to get back to normal out here, eh?"

"I think they are. I heard the Harris Teeter finally got a big delivery today. That's some great news. Everyone has probably eaten all the canned and dried food they can stand for a while."

He laughed. "My brother told me he's been eating dried fish from last year. He'll be first in the checkout line for sure."

There weren't any customers before or after his arrival. It was depressing and one of those things that always happened when I wanted to take my mind off of something. I dusted and reorganized the shop until there was nothing else to do but wait. Finally, I went out on the boardwalk to look at the sound.

A few seconds later, Trudy joined me on the bench. She told me her business was dead too. "People don't worry so much about their hair and nails when they have holes in their roofs," she said.

"That must be one of those words of wisdom," I agreed. "Maybe you should send it to someone and make some money."

"No one else would appreciate it unless they live someplace like this." She shrugged her slender shoulders under the pink and blue nylon jacket she wore. "What's up with you? You sound kind of down. Is it the murder thing?"

"Yeah. Pretty much." I didn't tell her about the gun I was expecting. There was no reason for her to worry too. I told her instead about my single big sale for the week. It was exactly the right thing to say. We talked about it through our early lunch at Wild Stallions, and she shared her new plan for making her business more successful.

"I'm going to have a massage therapist come in once or twice a week," she told me. "Like those full-service spas. I think it will bring in some new customers. We'll be the queens of the Duck Shoppes boardwalk yet."

We both laughed and enjoyed our time together. We talked about losing Phil and the coffee shop—something we both hated.

"Can't you recruit a new coffee shop?" she asked. "You're the mayor. This is a big issue for our community. Just think of how many citizens will vote for you if you bring back their triple-shot mochas. Mad Dog can't stand up to that kind of competition."

"Point me in the right direction, and I'll be all over it," I promised. "Everyone in Duck deserves to have at least one mocha every day. And as mayor, I swear to make it happen."

It was all silly talk, but it was exactly what I needed—a distraction. I'd expected Chief Michaels to be at the shop first thing in the morning. Instead, here it was lunchtime, and there had been no sign of him. I'd been prepared for his visit when I left the house this morning, but now my resolve about touching the gun was beginning to wear thin.

We finally decided we'd wasted enough time and paid our bills. One of Trudy's regular clients called and asked if she had an opening for a cut and curl. Trudy rolled her pretty eyes at me as she pretended to check her empty calendar on her cell phone. "Come on in, Mrs. Flowers. I'll make time for you," she said.

As we walked out of the restaurant, I saw Chief Michaels talking to August Grandin at the Duck General Store. Sheriff Riley was leaning against the railing along the boardwalk.

"Looks like you have customers too," Trudy said. "I guess lunch was good for both of us."

I agreed with her, but my heart plummeted. I felt a little sick and my hands were shaking. I thought about just saying no and not touching the gun that had killed at least three people. I thought about calling Kevin and asking him to come and get me. I wanted to run as far and fast as possible.

Then I thought about Sandi. She hadn't deserved to die. Her children didn't deserve to grow up without her. I knew it wasn't easy for Chief Michaels—let alone Sheriff Riley—to ask for my help. It had to mean they didn't know where to go in the investigation.

"Mayor." Chief Michaels nodded to me as I reached him.

"I thought maybe you'd changed your mind," Sheriff Riley said.

"Mayor O'Donnell, I'm glad to see you," August began. "Did you know Phil is closing the Coffee House and Bookstore? While we might get by without the bookstore, I don't think Duck will be the same without a coffee shop. I hope you have something in mind for this."

"I'm looking into it, Mr. Grandin," I said. "I'll let you know when there's news."

"Thanks, Mayor. You always know what to do for us." He smiled and nodded at the two lawmen. "Gentlemen."

"Shall we go inside?" I invited the two men in. I looked at the brown cloth bag that I felt sure held the weapon. I stiffened my backbone and told my knocking knees to cut it out. "Let's get this over with."

Chapter 42

After the three of us were inside the shop, I closed the door and locked it. I didn't want to worry about any customers coming in. It would be just my luck to suddenly have a few stop by after not seeing a soul but Stan all day.

"Is that the gun?" I asked Chief Michaels.

"Yes." He handed me the whole bag.

"I'm just going to sit over here and take a nap," Sheriff Riley said with a yawn as he took a chair near the door. "I expect you know what I think of all this hoodoo stuff. If you can't solve a case using good, God-fearing detective work, you don't deserve to solve it."

"Tuck, you're not helping matters," Chief Michaels said. "I haven't heard any better ideas from you. But if you have one, tell me now. Let's go track down the killer."

"You know I don't, Ronnie, or I wouldn't be here."

"Then shut your pie hole and let Miss Dae do her thing."

They both looked at me expectantly. I had a moment of performance anxiety I'd never had while finding missing change or lost cuff links. What if I couldn't tell them anything about the murders? What if all this speculation about what would happen to me if I held the gun made me unable to see the killer?

Chief Michaels just stood there, looking at me. Waiting. Sheriff Riley sat forward and laced his calloused fingers together. Waiting.

I took a deep breath and opened the cloth bag. The cloth was shielding me from the weapon as if I were wearing gloves. I looked into the bag and wondered—feared—what the gun would show me.

The weapon was surprisingly warm to the touch. Probably still holding the heat from where the chief had carried it. I turned it over in my hands and closed my eyes.

Wild Johnny Simpson was working on a letter to the woman he loved when the door behind him opened and the killer slowly moved into the tiny room.

"You have something of mine," the man holding the gun whispered in the quiet hotel room. "I want it back."

Johnny didn't turn around. "Yeah? You owe me money. Think of me as a pawnshop dealer. You pay me—I give it back to you."

"I want it now. Right here. Right now. Or the devil will be collecting your soul tonight."

"You don't have the guts to shoot me. Might as well go back home. I'll give it back to you when you pay me. Don't come back without the money."

"I'm not fooling around, Johnny."

When Johnny ignored him, the man with the gun shot him in the back of the head. Johnny slumped over. The killer took two boxes from the desk where Johnny had been working. He didn't wait to see if Johnny was dead—just closed the door as he left the room. The rest of the Blue Whale was empty around them. No one close enough to hear the single shot fired.

The killer threw one of the boxes into the bushes behind the Blue Whale and took the other box with him.

Chapter 43

I came back to myself lying on the burgundy brocade sofa with two worried faces staring into mine. I realized I must have lost consciousness. The gun was on the floor near the door to the shop—probably where I'd dropped it.

"Dae?" Chief Michaels whispered, chafing my hand with his. "Are you okay? Do you need some water?"

"She needs an ambulance," Sheriff Riley snarled. "I think she hit her head when she fell. Let me get on the line and call—"

"No! I'm fine. No ambulance—no paramedics necessary. Sometimes it's like this when the emotions inside something I touch are strong. But I'm fine now. Really."

I could hear footsteps running heavily along the boardwalk. Fists started pounding on the door and Gramps was shouting to be let in.

"Did you call him while I was moving her over here?" Sheriff Riley demanded.

"He's her only living relative. What else did you expect me to do?" Chief Michaels yelled at him as he went to open the door.

Gramps was in like a shot. He knelt beside the sofa and took my hand as the chief had. "Are you okay, honey? Do you need the paramedics?" He glared at Chief Michaels. "I can't believe she passed out and you called *me* instead of the ambulance."

"That's what I said," Sheriff Riley joined in. "She needs medical attention."

"I don't need anything," I told them. "Well, maybe a cup of tea."

It was amusing watching all three men scramble to make one cup of tea. I wasn't sure if my teapot and cups could handle all the clattering. Sheriff Riley and Chief Michaels kept butting up against each other. Gramps looked for sugar and I finally told him that I take honey in my tea.

Within a few minutes, I had a cup of tepid tea in my hands. I smiled at all three men, who'd found places to sit down.

Sheriff Riley wiped a red rag across his forehead. "I don't know about you all, but I need something stiffer from Wild Stallions after this. Is this what you go through all the time?"

I sipped my tea—glad that they were scared. "Sometimes. It all depends."

"We should never have asked you," Gramps said. "*I* shouldn't have asked you. I'm sorry, Dae. Are you sure you're all right?"

"I'm fine."

"I hate to ask, but did you see anything?" Chief Michaels inquired reluctantly. Sheriff Riley and Gramps looked at him like he'd grown another head. "Well, it would be a damn shame to have put her through all that and she didn't see anything. Wouldn't it?"

I described Johnny's death scene at the Blue Whale. "I'm

afraid I didn't see the killer." I put the cup of tea on the table next to me. "But he was scared. His hand was shaking when he fired the pistol. He killed Johnny and took two wooden boxes from him. One of them was the music box Johnny had planned to give Miss Elizabeth. The other was hard to make out. I'm not sure."

"We already knew that gun killed Simpson," Sheriff Riley said in a defeated way. "That's not what we needed."

"I picked up a few other details that weren't so clear." I tried to focus on those other things, but they kept drifting out of my grasp. There was something important about the box the killer had taken with him. I just couldn't quite see what it was. "Someone else has fired the gun twice since then. I'm sure it was a woman. I don't know if she killed Sandi and Matthew."

"Did you get her name and address?" Chief Michaels had his notebook ready for the information.

"No. I'm sorry. It's not that precise."

"How about her motive? Could you see into her head?" Sheriff Riley questioned.

"No. But I think it might be obvious."

The three men looked at me expectantly—I guessed it wasn't obvious to them.

"Matthew wanted to leave Sandi," I explained. "He didn't want their breakup to affect his career, so he was dragging it out, waiting for the right time. His girlfriend got sick of waiting. She killed Sandi to get on with it. I'm not sure why she killed Matthew."

"Do you have any proof—besides the hoodoo—any proof at all?" Sheriff Riley asked.

"Maybe your experience is different than mine," I said. "But usually a man doesn't risk everything to get rid of the only woman in his life. Matthew was worried about his job but still willing to break up with Sandi. That says to me that he had another woman."

"Anything else?" Chief Michaels asked.

"I think that's it, at least for now." Gramps took my arm and helped me up. "I think Dae needs to lie down for a while at home. You'll have to excuse her."

I didn't mind him taking over. My head hurt and my eyes were blurry. I was ready to go home. But I had one last piece of information for them. "There was something else I felt about the man who killed Johnny. I could feel his fear and anger. He was desperate to get that box back. I keep feeling like there's more to tell—I just can't seem to pick up on it right now. I'm sorry."

The chief and Sheriff Riley started blasting out more questions. I could feel them like arrows piercing into me. I needed to get away. Gramps and I started to go, but then I remembered my conversation with Cole and Molly Black last night. I turned back to the chief and the sheriff. "It has nothing to do with the gun, but did you know Shawn Foxx was seeing someone else too?" I told them what Cole and Molly said last night about seeing him at the restaurant.

"That's the first I've heard of it," Chief Michaels admitted. "You say the woman he was with might work at Carter Hatley's place?"

"We might've been barking up the wrong tree," Sheriff Riley said. "You rest up now, Dae. We'll take it from here. And don't worry your pretty head that the intel you got from the pistol was useless."

Gramps hustled us out of the shop after that, and we got into a shiny new golf cart in the parking lot.

"Where'd you get the new transportation?" I asked.

"I borrowed it. No telling when our insurance claim will come through."

We careened out of the parking lot. A delivery truck barely missed us and a car blared its horn. That was Gramps's driving. I was never sure if he was still pretending he was driving the sheriff's car on a high-speed chase or what. That's why I preferred to drive.

"Don't you ever listen to me asking you to do something like that again," he said. "You scared me to death back there. Your face was as white as a sail. You should've told me there could be a problem."

"You said you thought it was my duty."

"Horsefeathers! Don't pay attention to me. You do what you think is right. What do I know? I'm just a crazy old man."

He stopped hard in the driveway when we got to the house. I hugged him, and we sat together in the golf cart for a few minutes. "You're not crazy. You just want to do what you've always done—make Duck a better place."

"But not at the cost of losing you. You mean everything to me, Dae. And if I haven't said it enough—I love you. If you want to bring your father home for dinner, I'll make the stew. And you just ignore Mad Dog about Kevin. If he makes you happy, that's all that matters. You don't have to be mayor if you don't want to."

I laughed. "I guess I need to pass out and look pale more often. If I'd known it worked so well, I would've done it all the time when I was a teenager."

"You always were a sassy girl. Just like your grandmother. I should've warned Kevin from the get-go, only I felt like the two of you would be so perfect together. At least I was right about that, huh?"

"You're right about a lot of things, Gramps. I just try not to let on." I got out of the golf cart, and my knees gave out on me. Gramps came around and helped me up. We went up the stairs together, and I lay down on my bed.

"I'll get you some tea, honey. You just lie there and take it easy."

I'd been around Rafe so much in the last few days, I could feel his presence before I could see him. Gramps was barely out the door when the pirate showed himself.

"God's teeth, that was stupid and witless, girl! Just when

I think my blood must be running strong in you, ye do something ridiculous. What if you had been killed? What if you had been lost in those past moments?"

"Don't even pretend you care—except for the fact that I couldn't help you if I'd been injured."

"That's enough for me. It should be enough for you too. Who cares who killed that silly female and her lover? You have a once-in-a-lifetime chance to clear your blood relative's name. That should be enough to occupy your silly female brain."

"Go away," I told him. "I have a headache. I don't feel like talking to you."

"Bah! You don't know if you're up or down. I'm going to have some rum."

Chapter 44

Gramps coddled and fussed over me the rest of the day. He even skipped his newly restarted pinochle game to stay home. We watched TV together, and I wondered if he'd told everyone to leave us alone that night—the phone didn't ring once.

It was nice and cozy—a good way to recover from the shock of emotions coming from the gun. Kevin had been right about the extreme passion, anger, hatred and fear.

But I pulled out of it, and the next morning I was fine. I'd slept well—no wisecracking pirates or fatal dreams about the past. I was ready to go to Missing Pieces when Mrs. Euly Stanley called me.

"Dae, you won't believe it! I think we've found the magistrate's descendant. Come down to the museum and take a look."

"I'll be right there," I told her and closed my cell phone.

"Is this it? Is this the diary?" Rafe demanded as I walked out the front door.

"I don't know yet. She didn't mention the diary—just William Astor's descendant. He or she may not live here anymore. We may have to call or email them to find out if the diary still exists."

"Go on with ye and your fancy blasted words. Tell me when you know where it is."

"Since you seem to hang around all the time and listen in on private phone conversations, I don't think that will be necessary."

I got a "Bah" for my trouble, but it didn't bother me. I was almost running along Duck Road—as excited as the pirate ghost that hovered near my shoulder.

Having him with me made me wonder how many ghosts were out there that most of us couldn't see. Was there a ghost following Luke Helms as he jogged by in the other direction, waving to me as he went? Was Cailey Fargo's Aunt Twinny whispering in her ear as she drove the fire chief's SUV to the station? How many ghosts were trying to communicate but we couldn't hear them?

Marissa was at the Blue Whale's mailbox at the end of the driveway as I went by—breathlessly walking now. "Morning, Dae! You look like you're in a hurry."

"I was until I realized how out of shape I am. How are the repairs coming along?"

We both looked up with our hands shading our eyes against the bright sun. Kevin was silhouetted before the brilliant blue sky, a pack of shingles slung over one shoulder. He waved to both of us, then disappeared over the crest of the roof.

"Pretty good. Another couple of weeks and it will be like the mayor's conference never happened." She frowned, her pretty face puckering. "Sorry. Not that it wasn't a good idea. You couldn't know there'd be a storm."

"Or a murder. But that's okay. I know what you mean. Maybe we'll try it again someday—if Kevin will ever consider it again."

"He'd do anything for you. It's good when a man cares that much. Not many do—at least not in my experience."

I smiled, recalling that Marissa was divorced after a disastrous marriage. "I think there's someone for everyone. I hope you find your someone too."

She didn't respond, just hugged the mail to her and walked back to the Blue Whale. I hated that terrible sadness I felt from her each time we talked. She was so pretty—it was hard to believe men weren't beating down her door. But maybe they were all the wrong men. Shayla seemed to have the same problem.

Rafe urged me toward the museum, and I burst in the door as the group was discussing the exciting implications of their new historic find.

"Come on in, Dae," Mrs. Stanley said, her faded blue eyes sparkling with the thrill of new knowledge. "There are sticky buns from the bakery and coffee on the side table. Help yourself."

But I wasn't hungry or thirsty. I sat down and peeked over Mark Samson's shoulder as he looked at a new family tree.

"This is awesome!" he raved. "Not that we didn't know there were magistrates that governed the islands during those early times."

"But many of their names and family histories have been lost down through the years," Andy Martin continued. "Look here, Dae. You can see where Magistrate William Astor married Mary Smith-Masterson. They had four children—two sons from her previous marriage that he adopted as his own. Mary and William had two more children together in the eight years they were married."

"What happened to her?" I asked with no prodding from Rafe.

"Not a clue at this point except that she died and Astor remarried and had two more children," Mark explained.

I felt let down. Mary was such a valiant woman. I wanted

to know more about her. I'd have to research her later. "Did any of the Astor children survive?"

"Yes. Two of the six survived—pretty good numbers back then with all the childhood diseases going around," Andy added. "Magistrates were a pretty big deal in the late 1700s and early 1800s, so they'd have had all the advantages that were possible."

"Can you tell which two survived and if they have descendants?" I asked, feeling the anxiety in the pit of my stomach.

"One of them was clearly Mary Masterson's child. It seems he took back his birth father's name after his mother died. He went on to become a governor in Jamaica. The other was from the second wife. He was hanged for murder. Pretty sweet, huh?" Andy teased.

"Not so fast, boys," Mrs. Stanley countered. "We have no proof as yet that this Mary Smith-Masterson was indeed married to Rafe Masterson. I've never heard that the pirate settled down and had a family—except of course from your perspective, Mark. We need proof before we can consider it history."

"And? What about now? Are there any descendants left of the son who was the governor of Jamaica, Mary's child?"

"Yes!" Mark jumped on that. "Thanks to the Internet and the library in Manteo, we know that the magistrate's descendant is—drum roll—Joseph Endy of Duck, North Carolina."

I've never seen two faces lose their excitement so quickly. Mrs. Stanley sat down and made a modest *humphing* noise. "Oh, *that* diary. You'll never get it from him," she said. "Odious man! I didn't know he was involved in all this. We've wasted our time."

I didn't understand the problem. I knew Joe. He was okay.

"We've tried for years to get even a glimpse of it," Andy

confirmed. "He won't even let us see the diary much less tell us who wrote it."

"He taunts us with it." Mrs. Stanley frowned. "He knows how valuable it may be to Duck history. He's refused all of our efforts to get information about it."

Mark looked more crestfallen than any of us. "We have to do something about it. This could be definitive. He can't hide history. Maybe we could appeal to him. He might've changed his mind. Why hasn't anyone told me about this before?"

"You haven't been a member that long," Andy told him. "Besides, it hasn't come up in years. I never thought about the diary Dae was looking for belonging to that old coot."

"But maybe this is an opportunity," Mrs. Stanley said in a sly way as she looked at me. "A chance to change his mind. Joe always liked the ladies. I remember when he and Wild Johnny Simpson and Bunk Whitley used to have contests to see who could take out the best-looking girl."

"Dae isn't bad looking," Andy said. "And she has a very winning way about her. She might be able to get a look at the diary."

"Good idea!" Mark patted me hard on the back in his excitement. "If anyone can do it, our mayor can!"

Funny how people loved you when you could get something they wanted.

Chapter 45

So thirty minutes later (after an approved clothing change) I was at Joe Endy's little house off Duck Road on the Currituck Sound side. The three members of the Duck Historical Society had taken me up to the Sunflower Fancy shop and purchased an outfit they felt would win Joe's heart—basically softening him up enough that he'd let me take a look at the diary.

I wasn't so sure about the change, and I had plenty of clothes in my closet at home. The clinging, apricot-colored silk dress wasn't exactly my style, and the extra makeup Mrs. Stanley put on me made me feel even less like myself. But there was no arguing with them. No talking on my part at all for that matter. They spent the whole time telling me what I should and shouldn't say to Joe.

I wasn't thinking about any of their instructions, though, as I knocked on the weather-beaten door. Joe's little house was like so many in Duck that were built in the 1950s, withstanding hurricanes and high tides. It had a little wrought-iron fence around an old flower garden. Weeds had mostly overtaken the late-season roses and mums.

I was trying to get my pirate ghost to back off. Rafe was even more insistent and louder than any of the museum members. I knew he was excited about possibly having the end of his long road in sight. But I wouldn't be able to concentrate with him shouting that way when I spoke with Joe. At least no one else could hear his tirade.

"Come on in," Joe called. "Door's open."

I remembered that he'd suffered a stroke a few months back. While there had been sympathy expressed by the town council, members were also relieved not to have him complaining at every meeting."

"Mr. Endy?" I called as I walked in. "It's Dae O'Donnell. I was wondering if I could talk to you for a minute."

He appeared in his wheelchair, a skeletal remnant of the man he'd been. His gnarled hands were clenched on the big wheels that moved him from place to place. "Mayor! To what do I owe the honor of this visit?"

I took out my next secret weapon that Andy had insisted I bring with me—cookies from the bakery. Chocolate chip was Joe's favorite. "Actually I was headed this way and my grandfather had these extra and asked me if I'd drop them off."

Joe took the cookies—but never took his eyes off of my cleavage. "Good old Horace! He's always been a good friend. We had some great times fishing out on his boat. Thanks."

"I'm sure he'd be glad to take you out again. The *Eleanore* is in dry dock for repairs right now, but she'll be up and running again in no time." I glanced around the tiny house. "I hope the storm didn't affect you too badly."

"Not at all." He chomped a few cookies. "I hardly even noticed. Slept right through it."

"That's good. We've tried to check in with everyone and make sure they're okay."

"You do a good job, Mayor. Not that I'm surprised. Your family has a history of community service to the town. In a way, not too different from my own family in times past."

Rafe managed to nudge me, and a few papers flew off the nearby table. "Get on with it! Quit dillydallying."

"Really?" I smiled and looked interested. "I didn't realize your family was involved with the town."

"You'd be surprised." He laughed in a way that made me wonder if I should find some oxygen for him. "They'd all be surprised. Those harpies at the museum with their fine and noble heritages. I've got the best one of all. But no one knows."

"I'm surprised you don't want them to know. Wouldn't it be fun to see how amazed they'd be?" I was careful not to push too hard.

"Who cares about them? They don't matter. The only people I want to share this with are what's left of my family. My granddaughter moved back here a few months ago. I hope she'll keep the family name alive in Duck. I've left her my property—including the diary those witches at the museum want."

"Well, I'm glad you have Marissa, Mr. Endy. I'm sure she's a comfort to you. I've met her at the Blue Whale. She's very nice and does a great job." I smiled even though Rafe was all but dancing a ghostly jig between us. "I'm glad to see you're getting around all right after your illness. Don't be afraid to call if you need anything."

"I'll do that. Thanks, Dae." He frowned for a moment, then said, "What would you do with a diary like mine?"

"I don't know. I guess give it to someone who'd appreciate it. It concerns us all, Mr. Endy. If a family had a diary that described early times and people from Duck, it would affect the whole town."

"You want to see it?"

"The diary? I'd be glad to take a look at it. Whose diary is it?"

"It belonged to one of the original magistrates—lawmen of their day. Back before Duck was a town or anything like that. The magistrates were judge, jury, and in some cases, executioners. This was a lawless place, worse than the Old West ever was. Pirates, cutthroats, press gangs and thieves. The magistrates cleaned up the islands and left their mark so the rest of us could lead decent lives. Kind of like you and Horace. That's why I'd like you to have a look."

"That sounds really exciting." My heart was beating hard, and my smile felt a little off center. I felt like Rafe did, but on the inside. I couldn't let my emotions show and scare Joe off.

"Great!" He looked around the cluttered room as I had a few minutes earlier. "Now where did I put that?"

"Blast and hellfire!" Rafe threw his tricorn hat on the floor. "Get on with it, man! If I'd been alive, I'd have skewered your liver by this time."

"Quiet!" I mumbled.

"What?" Joe looked up at me. "I know it's here somewhere. Could you help me look for it? It's in an old wood box with a crest on it. You can't miss it."

So we started looking—under beds, in closets, in the tiny attic and behind every door. Nothing.

"It's been here all my life," Joe said. "I know it has to be here. I just can't remember where I put it."

"I don't know where else to look." I was pretty sure the apricot silk dress wouldn't be returnable after all the dust and the grimy smears I'd just added to it.

Joe started to say something, then shook his head. "What am I doing? You're Eleanore's granddaughter! You can tell me where it is, right?" He rolled up close to me and held out his hands. "Not sure how this works exactly. What do I do?"

"You think about what's lost," I told him, taking his hands. They were cold and leathery. "Close your eyes and let's see if we can find it."

Being in someone else's mind searching for a lost possession was like looking through an attic full of memories and pictures. Most of them had nothing to do with what was lost. But if the person could hold the thought of the lost item in the front of their minds, the search was as easy as walking up the stairs and finding the item at the front of the crowded attic.

In Joe's case, the attic was so overcrowded, I wasn't sure I could find the old diary he'd hidden. Then suddenly, as he concentrated, there it was. I could see the old, scarred box resting in a pool of sunlight.

I opened my eyes to find him staring at me. "I think I see it." I glanced around the room again. The box was hidden under a tobacco humidor. "You used to smoke before you had your stroke. I think you left it over here."

The box and humidor were both near the window where the sunshine was flooding in from the beautiful day outside. I lifted the humidor with one hand and pulled out the box with the other.

On the outside of the box, still intact after so many generations, was the Forester crest. I recognized it from the makeup case William Astor had made for his adopted mother, Suzanne. My dreams seemed to have been right about this. I could hardly wait to see if the magistrate had chronicled his near death at Rafe's hands—and the revenge he'd taken on the pirate.

I sat down again near Joe. He smiled at me as I opened the box. I pulled out the worn, leather-bound diary. In an instant, emotions from the diary flooded through me.

Wild Johnny Simpson had rummaged through Joe Endy's parents' home looking for anything he could hold until Joe paid him back the money he owed him. He'd heard Joe talk about the old diary. Johnny laughed as he took it back to the Blue Whale.

He wasn't laughing as Joe shot him and took what belonged to him before leaving Johnny there to die.

Chapter 46

I came back to myself, slumped in my chair, the diary still in my lap. Joe was staring at me with a horrified expression on his face. I could tell he wasn't sure what to do.

"Are you okay?" he asked finally.

"I'm fine." I smiled and opened the diary again—Rafe prodding me to hurry.

"Go to the middle or so," Rafe demanded. "Find where that bastard murdered me."

But there was so much more. I could've gotten lost in it for days. No wonder the historical society wanted it. The rich history of the area was well chronicled by the urchin saved from death by Lady Suzanne Forester on the beach centuries ago.

She'd educated him—treated him as her son. She had no children of her own and never married. William and his surrogate mother were very close.

She'd died in a fall from a horse. William had been away

at the time and though she'd left him a fortune, he never forgave himself.

He never carried her name—her family had forbidden it. But he'd been raised with privileges he'd never dreamed existed when he was surviving on a pirate ship.

After Suzanne's death in England, William had come back to North Carolina and the Outer Banks where he'd grown up. *"Imagine my amazement,"* he wrote in the diary, *"to find that blackguard Rafe Masterson still alive and married to a fetching wench! He has children, no less. My mind is reeling with possibilities."*

It became William's obsession to kill the man who'd once tried to kill him. With his money, power and background, it was simple to become a sworn magistrate of the law.

But as such, he had to find a way to get his revenge without stepping beyond the bounds of what he thought of as justice.

He finally gave up on that idea when he realized no one else knew that Rafe was the same pirate who'd pillaged ships along the coast twenty years before. To everyone else, the big, gruff man was a simple trader. William hired two men to set Rafe up as a smuggler, then revealed that he'd also been a pirate.

He'd wanted to torture Rafe but had fallen in love with Mary Masterson. That emotion hadn't stopped the cruel magistrate from exacting punishment from her in exchange for Rafe's quick death on the noose.

William detailed every event in his life—his children, failures and successes. He died a very wealthy man with lands and holdings in both Carolinas. Though there had been a seed of evil in him regarding Rafe, he'd lived a good, long life.

"And there it is!" Rafe breathed a sigh near my ear that made me shiver. "There it is in his own bloody hand. I was not guilty of any crime when he hanged me. As my blood relation, I expect you to chronicle this event, girl. Tell that little man who is writing my glorious life story that he was right. I am vindicated."

I looked up in time to see the pirate begin fading away for what might be the last time. In a moment, there were only rays of sunshine where he'd been.

His trauma was over. I hoped he was reunited with Mary and their children.

But in the meantime, I was sitting across from the man who'd murdered Johnny Simpson more than thirty years ago. There was no way for me to prove it—at least as far as I could tell. It would've been better if I'd found the .22 pistol with the diary. What was I supposed to do?

The front door opened and Marissa came inside, a confused expression on her face. "Dae? What are you doing here?"

I wished I could hide the diary. Maybe if I could take it with me, I could think of some way to use it to prove what had happened that fateful night at the Blue Whale. "Hi, Marissa. I just stopped in to bring your grandfather some cookies. Would you like some?"

She closed the door and looked at the diary I was holding. "I'm sorry. I hope my grandfather hasn't been boring you with his stories. He can run a little long sometimes."

"I wasn't boring anybody," Joe snapped. "Dae likes history. I'm thinking about giving her that old diary. Nobody in my family wants it anymore. *You're* not interested."

Marissa smiled and smoothed Joe's silver hair. "Of course I'm interested. But we can't live in the past."

"Maybe not." I tried to tread carefully. I was either seconds from keeping the diary—or possibly never seeing it again. "I'm a member of the historical society. There's so much information in this that could be helpful in piecing together our past. I'd love to have it. On loan, if nothing else."

Joe made a spitting sound. "I hate those old biddies at the museum! If I'd known you were involved with them, I wouldn't have let you in the front door!"

"Simmer down, Grandpa. I'm sure the museum could make better use of the diary than using it to hold up that old cigar box." Marissa smiled at me. "Take it, Dae. The box too. We need to do some cleaning around here anyway. I hope you all get good use of it."

"You can't do that," Joe charged. "That's mine."

"I think Dae should leave now," Marissa said. "I think you need your nap."

I didn't wait to be invited again to take the book. I grabbed the box and stuffed the diary into it, then headed out the door. I felt bad for Joe. It had to be hard to have someone come in and tell you what to do with your possessions.

On the other hand, a man was dead because of Joe. Maybe there was some way to prove it.

I took the box to the Blue Whale. Kevin and I examined both items, then sat and stared at them. "If only the book could talk and its testimony be admissible in court," I said.

"Tell me again what you saw in the vision," Kevin instructed. "Even little details."

I started from the beginning and went through both visions I'd had—the one from the gun that had killed Johnny and the other from the book, which seemed to confirm that my earlier vision had been accurate.

"So Johnny was seated at the desk—just like we found him," Kevin summed up while he looked at the diary. "He had this box and the old music box on the desk beside him when Joe came to the door and shot him in the back of the head."

"That's about it."

"We should talk to the chief. There could be fingerprints and if we're lucky, blood spatter from the bullet when it entered Johnny."

"I don't think he'd want to do tests on it simply because of what I saw in my vision," I told him. "Believe me, he and Tuck Riley were not impressed that I knew the gun killed Johnny. They're only interested in who killed Sandi and Matthew."

"Nothing on that front, huh?"

"Nope. I know it was a woman. I can feel that much. But—"

"What?" he asked when I paused. "You know it was a woman, go from there."

"This may sound terrible. I hate to even say it. But Marissa is Joe's granddaughter. She had access to the gun."

He shrugged. "That's saying the gun was at his house and not at some pawnshop for the last twenty years. Why would she be involved with Matthew's and Mayor Foxx's deaths?"

"I don't know." I looked at the diary again. "It just seems coincidental. Maybe I'm all wrong."

Kevin put the diary back in the box and put both of them into a plastic bag. "One thing at a time. Before I have to look for another manager, let's see if we can pin Johnny's murder on someone."

"I'm game if you are. I just thought I'd mention that Sheriff Riley and Chief Michaels weren't very interested in that aspect."

But Kevin was adamant. We drove to the chief's house, where he'd just sat down to chicken and dumplings for supper.

"I can't believe you tracked me down to show me an old book," he said, not bothering to get up from the table. "Bring it to the police station tomorrow morning. Maybe we can waste some time finding Wild Johnny's killer before we go out and look for the important killer who's still walking the streets of Duck."

"I know you want to collar whoever killed Mayor Foxx and Matthew Wright," Kevin said. "But Dae risked her life for whatever information she could get from that pistol. She says there's something that ties this diary to that murder. I think you owe her an investigation."

Chief Michaels looked painfully at his dinner. "All right. I suppose this chicken can be warmed up. I'll take your book down to the county and let them have a look at it."

I reminded Kevin on our way out that I'd never said there was any evidence on the diary or the box. "That was your idea."

He grinned. "But the chief doesn't feel guilty about what happened to me. He was willing to listen, since he still feels bad about asking you to hold the gun. Which, by the way, was a really bad idea."

"I know. But somebody had to do it. And I don't know anyone else around here who does that kind of thing—except me."

He put his arm around my shoulder as we walked away from the chief's house. "Next time, there might not be *anyone* who does that kind of thing."

"Maybe. But holding the diary was almost as bad. I wouldn't have expected it—and neither would you."

"That's true enough. I don't have anyone staying at the inn tonight. Let's go grab some dinner at Wild Stallions. You get to buy since you ignored my important warnings about the gun."

"Is that how it works?" I laughed at him. "I think our relationship might be a little one sided in that case."

Chapter 47

Three days later, the ME in Manteo had compared Wild Johnny's blood sample to the bloodstains left on the diary and the box. Not only was it a match, but when the sheriff picked up Joe Endy, his fingerprints were actually sealed in the blood on the box. Joe's fingerprints were also on the music box that had become police evidence after we'd found Johnny's body last year.

It was an old murder, but once it was solved, Chief Michaels and Sheriff Riley were glad to take credit for putting the pieces together. I heard they'd held a press conference and a few TV reporters had shown up for it. They had to end the press conference abruptly, however, when one of the reporters started asking rude questions about the recent murders and why the law enforcement team had been unable to solve them.

Gramps told me Chief Michaels had questioned Marissa about Sandi's murder, since she was at the Blue Whale the night of the storm and presumably had access to the pistol.

But Joe signed a sworn statement that he'd sold the gun to a friend who'd died a few years back. He said he hadn't seen it since then. He also vouched for Marissa—saying she was with him when Matthew was killed. Marissa also passed a polygraph test. She was cleared of any wrongdoing.

I had to admit I was glad she wasn't the killer. She continued working as Kevin's manager, though she wasn't as friendly toward me. The coldness I saw when I looked in her eyes made an arctic blast seem warm in comparison.

I didn't blame her. Her grandfather was going to prison— if he survived the county jail until then. He was an old, sick man. I regretted that I'd been the one to learn his most desperate secret. Justice was hard to understand sometimes. Gramps said that was the pirate in my nature talking.

The town of Duck held its monthly town council meeting. The room was packed since three weeks had passed since the murders and the police had yet to arrest a suspect. Shawn Foxx and his girlfriend, Judy Starnes, were still under investigation, but Chief Michaels wasn't able to make anything stick.

The chief gave a full report, which was met with a few rude remarks from otherwise polite Duck citizens. I had to call for order in the room. It seemed ironic to me that the council's biggest heckler, Joe Endy, was missing this particular meeting because he was behind bars. I could only wonder what he'd have to say about inept police work.

I introduced a motion to reimburse Kevin for the money he'd spent housing and feeding so many people after the storm. The rest of the council agreed with me and passed a motion to give him the money and the town's thanks. The only dissenting voice belonged to Mad Dog. I was pretty sure that was more to disagree with me than anything else.

Mad Dog had argued that we should wait for the county to pay Kevin. We all knew this could take a lot longer. Even Mad Dog agreed with that. But we had a precedent for helping town businesses through similar circumstances and that's what got us through.

We began getting more phone calls at town hall regarding the closed coffee shop and bookstore than we had about storm cleanup. Nancy said that was a good thing because it meant the town was getting back to normal.

I happened to be friends with Phil's sister on Facebook. We chatted about him closing the coffee shop for good. She was surprised, since she'd been planning to move away from Atlanta anyway. Her suggestion—that she might like to help run the bookstore—was met with relief from Phil, who'd dreaded leaving but had seen no other way. They were already working together on remodeling and swore I'd saved the day. It couldn't hurt my reelection campaign.

The publicity from the storm and the murders resulted in a nice buildup of tourists. It wasn't exactly the kind of attention Duck needed—but I didn't hear anyone complain. The boardwalk was full of shoppers every day, and they spent a lot of money, even in Missing Pieces. August Grandin gave me a thumbs-up every time I saw him, and Cody from Wild Stallions occasionally threw a free lunch my way. Not that I'd had a hand in bringing the tourists—but I wouldn't argue that point either.

I was at Kevin's early Thursday morning eating homemade blackberry jam and corn muffins for breakfast. Marissa was going to her grandfather's arraignment hearing that morning. She didn't speak, giving me a diamond-hard look as she passed me in the doorway on the way out.

"She's trying to get him out on bail since he's old and not in good health," Kevin told me. "He's her only living relative and not exactly a threat or flight risk. I think the DA will work with her. She's got Joe's house to use as collateral for a bond."

"Mrs. Stanley told me that Marissa is suing the museum to get the diary back." I shrugged. "I'm glad I signed it over to them so it's their property when the evidence from the trial is released. I can always look at it over there. Joe said Marissa wasn't interested in it. That must count for something."

"I don't know. She could argue that she didn't mean that you could keep it—much less sign it over to the museum." He poured both of us more coffee. "I guess we'll see. In the meantime, I'm glad she stayed here. I know she needs the job, and I need her. I don't know how I got along without her."

"Oh? That makes me feel a little insecure."

"You look insecure." He reached across the table and wiped jam from my cheek. "But I'm glad you could come over for a few hours since she has to be away. Everything came together at one time—food delivery, ballroom repair and upstairs carpet cleaning. Being an innkeeper has its drawbacks."

"I don't mind helping. You're always helping me."

"Even though I'm taking you away from what might be your last big money-making day this fall?"

I smiled and held his hand. "What's a few hundred dollars? You're paying me for this, right?"

"Yeah. Right. I got up early and made you corn muffins since I know how much you love them."

"Mmm." I chomped, mouth full of the delicious muffins. "And lunch? You mentioned lunch, right?"

We both heard the food delivery truck pull up to the back service area.

"Gotta run. Food waits for no man." He picked up his supply list. "Call me if you need me. Thanks, Dae." He kissed me and was gone.

I finished eating and put the dishes in the sink. "Time to explore!"

I figured I could walk between the downstairs ballroom and the upstairs rug cleaning—still managing to peek into a few nooks and crannies. The Blue Whale had such a rich—and sometimes tragic—history that it made me want to touch everything from doorknobs to ceiling fixtures.

I was careful what I touched and limited myself to only a few items each time. So far there hadn't been anything emotionally overwhelming—like the diary—but I didn't want to have any problems either.

Mostly, my visions showed elegant parties with guests eating smoked salmon canapés in glittery dresses and old-fashioned tuxedos. Other objects revealed only how they were made and delivered to the Blue Whale. But a few of the items I touched had been smuggled in—that was interesting too.

I could hear the rug-cleaning people getting started on the third floor. I left the crew replacing the ballroom window that had been destroyed during the storm and went upstairs to make sure the right rugs were being cleaned.

I hurried past the small room where Wild Johnny had been killed by Joe Endy so long ago. I'd already seen too much of that history, though I had to admit that old Bunk Whitley appeared to have told the truth about not killing Johnny.

A cold breeze swept down the hall and rattled the light fixtures in the ceiling. I looked around, but saw no sign of Rafe. I hoped he was resting in peace by now—and worried a little that I might become a ghost magnet. I had a lot of dead family members to consider.

It was a little eerie—especially when the door opened across the hall from that little room. It happened so slowly, I could almost convince myself that a strong breeze had nudged it ajar. The movement could be rationally explained. It was cold outside, and all the windows hadn't been repaired as yet.

"There is more of gravy than of grave about you," I quoted Dickens's *A Christmas Carol* to reassure myself.

The door hadn't swung open all the way. Somehow that comforted me enough to look in the room. The bed had been stripped down, and a huge bucket of cleaning supplies sat on the floor, waiting to be used.

I stepped in—another breeze making the crystals in the old chandelier chime together. I saw at once that my rational self had been right. The window had been broken during the storm, and the ocean breeze was coming in.

The cardboard that had been taped over the window had fallen to the carpet beneath it. I didn't want to leave it that way, recalling my experience with the gulls flying in when we'd been looking for Sandi. Easy to fix—I went downstairs to find some tape.

The inn was fairly buzzing with noise and activity. I knew I could take care of this tiny problem for Kevin. I went into the room-size supply closet and turned on the light. The shelves held everything from cleaning supplies to extra bath products, and even rain gear was stashed here.

I found the masking tape and started back out. The tape had its own ideas, however. It dropped and rolled to the back of the closet. I had to feel around (hoping there weren't any large spiders lurking) on the old wood floor in the dark corners beneath the shelves. I grabbed the tape finally—but something was now attached to the sticky sides.

It was a photo, or rather a chain of photos taken at one of those kiosks at the beach. I didn't need to feel anything from it—though it was curious that I didn't. Each of the four images was slightly different, but they were all of the same couple. Matthew and Marissa. Happy. Smiling. Kissing.

Chapter 48

This doesn't mean she killed him, I thought. But it made all the pieces fit together. I sensed that a woman had killed Sandi when I touched the gun. Marissa was at the Blue Whale that night. Joe may have lied or forgotten that the pistol was still in the house. People who were guilty sometimes passed polygraphs. All of this made her look more like a suspect.

I wasn't sure what to do with the photo—besides the obvious. After everything else, I didn't want to be the one to openly accuse Marissa of murder. Especially since the police had already cleared her.

Deciding to wait until Kevin was finished with his food delivery, I put the picture in my pocket and started back upstairs. Maybe together Kevin and I could decide what should be done. My insides were churning. I felt like I was going to be sick.

I took some deep breaths as I reached the first-floor landing. I had to focus on taping the cardboard back in place so the gulls didn't fly in and make even more work. I tried to let go of all the unknown possibilities.

My mind wouldn't cooperate. Marissa was obviously the girlfriend I'd suspected Matthew had. She'd killed Sandi to get her out of the way so Matthew's career wouldn't be hurt.

But why kill Matthew? She'd done so much to clear the way to be with him. Had she confessed to killing Sandi and he'd rejected her? The questions were burning up my brain.

At the third-floor landing, I stopped to look out of the window. The food delivery truck was still there. How long did it take to deliver food anyway? I couldn't wait forever to tell someone about the photo.

I forced myself to think about fixing that window. My feet dragged as I went down the hall. I could hear the rug cleaners talking as they took a break at the other end. There was plenty of time, I told myself. I couldn't leave Kevin in the lurch.

I don't know exactly what made me put the tape down on the bed and take out the photo. Maybe I wanted to be sure that what I'd seen was real. Maybe I was just nervous and a little scared.

Whatever the reason, I was standing by the window looking at the picture when I heard the door slam shut. I thought it was that errant breeze again—but when I turned around, there stood Marissa.

With a shaking hand, I put the picture back in my pocket and stared at her. Did she know?

"Dae. You've been snooping around," she accused.

"I don't know what you mean."

"I think you have something that belongs to me."

I took a deep, steadying breath. She wasn't a ghost. She couldn't have looked over my shoulder from the door and seen the picture. I had to stay cool.

"I don't think so. I felt the breeze in the hall and saw that the cardboard had fallen down. I got some tape to fix it."

"You know what I mean! Don't lie to me. You took something from my room at the house. I don't know why you haven't done anything with it, but I want that picture back *now*!"

I thought about the picture. I knew it had been in the supply closet downstairs. Obviously, she didn't realize that she'd brought it here.

"I think we should discuss this," I said with a smile. "Maybe we should have some coffee downstairs."

"You stole from me—like you did from my grandfather. But I'm not in a wheelchair."

"Maybe you should call the police," I said, testing her. "Maybe they could sort it all out."

"Or maybe I could just take it from you—and they could find you on the ground outside—a tragic victim of your own good heart. These windows can be tricky up here."

I started to say something else—*anything else*—that would get me out of this room in one piece. Normally I wouldn't have been afraid of her. But how many times had I heard Gramps talk about the desperate actions cornered people were capable of?

Before I could react, Marissa launched herself at me. I tried to move out of the way. She was faster—fingernails curved like claws and kicking as she moved.

I was up against a hundred-year-old window frame. I knew it wouldn't be able to withstand both our weights pushed against it. The glass that still remained in the top of the wood frame began shattering, spraying us both with slivers.

She was pushing at me, trying to force me out of the window. I pushed back, thinking that if I could reach the bed and the cleaning products, I could grab something to defend myself. Mostly, I just wanted to get away from the window. I didn't want us both to fall from the third floor.

A cold wind swept through the room. I couldn't tell if it came from the gaping window at my back or from some other opening on the third floor. I decided that yelling might be a good idea—despite the noise from the rug-cleaning machines that had started up again.

Marissa clapped her hand over my mouth as I opened it. She was strong. Obviously, I needed to start lifting large buckets of cleaning supplies—if I survived this fight.

Then, it was as if the cold wind lifted and pushed Marissa away from me. She flew across the room and smacked into the sturdy wall near the closet. She dropped to the floor like a broken doll.

I slid down on top of the cardboard I'd intended to use to fix the window. I knew that had been no ordinary wind—even before Rafe appeared, staring down at Marissa with his cutlass in hand.

"Do I have to do everything for you, girl? Was it not enough that I moved that picture so you could find it? Then you go and try to get yourself killed."

"Thanks?" I could barely say the word. "I thought you were gone."

"Without fulfilling my end of the bargain? I am a gentleman of the sea. I promised you my treasure in exchange for proving my innocence."

"Oh yeah." Not only hadn't I thought about the treasure again—it seemed a little unimportant right now. "Where is it?"

"Bah! You'll never find it alone. Meet me at the docks. Midnight. I'll guide ye there. Then I'm gone from this world."

He disappeared again. The cold wind went with him. Marissa groaned and started to move.

I forced myself to my feet and ran out the door.

Kevin called the police when I told him what had happened. He brought Marissa downstairs and made sure she was all right.

I sat downstairs in the lobby with a blanket wrapped around me. My teeth were chattering—I was freezing.

Shock, no doubt. Marissa sat across the lobby from me. If looks could've killed, I'd have been dead.

Chief Michaels arrived a few minutes later with Tim and Scott. "The arraignment ended early. Old Joe had another stroke. He won't have to worry about being in any trouble for Johnny's death."

Marissa started crying—quietly at first. Then she yelled out, "She killed him! She's responsible. And now she wants to get me in trouble too. He was my only relative left alive. I'm going to sue you, Dae O'Donnell. You won't have anything left when I get done with you."

"So what's going on out here exactly?" The chief looked at me and Marissa.

"She's trying to say that I killed someone—like she did my grandfather. She went to my house and stole something personal that she thinks proves something." Marissa kept sniffling and crying until Tim brought her some tissues.

"All I did was find a photo in the supply closet here," I said, defending myself. "I didn't get anything from her house, except the diary."

"Liar!" Marissa jumped out of her chair.

"Just take a seat, Ms. Endy," the chief said. "Let me take a look at that photo, Mayor."

I gave him the photo from my pocket. I could tell from the look on his face that it affected him the same way it had affected me.

"Tim, Scott—you two stay here with Ms. Endy. If you'd come with me into the kitchen, Mayor . . ."

I followed the chief out of the lobby. He waited to speak until we were alone. "Dae, I need you to tell me *exactly* what happened here. Don't leave anything out."

I knew I couldn't do *exactly* as Chief Michaels asked, but I told him how I'd found the picture (not that a pirate ghost had purloined it from Marissa's house) and that she'd attacked me upstairs when she got back from the arraignment.

"This is some mighty compelling evidence with everything else we have," he said. "I just had to make sure there was no hoodoo involved. You'll have to testify in court, you know. It would look bad if you explained that you'd held her hand or something to find it."

"I was just looking for some tape, Chief. And I'll be glad to testify to that, if you need me."

"All right then. I think we have our killer."

Chapter 49

I brought Gramps with me to the docks that night. I didn't like the idea of being out at sea in the middle of the night by myself. Besides, without him, I would've had to take a rowboat. Having Gramps there meant we could take the *Eleanore*—fitting since Rafe was related from the Bellamy side of the family.

The air was very cold—icy winds blowing off the sea— as we waited for Rafe to make an appearance. It wasn't easy explaining all of it to Gramps, but the fact that he'd lived with two women who were gifted was enough to make him a little more open-minded. He'd loved my grandmother. Her gift for finding things had made my life easier.

"Are you sure your friendly pirate ghost meant tonight?" Gramps stomped his feet and blew on his hands.

"Yes. But maybe they have a different sense of time than we do. Let's give him five more minutes. I'd really like to close all of this out between us. You can't imagine how awkward it is not knowing if a giant pirate ghost is lurking invisibly while you're sleeping or taking a shower."

Gramps cleared his throat and smiled. "I suppose that would be true. Your grandmother would've loved this. I always thought she was part pirate."

A minute later, Rafe's ghost appeared. "He's here," I told Gramps. "I wish you could see him."

"That's fine. Don't wish too hard. Just have him tell you where we should go."

"I see you didn't come alone," Rafe snickered. "Aye, you talk a good fight, but you lack the backbone, girl. That's as well. Get in yer vessel and follow closely. There are rocks hidden beneath the water as you get close to the shore. Be sure to give the captain my regards."

I told Gramps what Rafe had said. We climbed into the *Eleanore* and were able to follow Rafe only because I could see a dim fluorescence around him. He floated right at the bow of the boat and kept us going straight in the night.

The beams from the island lighthouses played across the dark, cold water. The boat was tossed a little roughly in the waves coming up. Autumn was a time of sudden storms. I hoped we wouldn't run into one as we went to retrieve Rafe's treasure.

"How much treasure are we talking?" Gramps asked. "Maybe we should've brought Carter Hatley's boat out. It's much bigger."

I pulled my jacket and rain poncho more tightly around me. My fingers felt numb with cold. I wished I'd worn gloves. "I guess if it's too much treasure, we'll come back out for the rest. It's been there for three hundred years. Another night or two probably won't matter."

Rafe's form stopped, standing near one of the smaller islands that surround the Outer Banks. He was pointing toward a cove that was frequented by tourists. It was hard to get to but a nice place in summer to paddle around in the shallow water.

"Is this it?" Gramps asked. "No way we can take the *Eleanore* into Pirate's Point. There are too many rocks. Even during the day when you can see them, you can only take a dinghy in there."

I knew all that, of course. It suddenly struck me—Pirate's Point. There was a reason for that name, and Rafe probably buried his treasure here because of the rocks.

"I can't stay past tonight." Rafe was suddenly standing beside me in the boat. "You'll have to come ashore so I can show you where the treasure is buried."

I looked at my watch. It had taken us almost three hours to get out here with the wind against us and the heavy fog bank we'd encountered after leaving the island.

I knew Gramps had an inflatable dinghy. It looked like I would have to row to the treasure anyway. At least the *Eleanore* had gotten us this far.

Gramps was skeptical when I told him what I had to do. "You're sure about this, Dae? This pirate isn't leading you on a wild-goose chase, is he?"

"I don't think so. He didn't have to come back. He wanted to keep his word to me. I'll be fine. It shouldn't be too bad from here to the shore."

We both knew it was going to be treacherous—especially in a rubber dinghy. No boat would ever come out on top after scraping one of those sharp rocks that I knew lay between me and Rafe's treasure. But I had to try. It would be nice to be rich and even better to find a real buried treasure chest.

I took two flashlights and threw on an extra poncho for warmth. Gramps found me some old gloves. We launched the dinghy, and I climbed down to it.

"Careful with the motor," Gramps shouted. "It can be a little temperamental."

"Okay. I have my radio and cell phone. I hope one of them works once I get there."

"I'm giving you thirty minutes," he said. "After that I'm calling Gus to bring out the Coast Guard rescue ship."

I laughed—but he was probably serious. Anyway, thirty minutes should be plenty of time. I got the little outboard engine started and held tightly to the rudder to steer it toward shore.

Gramps shone a spotlight from the *Eleanore*, but once I was out of its range, the water and the night around me were pitch black. Out here there were no streetlights—not even any lights from houses. No one lived out here. I remember someone telling me once that it was owned by the government as part of an offshore training area. I didn't know if that was true, and if it was, how it would affect claiming the treasure. The government might want a cut.

"Steer a bit to port," Rafe said, sitting next to me in the boat. "There's a big rock you could end up on top of in this little craft."

I did as he said. If he could see rocks in the water, he was doing better than I was. "Thank you for saving my life. I thought Marissa was going to push me out the window."

"Don't be daft! You're a fair, strapping girl. You were just afraid to do what ye needed to."

"What was that?"

"Why, punch her in the mouth. Slap her silly. Kick her in the knee. Nothing more satisfying than hearing a knee crunch. Hard starboard now."

I turned the rudder. "Maybe you're right. I really didn't think about hitting her—but I did think about getting to those cleaning supplies on the bed."

He laughed. "That's my girl! You'd have made a fine pirate."

"Thanks. But I'm afraid I have too much O'Donnell in me to be a great pirate."

"You may be right. O'Donnell was one of the worst pirates I've ever known. Stop here. Let the current take you into shore. The water runs past the rocks now. That little noisy contraption will only put you in harm's way."

I cut the engine, wondering what Gramps would think—

hoping he wouldn't call the Coast Guard just yet. "So what happens to you now?"

"Blast if I know. There aren't any rule books for this. One minute you're dead and the next you don't know where you are."

"What about relatives? After I found out you were innocent, did you go someplace nice and have lunch with Mary?"

"You're a dreamer, girl. If my Mary is out there, I've not seen her. I feel certain I will roam the seas for eternity. A man makes his choices. After that, he must abide with them."

It sounded depressing to me. I'd always hoped I'd see my mother again, either here or in that other place. But if Rafe and Mary weren't together, I had my doubts.

The boat bumped up against the shore. I jumped out quickly and secured a line to a large tree root sticking out of the sand. The flashlight was only so much help in this kind of darkness. Rafe floated before me with a kind of glowing light that helped me know where to put my feet. I grabbed the collapsible shovel from the dinghy and quickly followed him.

"All the kids in the area have been here at one time or another," I told him. "It's hard to believe anything could be buried here that the government or teenagers didn't find."

"Trust me. It's here. You're standing on it right now."

I looked at the sand under my feet. It didn't look like anything special. There were even some blackened leftovers from beach parties held here recently. I took off my extra poncho and unfolded my shovel.

Lucky for me, the sand was soft and easy to dig. There were some rocks and tree roots that slowed my progress. I wished I'd brought an ax or something stronger than the shovel I had. But Rafe was insistent that we find the treasure right away.

My pirate ancestor hovered over the tip of a rock about five feet from where I was digging. Oddly enough, it was shaped like a duck head. I was surprised by how accurate my dreams about him had been.

"What will you do with the treasure once you find it?" he asked as I dug. "I always imagined buying me a big house in Barbados with it. I'd have a hundred servants and a gold sword to carry. Maybe even a ship with a crew to take me wherever I wanted to go—without pillaging to get there, you know?"

"Why didn't you come and get the treasure so you could spend it after you and Mary were together?"

"Too many cursed eyes watching me," he snarled. "I couldn't risk showing them the way."

It seemed to me he hadn't gained anything from the treasure—if he never had the opportunity to spend it, what was the difference if someone else got to it? But I guessed the treasure meant more to him than just the gold, and possibly jewels, it contained.

"I suppose you'll be decking yourself out in some fine doodads," he suggested. "You could take a trip around the world. Or you could help yer old dad."

"I'm not making any plans yet." As I said the words, the shovel hit something hard and solid. I couldn't tell what it was. The horizon was getting light, but not enough yet for me to see by. I could barely make out the shape of the *Eleanore* where she rode anchor off the island.

"That must be it," Rafe said. "I think that means it's time for me to leave. It's been grand meeting you, girl. I'm proud to be your relation."

"You could at least wait until I bring the treasure up."

"I could—but that sunrise can't wait. Good luck to you." He looked up toward the pale sky showing at the horizon. He smiled and held out his arms. "Well, look here. It seems you were right. I see my beautiful Mary coming for me. After all these years of being alone."

I followed his gaze but couldn't see anything. When I turned back toward the duck-shaped rock again, he was gone. I sighed, hoping it was as he thought—Mary was coming for him and they would be together again. Then I dug some more until I saw the outline of the old wood chest Rafe had buried here three centuries ago.

I thought about the mates he'd left here after the treasure was buried, and got a little creeped out. I called Gramps on the radio to let him know that I was all right. "I don't know if I can pull this chest out of the sand. It's big and probably waterlogged. Any ideas?"

"I have a few. Can you hold on until I get back? It shouldn't take more than an hour each way with the fog gone. I can get some equipment and a few spare hands."

"Yeah. That's fine. It should be completely light by that time, so we'll be able to see everything. Bring back some coffee and biscuits with you, huh? All this predawn work is making me hungry."

I worked for a while longer after I heard the *Eleanore*'s engines leaving the area. I sat down on the hard, damp sand when I just couldn't dig anymore. My shoulders ached and my hands burned. Probably blistered, but no one ever said finding treasure was easy.

It was sunrise—pink and orange streaks running across the sky. I watched a few ships going by and enjoyed the antics of some seagulls. The island was a beautiful place. Who knew pirates and treasure lay buried here? If anyone had known, no doubt the wood chest would've been long gone by now.

I finally heard the *Eleanore* return. Gramps called to let me know he was back. I had dug enough sand so that the box was visible, but the bottom half was still embedded.

I wasn't surprised to see Kevin with Gramps when they brought the second dinghy to the island a short time later. They tied up to the same spot I did and came toward shore with block and tackle and sturdier shovels.

I kissed Kevin when he handed me a large coffee and two biscuits. "Still warm! You are a wonder."

"I have to keep up with you," he said. "You could've told me you were following the pirate ghost out here looking for buried treasure."

"I thought you'd had enough to do the last few days. I was going to surprise you."

"I'm surprised." He looked down into the hole I'd dug. "That's bigger than I expected."

Gramps looked at the chest too. "That could hold a lot of gold. Let's get started."

I attached the special rigging Gramps and Kevin had thought up to raise the chest. While I did that, they set up the block and tackle. I figured we might be rich by lunchtime. Maybe there was something to this talking-with-ghosts thing. I wondered why Shayla didn't make contact with some wealthy ghost who could show her where to find a fortune.

The wet sand under the chest sucked hard at the wood, making it strain against the rope that was trying to pull out the chest. Twice we had to reset the ropes and repair the block and tackle. But eventually, the island gave up its treasure.

Rafe's initials were scratched into the brass lock fixture. I looked at Gramps and Kevin, then hit the lock with a hammer. It fell open and Kevin pushed the top back.

"Yep." Gramps pushed his hat back on his head. "That's about what I expected."

"What is it?" Kevin asked. "It doesn't look like gold coins."

"I guess it's what Rafe thought was most valuable in the world." I dropped to my knees in front of the chest. Inside was an old sextant, covered in green mold. Beside that was a compass that didn't seem to be working anymore. There were some brass buttons and a silver knife and fork. And of course, there were three bottles of rum.

"Honey, I don't think this will even buy us lunch," Gramps said. "I hope you aren't too disappointed."

"No. Not at all." I smiled at him and Kevin. "I'm sure the museum will love to have this. And the whole thing isn't an adventure I'm going to easily forget."

Kevin put his hand on my shoulder. "Let's at least open the rum. I have some cups. This should be the good stuff."

"Sure. Why not?" I passed him a bottle. It took almost as much prying to get the cork out of the bottle as it did to get the trunk out of the sand. I held my cup up for the first taste.

But when Kevin upended the bottle, small stones poured out and filled my cup. They sparkled in the sunshine.

"Dae!" Gramps exclaimed. "The bottles are filled with gemstones! Maybe old Rafe knew what he was talking about after all."

I let the diamonds, rubies, emeralds and sapphires sift through my fingers, totally amazed. I thought I heard a touch of pirate laughter in the air around us—but that was impossible.

Chapter 50

The Duck Police had arrested Marissa and charged her with two counts of murder. I heard that she admitted to being Matthew's girlfriend—even to killing Sandi at the Blue Whale. But she never admitted to killing Matthew. The police didn't believe her, given the circumstances surrounding the crime.

People in Duck were satisfied that the killer had been caught—especially so since she wasn't technically from the area. They felt the entire incident was an outsider kind of thing that wouldn't have happened if Marissa hadn't moved to Duck.

I found the courage to invite Danny to the house for dinner one night. Gramps made stew and biscuits, and I made a cranberry apple pie.

Gramps was civil to Danny, if not warm and cordial. When dinner was over, Gramps took his coffee out on the back porch. I noticed he'd left the door open—the better to hear what we were saying.

There was only one thing on my mind. I told Danny that he was my father. I explained everything I knew about how I'd come to be born, and showed him a few baby pictures.

He seemed pleased. He jumped up and hugged me. We laughed as we looked at the old baby pictures and cried when we looked at pictures of my mom. I returned the smooth stone I'd found outside his van the night of the accident.

"Why didn't she call me?" he wondered. "Why didn't she let me know?"

The screen door squeaked open and closed. Gramps said, "It was me. It was my fault. I thought she'd be better off without you. Her mother was sick at the time. She died before Dae was born. I guess I didn't want to lose Jean too. I'm sorry, son."

Gramps held out his hand to Danny. For a minute it was touch and go. Would Danny accept this act of friendship after Gramps's admission and the passage of all these years? But he finally put out his hand and they both smiled. There was no hugging—not that I expected any.

I told Kevin about it. He didn't seem as pleased as I'd thought he'd be. He didn't say anything bad about it, or about Danny, but his silence said something about his thoughts on the matter. I didn't pursue it. Danny would be around from now on—a part of my life. The two of them would be all right.

Jamie and Phil reopened The Coffee House and Bookstore. We had a big celebration lunch for them at Wild Stallions. Then about twenty of us trooped down the boardwalk for a ribbon-cutting ceremony.

Nancy took lots of pictures as I cut the red ribbon with Jamie and Phil at my side. I was wearing the new necklace, bracelet and matching earrings made from the gemstones Rafe had left me. The federal government kept most of the gems, but I'd managed to put a few into the Duck Historical Museum coffer too.

We shook hands all around and went inside the coffee

shop for the rest of the celebration. The event wouldn't make the nightly TV news or even a mention in the paper, but it was fun and a good opportunity to bring the community together.

We were all standing around, congratulating ourselves at being able to drink lattes and espressos and order books from a local retailer. Kevin was at my side with his arm around my waist. He was wearing the new blue sweater I'd bought him as a thank-you for all his help.

I saw the woman start moving through the crowd as soon as she came in the door. She was tall and gaunt. Her face was pale, no animation under the straw-colored hair.

"Kevin," she said when she'd reached us. She put her hand on his arm and smiled. "I'm so glad I found you. I've missed you so much."

His smile faded when he saw her, though he finally managed to cover his shock with a pleasant expression.

I knew that look—it was one you use to hide your true feelings.

"Ann!" Surprised was a mild way to describe how he sounded. "When did you get here?"

"Today. Can we go somewhere and talk?" She glared at me. "*Alone.*"

"Of course." He looked at me. "Dae, this is Ann Porter, my partner when I was with the FBI. Ann, this is Mayor Dae O'Donnell."

I shook her hand and smiled despite the cold feeling of foreboding that overtook me. He hadn't introduced me as his girlfriend. Maybe it was just too awkward right now. I knew he'd never expected to see her again.

I was glad that I was still wearing my gloves when I touched her. There were stories in her dark eyes I hoped never to experience from her touch.

"Hello, Dae," she said. "I'm Ann—Kevin's fiancée."

FROM THE AUTHOR OF *A KILLER PLOT*

ELLERY ADAMS

❧

Wordplay becomes foul play . . .

A Deadly Cliché

A BOOKS BY THE BAY MYSTERY

While walking her poodle, Olivia Limoges discovers a dead body buried in the sand. Could it be connected to the bizarre burglaries plaguing Oyster Bay, North Carolina? The Bayside Book Writers prick up their ears and pick up their pens to get the story . . .

The thieves have a distinct MO. At every crime scene, they set up odd tableaus: a stick of butter with a knife through it, dolls with silver spoons in their mouths, a deck of cards with a missing queen. Olivia realizes each setup represents a cliché.

Who better to decode the cliché clues than the Bayside Book Writers group, especially since their newest member is Police Chief Rawlings? As the investigation proceeds, Olivia is surprised to find herself falling for the widowed policeman. But an even greater surprise is in store. Her father—lost at sea thirty years ago—may still be alive . . .

penguin.com